Also by Loryn Kramer Staley

The Righteous Enemy
1230 North Garfield
Briefly Borrowed
Thunder's Glory

Circus
of Angels

LORYN KRAMER STALEY

ARCHWAY
PUBLISHING

Archway Publishing books may be ordered through booksellers or by contacting:

Archway Publishing
1663 Liberty Drive
Bloomington, IN 47403
www.archwaypublishing.com
844-669-3957

Because of the dynamic nature of the Internet, any web addresses or links contained in this book may have changed since publication and may no longer be valid. The views expressed in this work are solely those of the author and do not necessarily reflect the views of the publisher, and the publisher hereby disclaims any responsibility for them.

Any people depicted in stock imagery provided by Getty Images are models, and such images are being used for illustrative purposes only. Certain stock imagery © Getty Images.

ISBN: 978-1-6657-4200-9 (sc)
ISBN: 978-1-6657-4201-6 (e)

Library of Congress Control Number: 2023906280

Print information available on the last page.

Archway Publishing rev. date: 04/19/2023

INTRODUCTION

In the early 1930s, a narrow dirt road known as the "Big Nine" veined north to Blue Goose Hollow, a company housing area for employees of an iron works refinery positioned alongside the Tennessee River. To the east of Big Nine, Onion Bottom, a low-lying area known to flood after an April shower, encompassed a dump site, a processing plant, and the county's largest slum. Pennies away from poverty, the area's residents lived alongside run-down and abandoned buildings, neglected lots, and vacant retail spaces. Storefront windows were busted out and, when city officials demanded, boarded up, only to be violated with graffiti gang members left behind when marking their territory. In the shadows, addicts and nickel prostitutes called condemned structures their "place of business." Over time, Big Nine attracted panhandlers, loitering, and petty theft, and its homeless population overflowed into muddy arroyos and littered streets.

DeShane Salliver, who is known on the street as Sally, is already crime savvy, and when day turns to night, the streets become his hunting ground. When the life of crime takes a day off, he returns to his mother's apartment, a single-parent environment he shares with Marshall, his younger brother.

Their building is the last structure edging Foundry Street. Abutting a drainage ditch, their building mirrors several four-story tenements overshadowing their run-down, three-story building.

Once an oasis for travelers, the train depot across the street shut down before the holidays and the lumberyard on the corner continues to post signs advising it is not hiring.

Sometime ago, when vandals defaced the green and white street sign, city officials made a so-so promise to replace it and the burned-out bulb in the street's only lamppost.

The daughter of a third-generation sharecropper, Ramona, DeShane's mother, escaped the hood when her mother kicked her to the curb. "A bad seed!" her mother shouted at her back while throwing an open hand to a rickety screen door. Now, each time Ramona narrows her eyes on DeShane, she repeats the names her own mother once threw at her.

1

"**S**uzanne, do you have a minute?" Gail asks, holding the phone close.

"I always have time for you. What's up?"

"Lewis is a coward. Always has been. Always will be. He is having an affair. When I questioned him about it, that stupid husband of mine went into details my heart will never forgive or forget," Gail shares in a low voice. "This chick wears spinners on her tatas. A sixth sense tells me Lewis is reaching for a way out. I could kick myself for not paying attention to his darting eyes. Now that I think about it, I'm surprised he is not cross-eyed."

"An affair? Are you sure? Given the dandruff he carries on his shoulders, I'm surprised any woman would take an interest in him," Suzanne lets slip.

"He met her at a casino," Gail shares, skipping over the insult her best friend threw at her husband. "He used our credit card each time he booked a room. Idiot kept the receipts in an envelope. I found them in our desk when I was organizing the drawers. When I asked him about them, he tried convincing me that it was just a fling and it's over."

"I am so sorry to hear this. I can't imagine the pain you are feeling."

"It's funny, but it's not pain I'm feeling. Pain is learning my mother was recently diagnosed with Alzheimer's. Lewis went on to tell me he had given this woman an engagement ring."

"Are you serious?" Suzanne asks, recalling the time Gail told her that when it came to happenings in the bedroom, Lewis knew only one position—spooning. "Are you certain he ended the affair?"

"That's the problem. I don't know. I'm ready to send his sorry self packing."

"I've never been in your situation, but my advice would be to wait it out. It's possible time will heal your open wounds."

"I've been such a fool. I believed he was spending his free time playing tennis. It never crossed my mind that he was playing house with another woman. When I slammed him with a wall of questions, he went possum on me."

"Possum?"

"Played dead. I could shoot myself for not staying single. I'm learning that life with Lewis is a crapshoot. I never know what's waiting around the corner. Take my advice—never marry a man known as One-Way Lewis."

"Not to worry. Glenn is stuck with me," she says, turning her eyes to her husband. "Something tells me there will never be another love like ours."

2

The Warehouse Row Clock Tower rings out eight bells, letting the people of Chattanooga know the city is open for business.

A parade of lawyers marches along at a pace hinting they were due in court yesterday. Shouldering cell phones, they race along East Third Street. Close observation lets curious onlookers know a smile is not to be found among them. Crammed together in their approach to the finish line, they travel the stairs to the Hamilton County Juvenile Detention Center, where youthful detainees await their arrival.

The center's walls are cracked, and dark circles left behind after a season of threatening rains freckle the ceiling. Given the center's tight budget is already at a stretch, repairs remain in the holding pattern.

Deep within the nurse's station, young DeShane runs a thick, wet tongue over a fresh cut on his wrist. Tapping his feet to the low music escaping the room's sound system, he licks at a pool of blood and picks at an aging scab a burning joint left behind. Nipping at the twisted appendage, he spits the flesh into the air. Twice in the last week, he asked the nurse in the white lab coat for ointment or painkillers—anything to ease his discomfort. Both times, her response was the same.

"If you're going to act out like a crazy man, you best be prepared to take it like a man."

Believing he is the victim of the courts and its reprimands and sentences, DeShane has little doubt his day in court will have a different outcome. A creature of habit and a kid who refuses to take no for an answer, he continues to keep after it.

"Give me something for the pain," he says, scratching at his ears.

"I'm no doctor, but that rash has me believing you're allergic to carbon steel or aluminum," the nurse says, limping to his side. "That's what those handcuffs are made of." Planting her feet and placing her fisted hands on her hips, she looks him straight in the eye. "One would think that alone would be enough for you to want to turn your life around," she says, giving her two cents' worth. "You also have a bad case of ear mites and scabies."

"Ear mites?"

"Common in dogs."

"And scabies?"

"Infestation of the skin by the human itch mite. They burrow into the upper layer of the skin, where they live and lay eggs."

"Get rid of them."

"Maybe you can nip at them and spit them into the air. Just so you know, a spit hood is on its way. How long have you had lice on your eyelashes?"

"Listen up, Gimpy. My lashes are my business. I'm guessing you are not paid to think," he sasses, running a hand over his eyes. "Don't think I won't use this," he says, throwing out his fist.

"Oh, but I am paid to think. Throwing out that fist will keep you here," she says, jabbing an inch-long needle into the beefy part of his arm. "Oops. My bad. I should have mentioned you might feel a sting."

Not to be outdone, he raises cuffed wrists to the air and, with the passion of a trained conductor, flips her the bird.

"Really? Like I've never seen that before. For what it's worth, my hip injury is a result of running dozens of marathons—something you'll never have to worry about, unless you're running from the law."

In the passing silence, a bulb in the overhead fixture flashes. A deafening buzz quickly follows.

"Am I being watched?" DeShane asks, searching the room for hidden cameras.

"Recorded. Every breath you take is recorded, and each time you shrug your shoulders or stretch your arms, a red light records your actions. Only a fool would be alone with you."

"A camera can't keep up with me. Can I get some gloves?" he asks, waving a bloodied wrist in the air.

"What kind of question is that? Are you taking psychotropic drugs?"

"It's a question you get paid to answer. As for the drugs I use, I don't see where that is any of your business."

"Yeah, yeah, yeah. Next time I'm at the mall, I'll grab a pair for you. Until then, move along. It's time for you to face the music," she says, pushing glasses up and over her forehead. "Something tells me I'll see you again. I've been told you are like a growing blister on an aging rooftop ... waiting to cause all kinds of problems."

"Believe what you will, but I'm never coming back to this hellhole."

"From your mouth to God's ears," she mumbles, folding her hands in prayer. "Be grateful you are not locked up in Alcatraz. I've been told the water's freezing temperature and its moving waves are alive with great white sharks. Looking at your slim frame," she says, pausing to study his thin stature, "I'm guessing those great whites will skip over you and go after fisherman's bait. The more blood, the merrier."

Uncaring, he shrugs his shoulders.

"There is a team waiting for you."

"Unless it's Perry Mason, I don't have a team."

"Once we step outside the infirmary, a duo of deputies will slap shackles on your ankles."

While DeShane drags his feet along the cold concrete, the deputies escort him through a maze of narrow, concrete halls, where they will pass him off to the state's attorney, whose job is to convince the judge that young DeShane's crimes are not worthy of prison time.

3

Judge Tafoya's courtroom is one of eight benches where juvenile matters are heard. Big on windows and without air-conditioning, the room's air is thick—typical for the river city from May through October. The gallery is packed tighter than a tin of dollar-store sardines. Circling overhead, a tired ceiling fan fails to rotate the air. Its constant screech keeps pace with the bailiff, whose job is to protect the judge and, when necessary, restore order in the courtroom.

Sipping coffee from a Styrofoam cup, Tafoya throws tortoiseshell eyeglasses to his slim face. After months of suffering with stiff muscles and constant twitching, he now struggles with swallowing and speaking. In recent months, he was diagnosed with Lou Gehrig's disease. Although his condition is treatable, he understands it comes with an early grave. In the passing minutes, he reviews the morning's docket. Other than the growing list of names, the docket always remains the same.

While the room is filled with silence and fear, an armed bailiff directs DeShane to a chair in the front row. Passing by a row of teenagers, DeShane gives a chin nod to Charlene, a young girl he knows from school, who appears to be expecting. It has been said she is like a library book—checked out easily and always returned. Word on the street hints she wants out of her mother's home and financial support from the state. Unlike the fool who planted his seed, DeShane knows to keep a safe distance.

Falling into the chair, DeShane recognizes a weathered woman in a wheelchair who, catching his eye, tries to hide behind a dog-eared paperback likely lifted from the shelf of a neighborhood shelter. Although her name is unknown to him, he is aware she lives in a tract house with Charlene and her mother, a woman who is often heard shouting expletives from the home's fallen porch.

On a good day, Charlene's mother is known as the hood's holy roller, always quoting the Bible, and her boyfriend is quick to jump at the opportunity to share the latest sports scores and rumors surrounding his least favorite athletes.

DeShane learned early on in his young years to cross the street when approaching Charlene's house if he wants to avoid stepping over used syringes and spent condoms.

In the far corner of the room, a young mother attempts to calm her newly hatched baby. A pungent odor floating on the air suggests a diaper change is needed. Turned heads from those seated nearby question if the old woman in the wheelchair is responsible for the odor. The court reporter stuffs twisted tissues up her nose, pulls at the sleeves of her knit sweater, and, believing her actions go unnoticed, slips her feet out of patent leather loafers.

Seated with his crooked spine pressed against the wall, an elderly man taps thin fingers against an oxygen tank. A walking stick rests at his side. He sits quietly while Judge Tafoya lectures his grandson, a high school dropout, who in his younger years was sexually and physically abused by his mother and her boyfriend, a known drug dealer. The local newspaper reported that both are serving long sentences in federal prison. Believing no one is watching, the old man looks down at his hands. He worries his grandson, a victim of crime for the better part of his young life, will likely return to the only life he knows if he is allowed to leave the center.

Lost in thought, DeShane jumps when a cell phone rings out.

"Please be advised cell phones are not allowed here. If a phone disrupts the court, the action will be treated as contempt of court. The violation comes with a steep fine and jail time," Tafoya advises, slamming down his gavel. "Next on the docket is *The State versus DeShane Joseph Salliver.*"

A young man dressed in a wrinkled blue-and-white seersucker suit lifts off his chair. He straightens his tie and opens a leather briefcase.

"Your Honor, I represent DeShane Salliver. Please be advised he arrived here on a 5150—involuntary hold in a psychiatric unit."

"His charges?"

"Skipping school and later expelled for smoking marijuana in the locker room. He is also charged with theft of personal and school property and a number of parking lot crimes."

"What are the parking lot crimes he has been charged with?"

"Smashing car windows, tampering with door locks, and begging for money from approaching shoppers."

"Was he armed?"

"When challenged, he waved a gun into the air. At the time of his arrest, a switchblade was found in his pocket."

"The issue of gun violence among our city's juveniles can no longer be ignored. I would like to believe this is a different kind of war, but our courts are seeing an increase in crime among the younger population. I'm aware DeShane Salliver was in a seventy-two-hour hold," the judge replies. "It disturbs me that there continues to be a rise in mass shootings. I would like to speak with Mrs. Salliver before you address the court. In the interim, please ask your client to remove his spit hood."

"Of course."

Hearing her name, Ramona Salliver eases up from the squeaky bench. A scar above her brow and deep wrinkles in her jowl-like cheeks own her face. Swinging an umbrella like she is walking the runway, she sashays over the worn floor to the waist-high podium.

"Mrs. Salliver, do you condone your son's behavior?"

"I don't know. What does that mean?"

"Accept and allow poor behavior to go unpunished."

"I leave that to the law."

"Do you believe your son's future is promising?"

"His actions tell me he doesn't have a future. I'm afraid of him. He sniffs out his next victim, and when the moment is ripe, he sucks the life out of them. I'm guessing he takes their dreams with him. Did I mention I'm afraid of him?"

"Twice now. Why is that?"

"His mind is soiled. That son of mine is evil."

"Fear is defined as an unpleasant emotion. I've heard it said that fear often depends on the zip code. You either choose to enter it or dodge it. Any offensive behavior goes with punishment and accountability. It's possible reform school is in his future."

"When it comes to my son, I've come to turn a blind eye," she says, deflecting the hostility in her voice. "He is capable of anything. Sometimes I sleep with my eyes open. He is always sniffing out opportunity and lurking in the shadows. I pray I'm not his next victim. I've heard it said there is a place in hell for people like him."

"And I fear you are part werewolf," DeShane interrupts. "Your Honor, I'll be so glad to be rid of that bitch. Even when I am souped up on drugs, she is still evil and ugly. She is colder than a witch's tit. And I should know. I've felt a few. One more thing—never walk behind her. She always has the walking farts."

"Blame it on Edna," Ramona throws out.

"Who is Edna?" Tafoya asks.

"She works in the plant's cafeteria. She doesn't wear an apron, and her hair is scorched at the ends. Skipping over the greens and fresh fruit, she loads our plates with beans. When the moon is full, she goes animal on me. I fear I'll need to fight her off with bug spray. Rumor has it she is related to the elderly woman who teaches German while rolling a piece of chalk in the palm of her hand."

"I'm sorry to hear this. I suggest we move forward in a positive direction. Mrs. Salliver, what is DeShane's full name?"

"DeShane Joseph Salliver, the second."

She begins to spell his last name, but hearing a snicker from the gallery, she forces the letters to the back of her tongue.

"Listen up, fatso. My old man didn't graduate from college, but he knew the streets and its numbers. Any numbers you tossed at him, he could calculate in his head. He would have made a great bookie," he says. "As for my mom, she always plays the victim. She will never admit it, but she turned her back on me long before she gave up on me. She will lie at any cost, even when it means she will lose her kids. She keeps us around for subsidized housing and welfare benefits," he says, eyeing her clothes. "She always dresses like she is channeling Johnny Cash," DeShane says, throwing his eyes to his mother. "And wipe the lipstick off your teeth. You look like a clown."

"When you say Johnny Cash, are you referring to the music artist?" the judge asks, eyeing the stain on Ramona's teeth.

"Yep."

"I'll accept *yes*."

"I'm guessing you watch *Judge Judy* too."

"I hear about her from my wife. Moving forward, please refrain from referring to your mother as fatso."

"Excuse me, Your Honor, but can we get back to me?" Ramona interrupts. "For all I care, that boy of mine can live on the street or in a storage unit. Life on the street is free. Should he choose to make the storage unit his home, it's on his nickel," Ramona adds, wiping a finger over her uppers. "I work in an environment where maintenance crews and factory workers get a ten-minute break, allowing them to tear into bologna sandwiches or chew away at skinless chicken drums. As for me, I prefer bologna. I fear a chicken bone will take my life. It happens, you know," she adds, picking at her teeth. "One day, I'm living the best life ever, and along comes this little hurricane, my little Charles Manson. Like I needed another mouth to feed."

"I'm guessing she was already lit when she passed through security," DeShane lets loose in a low voice. "She has a habit of telling whoppers and sticking with them. The bigger the whopper, the better. She acts like she is well read, but if you ask her about the weather, she rubs her hands together like a threatened mosquito.

When questioned about her hand motions, she folds her hands in her lap. When incoming weather appears iffy, she throws on a slicker and grabs an umbrella. She is a schmoozer but not in a friendly way. She tosses out words until she believes she will get her way or comes down a notch to settle a score," DeShane adds. "Our neighbors will tell you she's a lush. Once she clocks out at work, she hurries to claim a stool at Murray's Tavern. While the bartender mixes her drink, she slides into a public bathroom, where she steps out of her work clothes and slips into a dress one expects to see on Flora."

"Who is Flora?"

"She used to be a circus elephant, but she retired to the Elephant Sanctuary right here in Tennessee. Get this—her favorite food is watermelon."

"Interesting."

"Although my mom carries a few extra pounds, a bathroom scale shares she weighs several pounds more than her five-foot-frame can support. Once the clock's ticker strikes straight up five o'clock, she's drinking like she's living the life of one of our first ladies. I'll say this: she's always lapping up the sauce. Before the alcohol runs through her veins, she manufactures chaos. My old lady has a nose for booze. Wait for it. This is the best part. She drinks foot wine out of a growler. I keep waiting for her to start foaming at the mouth. When she's done drinking and eating, her teeth sleep in a jar."

While Tafoya struggles to ignore the laughter, the court reporter turns to him with curious eyes.

"Should I strike this from the transcript?" she asks with lollipop eyes.

"I don't believe that will be necessary. It's your job to document every word." Pausing, Tafoya turns to DeShane. "Let's agree to skip over the nonsense. As for the foot wine," he says, "I hope you will explain this to me."

"Don't you want to know about her teeth?"

"Let's agree to skip over her teeth. Please tell me about the foot wine."

"She stomps her bare feet on old and moldy grapes she lifts from grocery store dumpsters. Sometimes these grapes are hidden under discarded vegetables, stanky fish, and rotten tomatoes, but she doesn't waste any time throwing those old grapes into the bathtub."

"That's a lie. I'll agree I've had a lot of experience in drinking, but I'm not an alcoholic. And I don't shop the dumpsters for aging grapes. Do us both a favor and don't compare me to our former First Lady. Something tells me she could afford the best. Given my income, I'm forced to drown my sorrows with Mad Dog 20/20. Your Honor, don't pay him any attention. He tells stories out of the backside of his head. I worry he might just be the next Jeffrey Dahmer."

"The serial killer?" the judge asks, scooting forward in his chair.

"Just last year, DeShane was diagnosed with antisocial personality disorder. His teacher told me he suffers from Dunning-Kruger syndrome—he acts out like he knows more than the experts," she says, doling out information like she is the head of the neighborhood association.

"It's rumored my mom participated in the four-man bobsled. To be clear, I'm not talking about the Olympics," DeShane shares. "Did I mention hers was the only sled? I can't swear to it, but I was told they rode her pretty hard."

"I'm finding this foreign to me," Tafoya says.

"My mom hurries to shout out words. When she is cut off, she talks louder. I'm guessing she was silenced in her formative years." Allowing a grin to cross over his face, he turns to his mother. "You talk so much your lips sweat. My old lady never skips over the liquor. When she is not drinking, she talks about taking the stage somewhere in Hollyworth," he tells the judge.

"He means Hollywood. I can burp the alphabet. Would you care to hear it?" Ramona throws out with a sway of her hips.

"Although I find myself a bit curious, I'll wait until you open in Vegas for Wayne Newton."

"Don't listen to her, Judge. If there ever comes a time when I am given the opportunity to write a book about my childhood and the abuse I suffered, my mother and her actions will own the opening chapter, all the chapters in the middle, and a closing chapter she will argue until she is blue in the face. That said, her mouth runs more than a three-year-old's nose. When it comes to her, I prepare for arm-to-arm combat. I imagine her coming at me in camouflage clothing and camping gear. Having faced this my whole life, I learned early on to fight back with a smart mouth and a two-fisted punch. She knows only to talk trash. She poses like a good Christian, but you will never find her name in a church's member directory. If she had the money, she'd drink like a lounge lizard," DeShane lets slip. "For what it's worth, she calls me the *other child*."

"You're evil. There is nothing behind your eyes, and your heart knows only to be cold. You know only to kill or be killed," Ramona says, turning toward the judge. "That son of mine has a one-way ticket to crime. He is always knocking on hell's front door. I'm always left believing I should check his hands for gun residue."

"I'll ask that you keep in mind that rearing children isn't easy, and listening to you here today, I have come to understand you have faced many challenges. Perhaps you and your son can work to see the best in each other," Tafoya says. "I think we will agree it's in the best interest of this court to skip over inadmissible hearsay and whoppers. As for our former First Lady, she is now deceased. Let's stay on point. I suggest we draw a line and color it in."

"Forgive me, Your Honor, but you're a little wrong. I'm talking about the mayor's wife. In her brief time in the big house, she set an example for people like me who want the bartender to overpour our drinks. I believe you will agree we live in a time where criminals have more rights than law-abiding citizens. I'll admit my life is no Cinderella story, but I'm proud to say my family was the first to move into the East Lake Courts housing project. That was the first time we had running water and a toilet. On the flip side, I was shot at once while getting the mail. As for my drinking, I do cartwheels over the floor when the liquid meets the glass. When happy hour arrives, I wave at the bartender. When he throws a lime into my drink, I bite my tongue. What am I gonna do? I'm a boozer. Last I heard, that isn't a crime," she says, toying with a button on her blouse.

"Who are you kidding? Like I said earlier, you're a boozer, schmoozer, and a loser. You are your own frickin' trio. You drink cheap liquor from a plastic cap you rip from a can of hair spray," DeShane adds. "Your Honor, there are days when she displays all the symptoms of alcohol poisoning."

When the laughter breaks out, the bailiff positions himself near the judge.

"There will be order in the court," Tafoya reminds, slamming down his gavel. "My nerves are tired, and if the disruptions continue, all those present will soon have a lashing."

"She gets confused, vomits every minute on the clock, and the second she sits down on the couch, she passes out. Sometimes her skin turns blue. For real. Blue! Can you imagine that? She looks like a big ole bruise."

"Mrs. Salliver, if there is one ounce of truth in what your son just shared, you might consider seeking an intervention. That said, you might work to be a better role model."

"Pay no attention to him. On our best day, we would still be losers on *Family Feud*. All we know how to do is argue and throw punches. When it comes to DeShane, every minute is a challenge. As hard as I work to change him, he continues to execute poor choices."

"There you go using big words. What did you do? Lift a dictionary? And please stop nagging and hounding me. Don't your lips ever get tired? Your Honor, I've heard it said her motor runs hot. I'm not talking about her mouth," DeShane throws out. "Judge, when it comes to mothering, she is no Florence Nightingale. She mirrors Jack the Ripper. I'm pretty sure if she is ever given the opportunity, she would put a syringe in my arm and call it a day."

"Just so you know, the day is not over," Ramona says in a high shrill. "Something tells me my son will never write a thesis."

"What is that?" DeShane asks.

"I've been told it is a paper that will get a good student into college."

"Coming from someone who didn't finish the eighth grade."

"Listen up, you little snot. It's not my fault you came along and ruined my future."

"Mrs. Salliver, your actions and responses show that you wish to be dishonest and negative," the judge says. "Only you can decide the footprint you wish to leave behind. I understand DeShane was once booked into the county's juvenile detention center on suspicion of aggravated battery with a deadly weapon. Do you have any weapons in your home?"

"Just a leather belt and a cast-iron skillet, but they get the job done."

"Don't forget your mouth," DeShane says. "Don't pay her any attention. She is quick to throw out insults. Regarding weapons, I've been told hammers kill more people than guns. Ask her about the padlock she puts on the door."

"As for the insults, perhaps you can work at controlling your tongue," Tafoya suggests, turning to Ramona. "As for the skillet, I suggest you keep it in the kitchen and, if space allows, hide the hammer under the sink. Please tell me about the padlock."

"Between bus fare and groceries, I'm broke at the end of the month. When I'm not broke, I'm in the red. The walls in our unit are paper thin. Every chance I get, I complain to the property manager, but she brushes me off. When I press my ear to the wall, I can hear when my neighbor cracks his knuckles. The lady to the east of our unit needs something for her stomach. Maybe the state can send her a bottle of Pepto Bismol." Swaying her hips like she knows all and sees all, she paints a smile on her face. "You tell me how I should come up with the money to support and protect my kids when I'm living on help from the state?"

"I'm struggling to understand what this has to do with having a padlock on your door."

"I may not have attended finishing school, but I'm street smart. I'll be ready the next time something goes bump in the night."

Again, laughter breaks out in the courtroom. This time, Tafoya not only allows it but also joins in.

"I have to treat my little place like a rich man's timeshare—lock and leave. I can't afford one of those fancy alarm systems. You know what I'm talking about. You punch in a code, and all of a sudden, me and my kids are living free of fear. The folds of my thin wallet won't pay for a private security guard, so I have to keep a lock on the door."

"You always have money for fried chicken wings and a six-pack," DeShane whispers in a loud voice.

"Order in the court," the judge says. A questionable look to Ramona encourages her to explain the lock.

"I run a cable with a lock on it from the door to a hook on the wall."

"Please help me to understand. Is the lock inside the unit or on the home's exterior?"

"Inside, but only at night. I have to sleep too, you know. It keeps us in—well, me and Marshall anyways. Our little mansion doesn't have air-conditioning, and I'm afraid to sleep with the window open."

"Do you understand this lock on the door puts your children's lives in harm's way?"

"Let's all take a good, long look at the elephant in the room," she says, throwing her eyes to DeShane. "Lock or no lock, he's always in harm's way."

"Why do you think that is?"

"He's worthless. By that, I mean he is of no value."

"Are you aware one in five kids lives in poverty?"

"At least they have a roof over their head. My boys attend a Title 1 school. Lunch is free, and they can stay on the property until I get off from work. Is this a good time to mention I've been on the waiting list for something like three years now for an increase in my Section 8 housing voucher?"

"I'm sorry to hear this. To be clear, poverty means poor and without," Tafoya says, scratching his head.

"I thought that was the place over on Tully Street where the junkies and the misfits hang out. Did I mention we live in a one-bedroom unit on Leon Place? Damn place has sheet metal wrapping the lower half of the three-story walk-up, and the makeshift ramp goes missing every weekend."

The judge's audible sigh raises eyebrows among the young kids who, although sitting nervously, are enjoying the entertainment. "Well, this is certainly one for the books," he says, placing robed elbows on the raised desk. "Regarding the lock, what are you going to do should a fire break out during the night?"

Ramona rolls thick shoulders and places a frown on painted lips. She unbuttons the top button on her blouse and fiddles with the safety pin on the strap of her bra. Arms flailing about, she searches the air for answers. When none come, she widens her stance, purses her lips, and, seeking support, turns to the young men who wait along with her son to learn their fate. "Stop, drop, and roll?"

The roar in the room travels through dust-filled air vents and down adjacent corridors before coming to a screeching halt at the judge's bench.

"Surely you would want your children to escape a fire," he says, restoring order.

"DeShane picks the lock. He gets out all the time. He's like that Houdini guy—you know, that dark-haired guy who dated that blonde model ... Claudia something or other. He performs in Vegas. Not DeShane but the magician guy. I once seen him make an airplane disappear into thin air. Poof, just like that," she says, snapping her fingers. "Anyways, DeShane squirms his way out of everything. Sometimes when I leave, I put the cable on the outside of the door," she says, crossing her arms over her chest.

Rubbing a finger along the wide part separating his graying hair, Tafoya presses into his leather chair. "Mrs. Salliver, please uncross your arms. Your son is guilty of contempt. The bench warrant issued upon him is for his failure to comply with an order to meet with his probation officer. Do you understand he is your responsibility and is to be released to your care?"

Ramona raises her hands to the ceiling, lowers her head, and shakes it east to west before looking north. "Forgive me, Lord, but I don't want him." Whipping her neck, she locks eyes with the judge. "Your Honor, you are asking questions that require me to be sober."

"She always falls off the wagon," DeShane shares. "When it comes to me, she buries her head in a bottle."

"It's my head and my bottle."

"She's known as the neighborhood's bonesetter," DeShane says, rubbing a hand along his elbow.

"If you will, please explain," the judge says.

"She knows how to break a bone and reset it. She once left me at the grocery store. When the store manager chased her down in the parking lot, she told him I wasn't her kid. The police were called, and the store's surveillance cameras were studied. We both cried all the way home. She was crying because she was stuck with me. I cried because she pulled at my ear all the way home."

"Is this true, Mrs. Salliver?"

"Your Honor, if you have not noticed, he has ears better suited on Flora. I will admit that my head is never clear, and any words that roll off my tongue are a jumbled mess. If I ask anything, it's that you lock him up and throw away the key. If I'm asking too much, I beg you will keep him inside."

"What do you mean?"

"Jail. He's flawed, Your Honor. I can't have him stealing my hard-earned money and scrounging through my drawers and roaming the neighborhood. He has done these things more times than I can count. There is this lady down the street. She wears her hair in two cinnamon rolls like Princess Leia. She blames me every chance she gets. It's not my fault he doesn't know right from wrong. Why can't you just keep him here?" she asks, pleading with desperate eyes. Eyeing the gallery, she turns to her son with cold eyes. "We all know he'll be back," she says, pulling a thick lock of hair over her left eye. "I'm here to tell you he's dumb as dust. He just isn't smart. I think his wires got crossed. He steals newspapers from those big, old machines outside the deli on the boulevard and sells them down the street. If it's illegal, he has his hand in it. I'm telling you, he is no good. He is like a shark in dark water—always seeking his next victim," she says, giving DeShane's cheek a pinch.

Hearing a symphony of chuckles from the gallery, the bailiff takes a wide stance and places a steady hand on his holster. He canvasses the holding area with unblinking eyes. In return, he is met with turned-up chins and rolling eyes. In the space around him, nervous delinquents clad in standard-issue orange jumpsuits sit handcuffed while waiting for their case to be called. Forgetting their fun will be cut short once the judge delivers their sentence or reads the terms of their release, they laugh in unison like brothers from the hood.

"Are you suggesting your son becomes a ward of the state?" Tafoya asks.

"It would be a huge weight off my shoulders. Given that I don't want my son to come home with me, may I chew over these papers and get back to you? What do you say we visit next week?"

"I'm afraid that won't be possible. The court doesn't have a *chew box* in its program. Decisions and the court's actions will be determined today."

"I'm worried DeShane and his gang of street thugs will start shooting up schools and getting his baby brother hooked on black mollies. These kids know only to settle their differences with dueling handguns."

"To a young man of your son's age, it has been said growing old is a gift. It has been suggested that one should never waste idle moments. It has also been said regret should never take hold of one's last breath. Statistics suggest a troubled youth of DeShane's age has a steep hill to climb or a quick, and often fatal, downward spiral. Are you familiar with CASA?"

"I don't know. What is it?"

"The court appoints a special advocate for abused and neglected children and teenagers, especially those in toxic environments. It is the volunteer's job to make recommendations in the best interest of the child and those living in the same home. We can also assign a guardian ad litem to represent your son in court."

"Excuse me, Your Honor," the lawyer in the seersucker interrupts. "Most of what Mrs. Salliver has said of her son is nonsense. She is making defamatory statements to the court. I'm here on behalf of DeShane."

"I understand, but if you will listen closely, I believe you will agree Mrs. Salliver is making your case for you, and I'm making suggestions."

"While that may be true, I would like to enter the results of my client's evaluation. He suffers with antisocial personality disorder. It's believed he will never exceed beyond his birthright. It appears he doesn't have the life skills to grow his imagination. The evaluation results go on to report he has no redeeming qualities. He has indicators that show he has no respect for human life. Your Honor, I'm sure you are aware there are nearly seven hundred youth courts in the Unites States. That number continues to grow."

"It has been suggested and argued that the juvenile system should include youths older than eighteen. Research shows young brains continue to develop until the midtwenties. Our youth courts are in dire need of adult role models, including those youths and young adults who have turned their lives around," Tafoya says, shooting his eyes to Ramona. "An estimated two million youths under the age of eighteen are arrested in a single year. With this increase in juvenile crimes and illegal misconduct, this trend we are fighting is often referred to as the crib-to-cot train. This number would suggest the need for early intervention at schools and in the home. After identifying the problems, we should look for solutions. I might add that we have sixty-seven people on death row. Forty-nine of those offenders are from Shelby County, Davidson County, Knox County, and Hamilton. The oldest on death row is in his late seventies. He was found guilty of stabbing his estranged wife with a bayonet. The only female on death row is accused of killing a relative. The family argued that she suffered from severe mental illness and brain damage brought on by drugs and physical abuse."

"Judge, are you saying these facts for me or for DeShane? I don't plan on going to death row. The thought of being strapped into an electric chair gives me the shivers. Where is this death row place?" Ramona asks with genuine interest.

"Only, Tennessee."

"Fifty nifty United States and Tennessee gets it?" she asks, referencing a Ray Charles song.

"Only is the name of the town. If we can remain focused, I believe these facts might help heal your broken family. That said, the last person sentenced to death row is also the youngest. Mrs. Salliver, are you familiar with the juvenile justice system?"

"Believe me when I say this nightmare is not our first rodeo," Ramona throws out.

"It is the court's goal to rehabilitate our youths and enforce and encourage the supportive role their parents or guardians play in doing so. When it comes to the success of our youth court, I'm sure you've heard it said it takes a village to raise a child."

Slumped over, DeShane gives a slow side-to-side nod. When time allows, he will show his attorney and the rest of the world his *life skills*.

Hearing these words, a puzzling look comes over Ramona's worn face. "His test grades place him at the bottom of his class. He's never gonna be a brainiac. His teacher once told me he was caught throwing matches at spiderwebs and stealing shoes during naptime. He struggles to tie his shoes. Once he left kindergarten, his first-grade teacher warned he was trouble. I brushed it off, thinking he would outgrow it, but I was wrong. Hear it here first—Tennessee can have him for all I care." Turning toward her son, the lines in her face harden. "He's just like his dad—always busting up the house and throwing things. When he followed his meds with whiskey, he knew only to punch holes in the walls and call me names." Frustrated, she throws a hand to the air. "DeShane and his dad are cut from the same cloth. It's a tattered one, but it's the same one. They hurt animals and lie to save their—"

"Am I getting another butt chewing?" DeShane asks, interrupting. "She talks like she has a battery-operated voice box."

Fearing her string of curse words might get her into trouble, Ramona bites her tongue. "Anyways, his father is a hood rat who ends each day with alcohol on his breath, and when he survives the night, greets many a mornings with blood on his hands. It's no secret he spent a few years in the big house. You know, prison," she says, lowering her voice to a loud whisper. "He never calls it prison. Anyways, he took a bullet to his head outside Velvet Liquors, a seedy place somewhere near the highway. It's right at that twisty turn near a funeral home. You know, the one with that covered opening you can drive under to stay out of the rain. He was worthless the day I met him, and now, with the left side of his head blown away, he is less than worthless. Other than pumping gas in his teen years, he has never held a job. I've been told he spends his days hanging out down by the river. He's a drifter. The only time I hear from him is when he needs a dry blanket or a quarter to watch peep shows and window porn at a place I don't want to hear about. I wouldn't be surprised to learn he's incarcerated." Returning to the matter at hand, she places her hands on the table. "DeShane is dangerously curious and possessed by demons—nothing but angry, bitter, and mean-spirited. He knows only to disappoint. There are days I wish I had walked away with his father," she says, turning to the parents who wait nearby. "I'm telling you, that boy of mine is a bad seed."

"The one who abandoned us had the better gene pool," DeShane says, turning to the judge. "For what it is worth, I overheard my mom tell the manager of our building that she married on the fly. I also heard her say that they married and had a baby, but she can't say which came first."

"Your ears were not supposed to be listening," Ramona says, shifting her weight about. "Your time here is short-lived. From my mouth to God's ears, I pray you will never father a child."

Although his mother continues to throw him under the bus, DeShane's ears perk up. Perhaps this will be the day he learns something—anything—about his father, a drunken addict always high on peep shows, corner hookers, titty bars, and anything the courts deem illegal. On a sweltering September day, he walked out the door and into a new life. Not once did he look back.

When his mother refused to accept his father's mail, DeShane was all ears. Flapping her arms about and raising her voice for all to hear, his mother jumped on her soapbox, where she went on to tell the meter reader that her husband ran off in the dead of night to start a new family.

Although his mother rarely speaks of his father, she is always eager to jump at the opportunity when she has an audience. "He's a boy from Grundy County," she always says with a sneer.

What DeShane knows about Grundy County he learned from Dynamite Dean, a rough-talking, weak-walking firebug from Tracy City—a business district in Grundy, which over the years has fallen victim to dynamite blasts and dozens of fires set by unknown arsonists. Rumor has it Dean served time for criminal damage to property, possession of cordite, a smokeless propellant, possession of a controlled substance, and resisting arrest.

Throwing matches to dry fields rain never reaches, Dynamite Dean gets his kicks watching the city burn. Once known as the village idiot inside a growing cell deep within Chattanooga's Lupton city, Dynamite Dean is never without a book of matches and a burning fire in his dark, beady eyes. Every time he tosses a flicked match to his target, he raises illustrated arms into the air, where he pounds on his chest while letting go a screech falling just short of Tarzan's jungle cry.

"DeShane, please step up to the podium." Seated behind the raised platform, Tafoya flips through a thick file. A family law attorney for fifteen years, he has been a sitting judge for almost a decade. In recent years, he has become immune to the pleas and requests that travel over the room's cold floor to his gavel.

Dragging his feet, DeShane crosses over the old floor like he is heading to the guillotine. He has been in lockup for several weeks and does not want to stay one minute longer, even with the three daily meals his sentence guarantees.

"If you choose to continue down this dark path, I worry you will not like the end result. I have heard it said that there is a marked difference between respect and fear. That said, do you understand your release requires you to attend school?"

"Whatever," he mutters, shrugging narrow shoulders. "I'm not in lockup because I missed school but because the old lady in the house down the street came home while I was rifling the drawers in her apartment. She should bear some fault for not putting a padlock on her door."

Hearing his words, the young kids who wait to learn their fate exchange a laugh and high fives.

"Order in the court," Tafoya orders, throwing down his gavel. "*Whatever* is not an acceptable response. I'll accept yes or no for an answer."

"Yes."

"Mrs. Salliver, I hope you don't mind my asking what type of environment you were raised in?"

"There was a tree in the middle of the sidewalk, and we had snow in the winter. Our summers were hot, and miller moths moved in with us until October. It was awful. They did the backstroke in our soup and swarmed the outhouse. Did I mention my grandmother lived with us?"

"Not until now."

"She had a green thumb when it came to her tomatoes and cucumbers."

"Were both of your parents living in your home?"

"My dad worked at the rail yard. He left early in the morning and returned home just before dinner. My mom cleaned houses. She always wore an apron with a roll of tissue paper tucked into the front pocket."

"Are you an only child?"

"I have two brothers and a sister who is worthless. She knows only to pop out kids. Other than prostituting, she has never had a job. The state takes care of her and her kids."

"And your brothers?" the judge asks with genuine interest.

"Cedric, he is my oldest brother, works the graveyard shift at a beef-packing plant. Alden is a groundskeeper at a cemetery in Nashville. You would like him. He takes pride in his work. Don't get me started about his wife."

"DeShane, let's talk about your mother. When you were a young child, did she read to you? Take you on walks? Did she tuck you into bed and tell you bedtime stories?"

"She is always drunk and disorderly, and although she argues the truth, she likes pornography. She pretends to be a widow so she can get more money from the state. If she taught me anything, it's a short list. More than once, she reminded me to remove my watch before wiping my ass. We always have toilet problems."

"Not the best advice but one you should adhere to."

"When she got tired of looking at us, she dropped us off at the library. Hell, we weren't old enough to read. She would roll in at closing time, and I'm pretty sure she was either stoned or drunk—possibly both. She barked so much, her teeth jumped out of her mouth."

"I'm sorry to hear this. DeShane, I understand you are abusing drugs. You tested positive for marijuana, spice, fentanyl, and cocaine. Did a doctor prescribe the fentanyl?"

Fearing his words will come back to haunt him, DeShane looks away.

"I'm waiting for an answer," the judge says.

"I get them on the street."

"Are you prepared for an overdose?"

"Overdose? It's not like you can buy fentanyl off the shelf at the grocery store. It moves on side streets, dark alleys, and left in bus station lockers," DeShane shares with a grin. "On a slow day, we target playgrounds and school yards."

"Fentanyl is quickly becoming the number one killer of our young adult population."

"I thought guns and unthinkable crimes held that title."

"They are a close second. Spice is unfamiliar to me."

"Powder or crystals," DeShane offers with a grin. "Easy to move."

"What is it you do when you are not in school or moving illegal drugs?"

"As little as possible," he says, shooting his eyes to the kids who wait in the courtroom's gallery.

"I understand you participated in the center's juvenile art auction. I'm also aware you painted a picture of your mother."

"Bitch was smokin' a joint."

"I have been told yours was the only piece without a bid," the judge says.

"I'm guessing he was stoned," Ramona interrupts. "He thinks he deserves to attend a magnet school. You know, one of those Nelson Mandela high-class public schools."

"Don't listen to her. Every time she opens her mouth, junk falls out," DeShane warns.

"Prior to his time here, how often was he attending school?" the judge asks, ignoring DeShane's outburst.

"He stands in the corner longer and more often than any kid in the entire school district. He has been suspended four times. I'm guessing he was schooled by Hitler. After the last suspension, he never went back." Shuffling about, she missteps when she catches her foot on her umbrella. "It always looks like rain when he's around." Turning toward DeShane, she plants a frown on her face. "Why can't you do white-collar crimes like racketeering, money laundering, or receiving kickbacks?"

Turning away from the judge, DeShane gives his mother the stare down. In her, he sees his future. Together, they are going nowhere. Each time she curses at him, he lets loose the words he knows will send her over the edge and him into hell's raging fire. *Your blood is the poison that runs through me.*

He was just a toddler when he learned to appreciate the picture books his mother lifted from the local library. When he asked her about his father and his absence, he expected to hear his father was away on *Curious George* adventures or diving the Great Barrier Reef with sharks and moray eels. Instead, he was met with a curled lip.

Memories of the year he spent in Mrs. Romero's sixth-grade class flash before his eyes. He wanted to learn from her, and although the opportunity was always present, he failed to grab it. It was by happenstance that he took an interest when she spoke of places far away from Onion Bottom. When she shared a story about her first visit to Memphis while humming her favorite Elvis song, he came to understand staying idle was not in his future.

After an unsuccessful semester in Mr. Martinez's physics class, he was told he would never be inducted into the school's Einstein Club. Days before school let out for the summer, he learned his low grades prevented him from participating in basketball and cross-country, the school's off-campus activities. He accepted he would never be in the top 10 percent of anything until judges handed out trophies instead of warrants. Still, what he wanted most was to cut all ties to Onion Bottom and find a different lot in life.

A cough from his lawyer returns his thoughts to the hearing.

"Mrs. Salliver, I am not in a position at this time to make your son a ward of the state. I suggest you consult with a lawyer or social services," the judge offers.

"I can't afford a lawyer. My son is a predator. Crimes call out to him. He doesn't wait for the light of the moon to travel the streets to sniff out opportunities, and he has no problem committing crimes in broad daylight. After a mass shooting, I'm guessing he will want his mug shot to hold up the wall at the local post office."

"If you are not content with the attorney assigned to your son, there are other attorneys who can help you. When you leave here, take the elevator to the lower level. The clerk at the front desk will be able to assist you."

"Like his tongue, DeShane knows only to lie. Why can't I just immolate him? And what about foster care?"

"She throws out orders like she is the second-grade line leader," DeShane says under his breath. "When I look to my future, I don't see her in it."

Tired of the prattle, Tafoya hurries to end his line of questioning. Years on the bench tells him foolish talk leads to nowhere. A glance at the calendar on his desk reminds him he has twenty-two cases on the docket—the same number as yesterday—the same number each and every day in the foreseeable future. "Mrs. Salliver, I believe the term you are referring to is emancipate. Unfortunately, I can't rule on this today."

"Judge, you're missing my point. He's been riding the crime wave from the day he took his first step. I don't want him in my house. Can I leave him with you?"

"No, ma'am. Please understand there is a marked difference between missing your point and not agreeing with it," he answers in a low voice. "I believe you will agree it's time to focus on family restoration. We are working to expand our facility, and we have a line waiting outside the door and around the corner. It continues to be our goal to rehabilitate the youth who enter here and, when applicable, preserve the family unit. That said, your son is to be released to your care. Please be sure he checks in with his probation officer as instructed," he says, throwing DeShane a look he is to understand means business. "Mr. Salliver, these forms indicate you are sixteen. Is this correct?"

"Yep."

"Again, yep is not a word. We say *yes*."

"Yes."

"When you arrived here, you were searched, processed, and outfitted in the standard-issue orange jumpsuit. Our goal was to help you learn the skills to treat others with dignity and respect. It appears in your brief stay here that we failed to rehabilitate you. I worry the next time you come before the court, the charges against you will be criminal. Given the seriousness of your offenses, I worry you will stick with a routine you believe works in your favor—lather, rinse, repeat. I will say this: we have failed to see anything good or positive in you. This is where you decide if you are going to stop at the corner or run the red light," Tafoya says, shooting tired eyes to Ramona. "I hope when your son walks out of this courtroom, he will embrace a better life—one filled with wise choices. Should he choose a different path, I worry he will go from being a juvenile delinquent to fugitive status. If he continues on this journey, it is likely he will run out of people who care about him."

"Ain't that the truth," Ramona says, waving her arms about.

"When it comes to our family and breaking bad news, my mom slides into the role of a switchboard operator," DeShane shares without guilt. "She would rather share our problems than work to fix them."

"Your Honor, he has been coddling his whole life."

"I believe you mean coddled. Do you know the meaning of coddled?"

"I'm no Noah Webster, but I believe it means he has been torturing animals and stealing from the neighbors."

"I suggest we move on. Mrs. Salliver, it appears you have surrendered your role as a parent. I hope our time here today will have you stepping up to the plate. Children and teens need structure and routine. It is also vital that they receive love, encouragement, and support. Perhaps you should consider family counseling." Pausing, the judge closes the file. "Before you leave here, check in with your son's probation officer. There will be forms to sign and conditions to follow."

4

Shuffling about in tired shoes several sizes smaller than his feet, DeShane steps out of the courthouse, where he kicks traffic cones and window peeks into several parked cars. Painting a smile on his face, he casually walks his way into freedom and onto a waiting bus that will return him to his home in the hood. Biting his tongue, he curses his mother and the life he was born into. The look on his mother's face tells him she has already forgotten about the legal help the judge mentioned. Instead, she is counting on fingers his many shortcomings. When she turns to him, he shoves a finger in his ear.

"You will never amount to anything," she throws out, chewing on a toothpick. A two-pack-a-day smoker, Ramona has not stopped for a breath of air since she landed on the sidewalk. Upset that she is forced to keep him under her thumb, she gives him a wallop upside his head.

"Knock it off," he barks, dodging her open hand. "And get off your soapbox."

"You don't talk to me like that," she orders, popping him on the mouth. "When you act like this, you don't deserve anything—no dinner and no warm bed."

"Ketchup on a cracker isn't dinner. And quit screaming at me like you're coming off the pages of *Chicken Little.*"

"I don't know *Chicken Little*, but that witch should know it's my house and I make the rules," she says with a puzzling look. Before taking her next breath, she circles around him like she is drawing a chalk line. "You will never be the pretty boy at the prom. You are ugly inside and out."

"I don't care about prom. As for dinner, even on your best day, our meals come out of a tin can."

"It's my can."

"Are you ever going to do the laundry? I've worn these jeans for three weeks."

"When you fill your pockets with quarters, you can wash your own clothes. You should be grateful for the Laundromat we have. When I was your age, we threw our clothes over a thin clothesline. Sometimes our clothes—underwear included—went missing."

"I'm tired of sleeping in Marshall's pee. I've become a puddle jumper. I wake up smelling like that metal shed near the river. Maybe you should put him back in those plastic bags you used for diapers. And why are you so cheap? You never buy our school pictures."

"I know what you look like. Like I told that judge, I'm guessing there will come a time I will admire your *wanted photo* on a post office wall. And you wet the bed until you were ten."

"That was because I was afraid of you."

"Listen here, you best button your lip. If you don't like it here, you can march right back to juvie," she shouts, "and if you don't like that arrangement, you can live under a bridge for all I care."

"Tent town?"

"Yep. Do we understand each other?"

"You heard the judge—*yep* isn't a word."

"Don't you get smart with me. When you leave, you can take Marshall with you. I'll find a way to love him from a distance."

Feeling the sting, he raises his hand to strike but backs off when she waves his release papers in his face.

"You take one more step, and I'm calling the cops."

"Whatever," he says. "I'm not going back to juvie. If you put me out on the street, your monthly check from the state will take a hit."

"It will be worth it to be rid of you."

Familiar with the route, he knows the bus will make several stops before he can escape his mother and her never-ending criticism.

"I'll say this: if that judge thinks he has seen the last of me, he has another thing coming," Ramona whispers for all to hear.

Catching DeShane by surprise, she grabs his ear and gives it a forceful pinch. "You better start looking for a place to live. And don't be thinking you can take anything with you."

"You just said I could have Marshall."

"Boy, you are asking for it, and you're about to get it."

"Like I would want a soiled mattress or the sheet covering it. You are always raising holy hell about something. You are quick to point fingers, criticize my actions, and ready to throw me to the curb. I'm guessing you didn't take any parenting classes."

"If you think things are so bad at home, I'll ask the bus driver to drop you off at a shelter."

"At least I will get a hot meal and sleep in a dry bed. I'm gonna buy me a pop-up trailer and travel the world. Just you wait and see."

"Listen up, you little gangster. You came into this world crying like a sissy, and I'm betting my bottom dollar you'll leave the same way."

"I'm guessing it's true: *mama always loves the baby.*"

5

Always on the hunt for a set of wheels, DeShane crosses over a nameless road littered with sinkholes and fallen branches, leading him to Onion Bottom, an area known for its drug dealers and punk street gangs. It is not on any map, but its visitors know it well.

He is resting on a bench at the city's park when a group of middle schoolers catch his eye. Left unattended, the children dash over the worn grass, dumping trash cans along the way. Minutes later, when they scramble, DeShane lifts off the bench and shuffles over to the crime scene they left behind. Raising a foot, he drop-kicks a traffic cone into the street.

Up ahead, he is drawn to a woman who is dotting an art canvas with a brush she dips into the paint palette resting on a folding table. Picking up his pace, he crosses over to the woman, where he flips the easel on its side.

"What are you doing, young man?" the woman asks.

"Give it up. You ain't no Van Gogh."

Startled by his actions and his words, the woman grabs the canvas and the easel and races off to the safety of her car.

Out of the corner of his eye, DeShane spies an elderly man resting on a weathered park bench. He is drawn to the cigarette pinched between his withered lips and the beer can in his aging hand. Filled with curiosity, he watches the old man fish the park's shallow lake. Canvasing the area, he makes his way to the water's edge.

"Give me that," he says, pointing to the fishing pole.

"Young man, I need this old pole. This is how I eat."

"I said give it to me. I need to eat too."

Feeling threatened, the old man drops the pole and steps back.

Baiting the hook, DeShane hurries to cast the line. His first attempt catches a tree's slim branch. Minutes later, when the hook pierces the water, he reels in a small carp. Balancing on the lake's rugged bank, he pulls the hook from the fish's upper lip and tosses the rod aside. Knowing the old man's eyes are on him, he forces a fallen branch into the carp's mouth. When the old man cries out, he tosses the rod into the lake and slaps the fish against a tree. Giving a smirk, he heads out toward the street.

Crossing over the veins in the road, he makes his way to an area once known as Ross's Landing. In its heyday, it was home to employees of refineries once positioned alongside a shallow thumb of the Mississippi River. The yarn mill, a staple that once fed hundreds of families, is now a heap of long-forgotten memories and broken concrete. Left floating on the air, scraps of seasoned plastic embrace the property's overgrown weeds.

After the post office closes its doors at the end of the day, the Bottom comes alive with loitering and petty theft. With little police patrol, its growing homeless population now overflows into slim, dark alleys and long-forgotten streets, where crumbling bridges, tents, and cardboard boxes provide shelter.

For DeShane and his family, they know only to call their subsidized housing their home. As for his friends, they are thick as thieves and as heartless as serial killers.

Every step he takes leads him on the bumpy road known as trouble. Known as Sally on the city's roughest streets, DeShane was crime savvy—mostly petty thefts and threats—long before he reached puberty. Early on in his youth, he made the Bottom his feeding ground.

When the sun begins its descent, teenagers in short skirts display sleeves of tattoos. Flirting with their eyes, they mingle with interested patrons, giving special attention to the naive fools who hurry to open their wallets to prove they can afford the impending gifts they desire. In the rare times DeShane passes by, they huddle together, exchanging a joke he is likely the butt of.

Dragging his feet, he makes his way back home and into his mother's care, where he shares a cot with Marshall, his younger brother, whom the court recently labeled an "unruly child" after finding him habitually disobedient and truant from school.

Eager to learn the ropes and tag along behind his brother and the older boys, young Marshall will celebrate his twelfth birthday in the coming weeks in the company of the neighborhood's infamous juvenile delinquents.

The Sallivers' corner unit receives little light from the room's slim window. Months earlier, when Ramona worried the neighbors were catching a peek, she covered the unit's single window with a stained bedsheet she ripped from the walk-up's shared clothesline. The last of five towers situated along an area where grass gave up growing, the unit's window provides a view of the dumpster vandals recently claimed with graffiti and tenement housing that overshadows their run-down walk-up. Months earlier, when a tenant jumped to his death, the property's upper-level windows were covered with chicken wire.

In recent months, soon after vandals defaced the corner's green-and-white street sign, city officials promised to replace it, along with the burned-out bulb in the street's only lamppost. The city's lack of funds keeps the dark, narrow street unnamed to those who foolishly stumble upon it.

Raised in a duplex in the northern part of town where loud and angry voices were the norm and impossible to ignore, Ramona was the oldest of four children. Fearing her mother's wrath, she often sought refuge in the crawl space under the rental's slim porch. In the hours when she was forced to clean the unit, she dreamed of her future while watching reruns of *I Love Lucy* and *Charlie's Angels* on a boxy black-and-white television that came with the rental. Days after her fourteenth birthday, she experimented with rebellion. When her parents learned of her involvement with a hoodlum from the wrong side of the tracks, they threw Ramona and a plastic bag filled with clothes and distant memories to the curb.

A woman of strong faith, Ramona's mother ran a tight ship, and when someone rocked the boat, the whole family suffered. Standing five feet tall, she applied a strip of duct tape to her bangs each night before going to bed, and in the morning, she smeared a thick layer of wax over her thin brows. Each time she stepped into the sunlight, she wore the look of surprise.

When the day came for young Ramona to meet the man who would later become her children's father, she envisioned a two-bedroom apartment with a working toilet, running water in the kitchen, and a color television with a remote control. If this mystery man was willing to put in a little effort, she wanted a porch with a swing and a ceiling fan. Pennies remaining would pay for a car with a running engine and balanced tires. When she stretched her dreams, she imagined a gold band around her finger and a flashy gold watch that kept time.

In the end, when the love of her life abandoned her for sharp needles, an endless supply of heroin, a carpeted refrigerator box, and the woman who would later saddle him with two negligent sons and a daughter who knew only to beg, borrow, and steal, she was left fighting syphilis, gonorrhea, and two monsters strapped to her leg.

6

Slamming the refrigerator's door, Ramona stomps over the floor like a Berber horse out to win a chariot race. Seconds later, when she forces her wide hips through the bathroom's narrow opening, she falls to the toilet seat, where, once her pants reach the bend in her knees, she stretches a thick arm for a pack of cigarettes she keeps tucked under the unit's cracked floorboard. Throwing her head back, she holds the first drag. Exercising yoga's downward dog, she eases tired shoulders. Leaning against the tank, she blows smoke rings into the air and chips the polish off unkempt nails.

Cigarette butts decorate the wall opposite the toilet. Those times when she was stuck on the toilet and desperate for a drag, she lit up a soiled stub she put out days earlier.

Sharp edges on the seat's torn cushion pinch tender flesh every time she shifts about. She intended to replace the padded seat when she moved into the unit years earlier, but DeShane and his menu of poor choices got in the way. Throwing her weight to the left, she looks out to the living room. She is surprised to find him where she left him.

"Mom? I'm home," Marshall calls out. "I'm hungry."

"They are supposed to feed you at school."

"They did, but I'm still hungry."

"Did you get breakfast?"

"Yeah."

"What was on your tray?"

"Apple juice, orange slices, and a waffle stick with an egg."

"I don't understand why you are complaining. That's more than I had."

"What did you have?"

"Coffee and a green banana. What did you eat at lunch?"

"Turkey and rice, cucumber circles, and carrots. The carrots were nasty."

"They are free."

"Still nasty."

"Did you get an after-school snack?"

"Only if you call jicama sticks a snack."

"What in the hell is a jicama stick?"

"I've been told it's a potato."

"There is food in the icebox," she shouts, exhaling a plume of smoke into the air.

"Where?" he asks, placing a jar of grape jelly on the kitchen's plywood countertop. "Why are you saving all of these safety pins?" he asks, eyeing the silver pins stuck in the wall.

"Use your eyes. That's why God gave them to you. And safety pins are hard to come by. There is a can of leftover noodles on the top shelf next to the mousetrap."

Straining to hear the commotion outside the open door, Ramona puts an ear to the wall. "Did you find it?"

"Nothing in here but a jar of mustard and a ball of fur," a soft voice answers. "After my trip to the emergency room, I'm afraid to eat leftovers. I'm tired of always being hungry."

"Hey, this isn't some fancy mansion. You best be grateful for the food in your belly and a roof over your head. If you keep complaining, I'll feed you ricin."

"Coming from someone who never skips the chow line," DeShane says in a voice above a whisper. "Given that you color your hair in the kitchen sink, I'm guessing this dump will never be featured in any design magazine. And stop serving us wet cat food."

"It's what I can afford. One can costs seventy-six cents."

"It's probably cheaper at the Tractor Supply store. Either way, I want real tuna. As for ricin, you know it will kill us."

"What was that, boy?"

"Nothing. I didn't say nothing."

"Don't you talk to me like that. God gave me these two hands so I can beat the shit out of you. One more word out of you, and I'm gonna serve up a can of whoop ass like you have never seen before. If you don't believe me, try me. If that doesn't suit your fancy, I have a tin of creamed possum. All you have to do is add water. While you are enjoying the comforts of this here castle—"

"Castle? We live in a mouse-infested unit some would call shoddy. This dump will never have air-conditioning, sconces on the wall, or shag carpet under our feet."

"What do you know about sconces?"

"Only that we will never have one. Every day, I'm reminded that we rely on welfare and food stamps. Can you once not overwater the grits and pull back on the salt you throw on those thin patties you sweep up at the corner market near the river? Every time I take a bite, I worry food poisoning will take my life."

"You ain't ever gonna say something I want to hear, so shut that big trap of yours. If you think your skinny ass can tell me how to run my house and prepare my meals, you have another thing coming. And stop kissing dumb girls. I worry you will get one of them pregnant."

"Don't go throwing dirt on me. I wasn't a bad seed until you planted me. And Shasta is not dumb."

"She has a baby!"

"No, she doesn't."

"I'm betting she is aiming for you to father her first child."

"Forget about her. Making a baby ain't happening. She wears a Mickey Mouse watch and listens to iTunes."

"When it comes to surviving, she is a leech. She pretends to be a victim born into a lost, greedy, and negative generation. When forced to answer for her mistakes, she knows only to cry fake tears. Santa's elves would kick her greedy ass to the curb. When the truth of her poor choices surface, she argues her right to public assistance and welfare. When you learn to control your private parts and make better choices, you might find a way to be productive."

"For real? Like you are one to talk. Every time your lips move, you burn a path of fire," he says, rolling his eyes. "You've never met with any of my teachers or taken an interest in me."

"You and Marshall were born during my marriage. To be clear, I didn't meet with your teachers because I was meeting with the principal, and later, when you carved out a life of crime, my hours were spent explaining your actions to your probation officer. We spent so much time together we spoke on a first-name basis," she says. "What I wouldn't have given to have been blessed with a daughter."

"Knowing your evil mind and your empty pockets, I'm guessing you would have pimped her out."

"If you know what is good for you, you best zip your lips and toe the line. Let me remind you I'm the one wearing the crown."

"Along with a few extra pounds," he mumbles under his breath. "Our *castle* offers a view of a train depot across the street, a bird's-eye view of prostitutes selling their goods on the nearest street corner, and a reminder that the abandoned trestle bridge stretching over the river is littered with used condoms, empty whiskey bottles, and a map of false promises. In case you have not noticed, the lumberyard on the corner continues to post signs letting the lost and lonely, and the unemployed, know it is not hiring. And I hate that skirt lamp," he says, pointing to the bent lamp his mother swept up from the curb just after dawn. "Most of my friends have a television. Are we ever going to have one?"

"There is nothing stopping you from moving in with them. As for the lamp, it was free, and it lights up the room."

"I hate the lamp, and the fringe shade is ugly. I'm guessing that is why the lamp was tossed to the curb on garbage day."

"If something is eating at you, tell it to someone who cares. I have my own set of problems, and you top the list."

"Game on," he says, throwing out the middle-finger salute. "And I would like a new pillowcase. Marshall boogers up my pillow."

"When I'm done here, I'll sew one for you."

"I wish Dad had taken me with him," DeShane says under his breath.

"It's never too late. You can probably catch up with him at a titty bar."

Unaware his mother is still on the toilet, he imagines her in the tub. The image of sagging breasts and rolls of fat makes him cringe. Now, each time he pokes a toe into the chipped, porcelain tub, a shiver runs through him. The water is always cold, and from Thursday through Sunday, it smells like pickled onions and sauerkraut. His mother is convinced the building's old pipes and runoff water have something to do with the odor.

"If I'm going back to school, I'll need running shoes. I want to sign up for track," DeShane says, lifting his voice.

"I'll knit you a pair," she answers with her usual sarcasm.

"Is that a no?"

"You don't need to run track. You can speed walk to school. If you don't like that, you can chase after the bus." A pull at the toilet's thin chain has Ramona cursing. "Damn thing never works right."

When the chain breaks from the lever and drops from her hand, she inhales the cigarette's last drag. Letting go an audible sigh, she drops the butt into the running toilet. When the toilet coughs up her deposit, along with those of their neighbors, a quick glance lets her know the chain is long gone.

"DeShane, run next door and tell old man Sweatt the toilet needs fixing again. While you're at it, tell him the icebox is on the outs," she yells into the small space between them. "Before you go, hide the cable behind the couch. No reason for rumors to get started."

"He hates coming here when you have a problem. Every time I knock at his door, he reminds me he doesn't work here and he doesn't have a box filled with tools and spare parts. Are we ever going to have a bathroom door? I don't like talking to you while you're sitting on your throne."

"Want, want, want. That's all I ever hear from you. Listen up, you little wise ass. You have been nothing but trouble since you escaped the womb. Do you wanna hear the words I'm holding on the back of my tongue?" she says, throwing down the iron hand.

"Am I gonna get a bar of soap on mine?"

"Listen here, smarty-pants. You are acting too big for your britches. When you have a place of your own, you can have as many doors as you want."

"I'm going to live on a grand estate with a helicopter pad overlooking the river where syringes, soda cans, and food wrappers don't litter the street. If space allows, I'm gonna build a fireplace like the one at the Izaak Walton. Keeping with tradition, it will be built with stones from every state. I'll host catered dinner parties where a band plays soft music in the living room's corner. When I'm not traveling the world, I'll play croquet on the lawn. When the weather heats up, I'll float in my pool. My kitchen will be the envy of every chef. The shelves in my refrigerator will be lined with food, and I might just have a pantry. Until then, I'll pay a visit to Ruby. She makes the best vegetable soup."

"Who is Ruby?"

"She lives in the unit next door."

"With old man Sweatt?"

"She is the lady with the stomach problems. She has a mannequin in her kitchen she calls Alice. She spent an hour trying to convince me Alice prepares all of her meals, including her vegetable soup. In her spare time, when her daily soaps are over and Judge Judy owns the moment, Ruby shops estate sales. The shelves in her apartment tell me she has a liking for tea kettles and coloring books."

"Where does this Ruby get the money to shop estate sales?"

"She works the food line in the school's cafeteria. Unlike you, she is making an honest living."

"What are you doing in this old woman's apartment?" Ramona asks, planting her hands on her hips.

"Slurping vegetable soup."

"Your future is flatter than a flit, and you will eat table scraps off the floor. What do you know about pantries? Don't bother with an answer. Your forked tongue knows only to lie to me. Only rich people know about traditions and croquet. Your actions tell me your lawn will be a concrete pad inside prison gates. If you ever get a job, you will be paid by the hour."

"Only whores and lawyers charge by the hour."

"Tell that to the next lawyer who throws down my hard-earned money to bail your ass out of jail. Other than securing the lock on the door and turning off the lights before bedtime, we don't have any traditions. Look around you. This hacienda is your castle. Until you win the lottery, you'll never have more than a shopping cart. If that's not in your future, you can canoe on down the river. Better still, you can get yourself a rubber inner tube from the tire repair shop over in the high-rent district. You know, the one near the grand estate you will never be able to afford. You won't be overlooking the river, but you will be floating on it. Hell, you'll probably bathe in it. If money is tight, you might just fish for your dinner."

"Just you wait and see." In a flash, his thoughts return to the old man and the fish he stabbed. "When the time comes, I will walk away from this dump and your constant criticism. Something tells me I'll never look back."

"Now, that is something I want to see. When the time comes, remind me to throw on my eyeglasses. If case you haven't noticed, we don't live in the land of milk and honey. Kids don't ride bikes, skateboard, or run barefoot through the neighborhood. Once the ice-cream truck silences its bell and hurries to pass over the streets leading him to Onion Bottom, he never lets go of the steering wheel. I've come to notice that UPS and FedEx never leave a package at our front door. The best we get is a sealed envelope offering a past-due notice and a request for payment."

"You don't have to remind me. I learned early on that we struggle in the zip code of single parenting, drug abuse, poverty, and unthinkable crimes. What is the legal age when I can run away from home?"

"When the day comes when you find yourself famous and your pockets full of money, you can run away and reinvent yourself. You can be darn sure I won't be throwing my hard-earned money your way. Have I made myself clear?"

"Crystal."

DeShane's thoughts turn to the day his mother returned home from work swinging a coiled cable at her side like a roping cowboy with a brand-spanking-new lasso. He watched in curiosity when she moved the thin cable through the door's slide lock. When she offered a bit of hocus-pocus, he rolled his eyes and turned away. When he looked back, a padlock appeared in her hand. She popped the lock with a thin key she pulled from the breast pocket of her blouse. Positioned like a bantam rooster, she stood all-knowing and ready for a cockfight.

"Why are you still sitting here?" she asks, giving his feet a shove. "Quit jackin' around. I told you to go next door. Don't make me get the frying pan."

"That's right up there in your book of dumb questions. As for the frying pan, I've been told it can be used for food other than bologna and onions."

"Listen up, you little shit. I'm not asking you to go next door. I'm telling you. If you know what's good for you, you'll get up off your ass and get moving," she says, throwing out her hand and pinching his cheek. "Something tells me you are not long on this earth. When we celebrate your death, you will leave here dressed in a wifebeater T-shirt and laid out in a rented casket."

"What are you smoking? You can't rent a casket."

"Oh, but you can. When your funeral service is over, your body will be cremated, and I'll flush your ashes down the toilet. To be clear, I've washed my hands of you and your string of mistakes."

"The toilet is not working."

"Best not cop an attitude with me. You sass me one more time, and I will bury your ass deep inside the city dump."

"You are the reason my dad isn't here," he says, recalling the penciled words his father left behind. "He couldn't take one second more of your constant nagging, yammering, and mean-spirited words. Do not get me started on your fried foods and skillet meals."

"Don't go pinning the blame on me. I don't nag, and I sure as hell don't yammer. You wanna know the truth? He couldn't take one more day with you. All you did was cry. Doctor said you had colic. A bullet to your father's head had him running away from his obligations."

"I was sort of hoping you would say *his family*."

"Don't kid yourself. Family means nothing to him. All he wants is a peep show and a needle in his arm. He's always catting around."

"I'd settle for that. I'd give anything to get you off my back. I'd consider it a gift."

"The needle in your arm is gonna be a gift from the state."

Careful to hide his anger, DeShane lifts off the sofa. "Come on, Marshall. Walk out with me."

Trained to trust his older brother, Marshall rocks off the couch.

"Listen, I'm going out for a while. Whatever you do, don't let Momma put the lock on the door," he whispers on the flip side of the door. "Don't worry. I'll be back."

7

The city is celebrating Labor Day weekend when DeShane is summoned to the Village, a crime-ridden region leading to nowhere. Empty promises and the threat of bodily harm welcome those who dare to enter.

Years earlier, when a gang of social misfits fired shots into a parade of youngsters on their way to the grand opening of the neighborhood's first playground, an order went down in the police station that the area was to be avoided at all costs. Today, children skip alongside drug dealers and strung-out users.

Often compared to a garden gnome and with skin so white it glows in the dark, Pugs rubs at the whiskers on his chin. "Word on the street is that a stately house pushed up against the river and Prentice Cooper State Forest is unoccupied," he says, chewing on a bone the size of a puzzle piece. "We're moving in on a small troop arrangement. No need to alert the neighbors."

"The high-rent district? Are you saying we have neighbors to contend with?" Red asks through jacked-up teeth that rarely get a brushing.

"Can't agree or disagree. The house is on Browns Ferry Road," Pugs shares, reading off the address.

Years earlier, when Pugs fell into the life of crime, he did not give his criminal network a big, fancy name. Instead, he armed his thieves with .22 semiautomatics with silencers, crowbars, brass knuckles, and long-bladed knives. The nearest rival is across town in a poverty-stricken area much like the Village. The misfits near the rail yard are known for their extreme violence. On a slow day, when trouble takes a day off, they hone their skills by killing stray dogs and skinning feral cats and, when obedience training is thrown on the table, slicing up one of their own.

In recent weeks, its members fired loaded BB guns at moving vehicles. While people cried out in fear, they shot out storefront windows and ransacked big-box stores and neighboring boutiques. Target practice ended when a patrol car was shot up. A search of one of the shooter's pockets uncovered blotter paper tabs laced with LSD. When the young kid was questioned, he boasted the blotter paper was double dipped—a gift to the user. The crime lab reported the substance was a synthetic hallucinogen. The kid now spends his days awaiting trial and chewing away at thickened toenails.

"Red, take a car out for a test drive—just don't alert the owner," Pugs says, rubbing at bulbous eyes that hint of Crohn's disease. "Better still, grab a van. We might need the extra space." The creases in his forehead deepen, his jowls sway from east to west, and the ring of wiry hair hugging his head pirouettes like a ballerina's tutu. "Get a dark one. Search the strip center at the corner of McCallie Avenue and North Highland Park and hospital parking lots. An increase in badges over in Orchard Knob tells me we've worn out our welcome," he says, shooting his eyes to Hank. "Park near the forest. Take Sally with you. Stay low and go in from the back. The driveway wraps around the garage. It's wide like an alley."

"An alley?" DeShane repeats with a puzzling look. Years earlier, as a young boy, he watched his mother become a victim of a purse snatching. A knife at her throat left him hating back streets and gangway corridors. Each time he passes by a sketchy side street, he is reminded nothing good comes from traveling dark roads and forgotten streets. Today, his crime of choice is smashing car windows and robbing glove compartments and loaded trunks.

"A narrow road that often travels behind a row of houses, you idiot," Pugs says. "Flapping your wings about, you flit about from one place to another. I'll be the first to spit out that you are not a hummingbird. To be respected as a man, you need to learn the lay of the land. Gates and cameras are there for a reason. The homeowner is protecting his assets. He may not know it, but where I come from, his property is my target. I'm betting he has cash and jewelry tucked under the floor in his closet or in an air vent in a room he believes people like me would never search. Start with the laundry room. If that fails to offer cash or trinkets, move onto an office. If the house has one, search the nursery. Sally, what do you have in your tool bag?"

"I was hoping I'd learn how to hot-wire a car," DeShane says, looking down at his feet.

"You are still green behind the ears. This game is too big for you. I asked about your tools."

"I have a crowbar, pliers, a slide hammer, wire cutters, and a torch that burns through concrete."

"When it comes to hot-wiring a car, a smidgeon of error will have you pleading your innocence while your wrists are anchored in cuffs. It is rumored a shadow of doubt will not set you free. In the blink of an eye, the police will have you bending over. Before you can call your attorney, they will slap on spurs. You gotta know the difference between being patient and wasting your time. You also have to take a minute to revisit your life skills. Hot-wiring a car is not in your future, and if you know what's good for you, you will stop wasting my time."

"He's a burner," Red says. "He likes his marijuana and my fentanyl. I've been told he vapes."

"Sally, are you a coward or a sissy?" Hank asks, letting go a laugh. "We don't vape. We put a match to that bitch. I've been told you keep battery-operated hand warmers in your undies."

"Front pouch or backside?" Red asks.

"I'm guessing his backside."

Hank, whose given name is Juan Jurado, is a petty drug dealer. Red earned his nickname years earlier when he was teased about the fiery red hair he inherited from someone other than his parents. Sitting side by side, they exchange a high five.

Remaining in the shadows, Kleppy is the quiet one. He earned his name due to his fingering skills. Although DeShane has never met Kleppy's younger brother, who is known as *the rectal rocket*, he knows how he earned his name.

Red in the face, DeShane knows all eyes are on him. Although a chill runs through him, he feels the burn. Understanding the order is a reprimand, he lets loose his posture. Last week's close call with the police put him on Pugs's shit list. After several misdials, he learned any and all challenges come with a price he can't afford to pay. A pinch in his chest reminds him he does not want to put his brother in harm's way. He would give darn near anything to shrink into the shadows and escape unnoticed. Damp with worry, he tries to hide the beads of sweat traveling above his lip. The pounding in his chest is making his temperature rise. Afraid to wipe at the growing bead of sweat above his brow, he turns away.

"Wake up, boy. You don't think I see inside that nine pounds of empty space you carry on your shoulders? I was you once. My skin might not be the color of yours, but my heart is just as angry. The difference between us is I think before I act, and I've learned that both bullshit and experience are learning tools. You should know I've grown a spine. I'm never going back to a two-man cell, and I sure as hell won't count out my last days on death row. You need me to say it any clearer?" Stroking Bert, a dalmatian so fat he is often mistaken for a Holstein heifer, Pugs skips over a pause for a response he knows will not come. "You can be angry, but you better be smart. If you wanna stay in this action, you best wise up. And don't be like Stovall," he adds, referencing a punk kid who tried convincing him that a sandwich bag filled with freshly cut grass was marijuana. Never one to mince words or let a mistake slide, Pugs jabs a fat finger against DeShane's sunken chest. "Don't screw up this time, you hear me?"

"I hear you."

Feeling the heat and knowing all eyes are on him, DeShane turns his eyes to Bert. He has always wanted a dog, but his mother continues to remind him that they are too much work. She laughed in his face when he promised to care for the dog.

"Hey, Pugs. I'll take Sally around back if you want me to," Dynamite Dean offers, waving a book of matches in the air. "You should have seen that alley cat last night when I threw a match to his tail. He was running around in circles like he was on fire."

"Was he?"

"Damn straight."

8

A trio of streetlamps light up the night, the homes along Browns Ferry Road, and its neighboring park. The target house looks out at the Tennessee River. The home's grand porch stretches the length of a basketball court, and double doors wait to welcome invited guests.

Moving around to the garage, DeShane admires a Mercedes convertible resting on a bed of cinder blocks. A battered tarp meant to protect the car's canvas hood has seen better days. *HASBENZ*, the car's personalized tag, invites a chuckle, but because he is not car savvy, its humor is lost on him.

As the moon rises over the park, DeShane imagines the wealthy people who call this neighborhood their home. Something tells him they do not look like him. Taking refuge behind a row of budding magnolias, he checks the time on his watch. The timepiece tells him he is three minutes ahead of schedule. Lying low, he throws a match to Bad Betty—a strain of marijuana he has been warned will mess with his head.

"Go in just as we planned," Hank says, coming up behind him.

Hoisting a rock he lifts from a forgotten garden, DeShane pitches it against the door's paned glass. When he doesn't hear an alarm or the bark of a disgruntled dog caught by surprise, he elbows the window. When he finds the thumb-turn deadbolt—the dream lock of every burglar—he throws out a fist pump.

On the flip side of the door, he plants his feet and bends an ear. Hearing a rhythmic beep, he holds his breath. Fearing someone might come charging at him, he presses against the wall. When no one shows, he glances at his wrist. An upturned smile comes over his damp face. Unlike the gold timepiece he lifted weeks earlier from a nearby gym, the bling on his wrist is still ticking. Counting on fingers, a habit he learned from his mother and his first-grade teacher failed to correct, lets him know Red will arrive any minute, bringing with him the getaway van he was hot-wiring when Hank dropped him off at a hospital near East Third Street.

Laid out hours earlier with white chalk on a floor littered with fast-food wrappers and empty tequila bottles, the plan is to take what they can carry and easily sell. His job is to escape with televisions, computers, cameras, jewelry, and his personal favorite—weapons. Guns are easy to sell, and none of their buyers squeal when caught with a hot pistol. If the heat with shiny badges comes knocking, a hot trigger finds its way into the deep end of the nearest river.

Careful to stay low, he again turns his ears. He wants to believe they are alone in the house, but a pungent odor warns a different truth. A passing cockroach sends a chill up his spine. Images of dead rats, cats, and a web of leggy spiders have him on high alert. Although he is new to the game, he believes the house has already been ransacked.

Rounding the corner, his eyes fall on a muddied running shoe— its tongue tangled up in the laces. A tube sock hugs the wall. Catching his foot on an extension cord, he falls hard to his knees where he army crawls over the rug. Repeating the words he was instructed to put to memory puts a pinch in his heart. While his eyes adjust to the low lighting and the faint sliver the distant streetlight offers, his thoughts turn to the many differences between privileged people and those born into a life like the troubled one he hopes to escape.

Entering the kitchen, he allows the ice dispenser's low light to guide him along a narrow hall that appears to serve as a gateway to several rooms. In his next breath, he is slammed with the stench of rotting flesh. Working through dry heaves, he struggles to right himself. Shaking off an uneasy feeling, he wipes his shoes over the carpet. Inching along the hall, he is surprised when a door yawns open. He considers bolting from the house, but knowing Pugs will not offer understanding, he uses his elbow to widen the gap.

A thin slice of light peeks through a small opening in the curtains on the room's far wall. Creeping along, he is hit with an awful odor. Throwing a hand to his face, he pinches his nostrils. Though several thoughts rush at him, he believes a toilet has overflowed or Pugs has been here.

Pugs, whose real name is unknown to him but rumored to be Dwight, rules the Village. Resembling an alpaca, his halo of hair meets his full beard below his ears. A big man with rolls of fat under his chin, around his middle, and below his belt, there is never a time he does not smell of fried onions, garlic, and Sackie's Fish Market—a quick-stop shop Pugs once robbed. Although he found himself only three dollars richer, brandishing a weapon landed him in juvie.

Soon after joining the gang, DeShane heard Pugs made it all the way through the eighth grade before dropping out of the Title 1 school designed to educate students from low-income families. Pugs is often heard saying that living on the street taught him all he needs to know. Never a good student, he walked off the school's campus and away from education at the onset of his freshman year. Pride, along with recurring nightmares of his time spent in detention, keeps him from going back.

Needing both hands to carry valuables he has yet to secure, DeShane pulls the collar of his shirt up and over his nose. When a rancid odor fills his nostrils, he swallows back vomit. Recalling the afternoon when he stepped on a decaying rodent in the dry ravine behind his apartment, he again forces bile down his throat. The rat's lingering odor forced him to toss his only shoes into the dumpster.

His movements now swift, he searches the bedside table. When he finds the top drawer empty, he pulls at the drawer nearest the floor.

A can of nasal spray, a worn emery board, and a book of matches from Fat Freddie's, a tavern near the westbound train station, stare back at him.

A flip of the switch has his eyes growing wide and nostrils flaring. A bedside lamp is overturned, and the bedsheets are torn from the mattress. Crossing over the unmade bed, he throws open the side table's slim drawer. Finding it empty, he pulls the drawer from its tight hold and throws it to the floor. Shards of glass below the window lets him know somebody beat Pugs to the job.

"Hank, you might want to see this," he shouts down the hall.

"What the hell?" Hank asks, entering the room.

"Turf battle."

"What does that mean?"

"Marking their territory. Pugs isn't going to be happy about this. If he learns he was double-crossed, heads will roll, and there will be hell to pay. I hope he lets us keep our limbs."

In a room down the hall, a built-in television cabinet holds dust, a collection of *Kill Bill* videos, and a smear of fingerprints but no television. Overturned chairs and throw pillows litter the floor. A kaleidoscope of gang symbols sends a message meant to instill fear.

Damaged paintings and portraits and deep cuts in the drywall send a shiver through DeShane's thin frame. A crimson stain on the area rug has his stomach in knots. Looking to the bed, his heart suffers a painful pinch before skipping a beat. He wipes at uncertain eyes and moves toward the bed. His eyes travel over the bloody arm peeking out from under the bedsheet before taking a crash landing on the naked body. A pool of blood suggests the young boy had been emasculated and left for dead.

Racing from the room, DeShane catches his sleeve on the jimmied doorjamb. Losing his balance, he is thrown to his knees. A warm flow traveling along his leg tells him he skinned more than his arm. A jolting sensation up his leg confirms his knee has taken a blow. Pursing his lips, he curses his bad luck. One thing is certain—a single drop of blood is sure to stir up trouble. Breaking and entering will land him back in juvie, and a dead body will have him strapped to the electric chair. Moving at the speed of lightning, he hightails it out the door.

9

A blend of sweat, skunkweed, and a thick cloud of flatulence drifts freely throughout the house on Gunbarrel Road. It is only now DeShane recalls hearing the many reasons the city deemed the house condemned. In recent years, gangs and drug dealers have controlled East Brainerd, an unincorporated community consisting of roughly four thousand families. Murders and burglaries happen daily, and although it is not always reported, rape and child trafficking are on the rise.

"We were late to the job. The house was ransacked, and a dead body was left behind," Hank says. "They slashed the walls and destroyed the art."

"You gotta be kidding me. Those paintings were worth a fortune," Pugs says, waving a fisted hand through the air. "I was told there were works painted by Michelangelo, Monet, and Henri Matisse."

"Place was tossed and messed up. Gang symbols painted the walls."

"You recognize the work?"

"I'm pretty sure Finch had his hand in it. I've been told he is the best porch pirate in town."

Hearing Finch's name, DeShane looks about the room. He met Finch months back, but his name has not been mentioned since Pugs kicked him and his cheating ways to the curb. It takes only a moment for his mind to race with images of the actions Pugs will take should he get his hands on Finch. History reminds that brass knuckles thrown to Finch's face will freckle the walls with blood, tender bones will break, and any begging Finch can manage through a broken jaw will go ignored. What little is left of Finch's body will likely be turned over to Dynamite Dean.

"Hank, go find that little bastard and bring him here. Take Sally with you," Pugs orders. "I'll give Finch an ass whooping he will never forget. You can be damn sure he will never double-cross me again. You might visit his old lady. If she doesn't get all pissy, you might suggest she should start planning his funeral. You might mention Dead Man's Park. It doesn't require a casket. What's left of his body can be buried in a shallow grave filled with sand or dumped into the Tennessee River. As for you, Sally, if you mess up, I'll give your ass the same whooping I'll be giving Finch."

"I think Sally would prefer the shallow grave. I hear he can't swim to save his life," Hanks says, thinking about the possibilities.

"When I'm through with him, there won't be any life to save," Pugs says, stroking Bert.

10

While their hearts are breaking, Glenn and Suzanne Urling stand shoulder to shoulder in the hospital's critical care unit.

Each time the nursing staff locks eyes with Suzanne and Glenn, they hurry to look away. The words they offered hours earlier were not filled with hope and promise but love, support, comfort, and understanding. Losing a loved one is not new to them, but in this case, they share Suzanne and Glenn's pain.

11

In the distance, a train's rumbling whistle interrupts the silence. Waking from a drug-induced sleep, DeShane rubs dry and filthy hands over his face. He cannot be certain which hurts most—the cramp in his arm or the pain in his knee. A dry swallow reminds him his tongue is thick with pot residue, and his breath smells of greasy burgers and cheap beer. A lick of his lips hints a sip of water just might be the cure his aching body needs to heal open wounds.

Getting his bearings, he turns over onto his side. Arching his foot and stretching his toes, he allows a wide yawn to open his face. A timely glance in the mirror exposes bloodshot eyes, chapped lips, and a mop of unkempt hair. Struggling to recall the night's unfolding, he pulls at the crusty nuggets in the corners of his eyes. Ignoring the pain in his arm, he sits ready to face the day. Given last night's adventures, he continues to battle stomach cramps and lifelike nightmares.

Shuffling over broken tile, he steps up to the window. Peeling back a corner of damp cardboard, he allows a slim ray of the midmorning sun to filter in. A grumble from his stomach reminds him he missed breakfast. Craving buttermilk pancakes and his mother's skillet-fried bologna, he searches his pockets for cash. His clenched palm returns with a ball of lint and a crumbled paper from a cookie he stole days earlier. "A quiet evening with friends is the best tonic for a long day," the fortune promises. Reminded that living on the street is not easy, he curses the slim paper. Struggling to recall his reason for saving the cookie's slim strip, he tosses the lying paper to the floor. Forced to look to his future, he calls his new batch of friends a brotherhood of thieves, a slew of hoodlums, and in recent days, trailblazers.

Moving about like a ninja, he scavenges the floor for a morsel of food. He throws back a bottle of water one of his crazies tossed aside when the drugs and booze took over. He is shoving soggy fries into his mouth when he remembers this is the day he is scheduled to check in with his probation officer—a balding man whose Coke-bottle glasses rest against pocked skin.

He grows angry every time he is forced to make the visit. After all, he served his time. He hates that the system continues to treat him like a common criminal now that he is outside their armed compound.

In the room's far corner, Rooster, a young kid from Hurt Ward who is always crowing about something, mumbles in his sleep. His words are unclear, but it appears he is craving moon pies and buttered popcorn.

In his effort to escape the house, DeShane stumbles over empty vodka bottles, a digital scale, and a tactical vest. Crouching low, he searches sleeping bodies. He steps over pages torn from porn magazines and clothes turned inside out while searching pockets for cash or credit cards. Just as he slips his hand into Red's pocket, he hears a cough. Glancing about the room, he is drawn to Pugs.

Propped against the wall, Pugs's shoulders slump over his woolly belly, and his back rests against a pony keg. A stream of thick saliva oozes from his open mouth into the folds of his chin. His folded hands hold a prepaid burner phone and a crack pipe. A hint of clear plastic peeks out from under his armpit. DeShane knows all too well what is in the bag—*Snow White*—street slang for pure cocaine, and woolies— cocaine mixed with marijuana, heroin, or ecstasy. He also knows where there is cocaine, there is cash, and within arm's reach, a loaded Glock with an XS Big Dot front sight and a SureFire suppressor.

Running his tongue over his lips, he calculates his next move. Stealing from Pugs is risky business. Some might call it a death sentence. When caught, he will be given only seconds to explain his actions. When Pugs grows tired of his lame excuses, his actions will become a learning tool for the rest of the gang and the consequences they will surely suffer should they attempt to double-cross him or surrender to temptation. Anyone who has tangled with Pugs knows his bite is far worse than his bark.

Rubbing a hand through his hair, DeShane recalls hearing that after fleeing the hood, Pugs hid in the shadows of Louisiana's Caddo Parrish. That was until the lure of opportunities beckoned him back to Chattanooga. DeShane is also aware there is an endless debt in his revenge. In recent weeks, he watched as Pugs's minions punished those whose actions led to disappointment. A virgin to unthinkable crimes, he turned away when blood sailed through the air and vomit rushed his throat. One thing becomes certain—a soft heart and a sensitive stomach are not an option if he is going to survive.

Balancing his weight in high-top sneakers he lifts from the floor, DeShane holds his breath. With a magician's wave of the hand, he swipes the plastic bag, a roll of cash, and the Glock. Faster than a common purse snatcher, he hightails it out the door.

12

"**P**lease, Glenn, just one more day," Suzanne Urling begs.

    Stepping around sealed boxes movers will soon stack in a trailer pulled by an 18-wheeler bound for Tennessee, Glenn pulls his wife close. While the sweet scent of vanilla envelops him, pain keeps his heart at bay. "I promise we will visit as often as we can."

"I don't want the children to forget her," she says, struggling to maintain her composure.

"We won't let them."

"My heart tells me I'll need to return here."

"I promise I'll come with you."

"You mean it?"

"Of course. I loved your sister."

The drive along Lizbeth Road seems longer than its four miles. Focused on the two-lane blacktop ahead of him, Glenn bites back tears. It damn near kills him to watch Suzanne shrink away. When she gives his hand a gentle squeeze, a lump forms in his throat. Patterson County has always been their home, and as much as it pains them to leave family and friends, he knows a fresh start will be good for them.

"Thank you for doing this. I visited yesterday, but it wasn't enough," Suzanne says, rotating her wedding band—a habit she has come to find comforting in recent weeks. "It never is."

"I understand."

Although she tops off at five feet, Suzanne's personality is ten feet tall. Always poised, she walks the earth with confidence he admires, and if his pain finds a way to rest, he hopes to emulate her in every facet of his life.

Slowing the car's engine, he turns into Eastwood Gardens. When the gates up ahead come into view, a familiar pain pulls at his heart. He exchanges a nod with the elderly groundskeeper, who, throwing out an arm, waves an eight-by-ten map of the sprawling property. Returning a wave, Glenn continues down the road. In recent months, he has come to know the cemetery's layout like the back of his hand.

A deep sigh follows Suzanne's whimper. In recent weeks, acceptance has come to replace anger. Looking ahead, she scans the rows of headstones. When her eyes fall on the flowers she placed on her sister's grave days earlier, her face falls into her hands.

"I know how difficult this is for you. It's never easy to lose a loved one. Maria is in a good place. Something tells me she has made a circle of genuine friends."

Giving a soft smile, Suzanne reaches for his hand. "Heaven gained an angel."

Born in Nebraska, Suzanne is the first of three daughters born to Maeve, whose apron is always stuffed with tissues, and Joseph Tenery. Dedicated to the tradition of passing down family names, her parents toyed with Josephine, but in the final hour, they agreed to call her Suzanne, a deep-rooted name in her family tree.

While Joseph served in the United States Navy, Maeve served the Lord. Their single-story clapboard home offered a wraparound porch and a view of a deep-water pond with a sand bottom. Three miles east of the town's square, theirs was the first house assigned a rural route address.

Windowsills and bookcases displayed the clay pieces Suzanne and her sisters made in elementary school and the medals they earned in area tennis tournaments.

In the fall months, when football season was underway, Suzanne participated in the school's marching band. Although petite in stature, she played the tuba.

After some convincing from their mother, their father converted the old barn where he once tended to Cadillac, a quarter horse he rescued at a Saturday-morning auction, into a music studio. In the renovation, heat lamps and bales of hay remained, and folding chairs he borrowed from the porch anchored the dirt floor. Once the oval trough was drained of stagnant water, it was filled with sodas Maeve purchased at Clem's Dry Goods, a mom-and-pop quick stop located outside the city limits and a hop, skip, and a jump from their home. Clem's storefront window often displayed team posters meant to encourage support and harmless rivalry between the Fighting Tigers and Sacred Heart's Saders, the town's high school teams.

Weeks before Suzanne and Glenn attended senior prom, they were officially a couple. In the coming days, Glenn's letter jacket came to rest on Suzanne's slim shoulders. Soon after, a simple promise ring displayed their commitment to a long life together.

On the evening of their school's prom, Suzanne wore a pink dress her mother sewed for the occasion. A corsage rested against the boat neck collar, and white gloves met dotted swiss sleeves at the elbows. Her honey-blonde hair was pulled back with a white bow, and a small clutch fell from her wrist. A cheek-to-cheek smile she shared with the camera spoke of love and commitment. Looking sharp in a rented tuxedo, Glenn matched her smile. Dancing to the music the band played, he drew her close. Believing no one was watching, he gently kissed her neck.

When it came time for Suzanne to map out her future, she was torn between a career in teaching or attending nursing school. Months after flipping a copper coin to a carpeted floor, she enrolled in a small junior college, where she learned to take a patient's temperature, monitor heart rate, and, after several trial and errors, position a bedpan.

When a three-day break from school presented itself in early September, she passed on the road trip her classmates had talked about in the weeks leading up to the retreat. Although she was tempted to walk along Lake Michigan's shore and spend an afternoon under sail on its clear water, she wanted to spend her free time with Glenn.

On the long-awaited day of their wedding, steamy and oppressive heat followed unexpected rain. Worried their guests would be miserable, Suzanne phoned the church. Expressing her concern to the man who answered the telephone, she was assured a maintenance man would reset the thermostat.

While the bridal party tended to Suzanne, her mother stepped into the sanctuary. Believing great things awaited her daughter and Glenn, a warm smile crossed over her face as she gave thanks.

Suzanne and Glenn's first year of marriage was a busy one. While Suzanne focused on nursing, Glenn studied to earn his bachelor's degree in engineering.

In their free time, they enjoyed tennis and golf. When Glenn was busy studying for his master's degree, Suzanne joined her sisters in a game of softball, learning the rules of bridge and canasta, and spending Wednesday evenings at Bible study. On those evenings when she was asked by the church secretary to call out bingo's winning letters and numbers, she made herself available. Hours later, when she arrived back at their duplex, she would tell Glenn all about the activities in the church and the local gossip she learned from those rumored to be in the know. Hiding his envy, Glenn laughed at her innocence. With each word she spoke, he fell deeper in love.

When lack of money kept them at home, he never let on that he knew she cheated at cards. Enjoying her laughter and playful ways, he played along. Each time he was convinced she overplayed her hand and cheated his, he took her in his arms, giving thanks for the angel God had placed before him.

13

With little care, DeShane walks the gang-ridden neighborhood. Lost and alone and fighting his own battles, he is not aware the city's planners are about to kick off major renovations, which will include immediate demolition of the crack-infested whorehouses he passes by each day on his way to nowhere.

Months earlier, when the police cornered him on Dunbar Street, he enjoyed his last day of freedom. A United States senior district judge had not taken pity on him when it was learned in court proceedings that, prior to advancing his life of crime to include auto theft, he occupied a lone cell for assault charges and possession of stolen goods.

Sidestepping the cracks in the sidewalk, he shuffles toward Firestone Avenue. When he nears Tuhan's Barbeque, the aroma has his mouth watering and his stomach begging for sustenance. Resisting the urge to challenge the restaurant law known on the street as dine and dash, he quickens his pace. After all, his destination is Charmagne's apartment.

Everything about her makes her easy on the eyes. Chocolate-brown eyes dance with delight when he enters her one-bedroom rental. Before the screen door has time to slam behind him, Charmagne drops her baby into a cardboard box. When DeShane feels her hands patting his pockets, he knows she is searching for illegal candy.

"Hey, baby girl. Take it easy. You gotta feed the beast first. What's with the box?" he asks, ignoring Sly and the Family Stone's "Everyday

People" busting out from speakers likely stolen from an unsuspecting entrepreneur.

"Found it last week on my way home from T.J.'s." Believing the refrigerator box would make a nice playpen for her kid, she dragged it down the street to her rental. "I know you want to know where I found it. You thinking about doing a five-finger job? Hard to steal a frickin' refrigerator."

"I don't want your neighbor's refrigerator. I want their spending money."

In a passing moment, his thoughts drift to Paula Fields. He met her last month when he went out for a meat stick. Paula was working the late shift at a local gas station. Her deep cleavage was heavily inked and begging for attention. With a promising smile, she had given him a carton of cigarettes before allowing him to explore her body in the back seat of her Chevy Citation. One thing is certain: if Charmagne learns of Paula, she will have it out with her after turning on him.

"Where are you off to?" Charmagne asks with little interest.

"I'm heading to check in with my parole officer."

"You want a hit before you go? I also have a bag of cut adulterated drugs. In case you haven't noticed, these streets are filled with dealers."

"Who is your contact?"

"Snake," she says, squirming about.

"He hustles the cheap stuff. He's not that bright. He has crust on his brain, and he worms his way through the system. He has a long list of aliases."

"Snake is my man. I'm betting he gets high all hours of the day."

"How often does he get you?"

"As often as he likes. Correct me if I'm wrong, but I think I smell a bruised ego."

"My ego is never bruised. I need to use your bathroom. I'll likely be asked to take a urine test."

"Here," she says, offering him a tall glass of water. "It will dilute any drugs you might have in your system."

Exiting Charmagne's apartment, DeShane heads around back to the building's dumpster. Staying low, he weaves his way through the tall grasses where he hides the drugs and the Glock he lifted from Pugs.

14

Sporting the starter jacket for the Memphis Tigers he lifted from the passenger seat of a parked car, DeShane arrives at the meeting with his probation officer. Resting his eyes on Ted, his parole officer, he wrestles with the jacket's leather sleeves before falling into the chair opposite the officer's desk. Shifting about, he struggles to get comfortable.

Often compared to the late sports journalist Howard Cosell, Ted sports a preacher's comb-over and hair the color of midnight. Tortoiseshell eyeglasses own his narrow face.

DeShane wants to tell him he looks like an owl, but he is in a hurry, and a confrontation of a personal matter is never a good way to start a parole visit.

While Ted reads through DeShane's file, DeShane's eyes fall on Ted's short-sleeved button-down shirt and its plastic pocket protector that is stained with orange smudges.

"Have you ever participated in sports?" Ted asks.

"There was a time when I wanted to run track and cross-country, but I couldn't afford running shoes. On any given day, my family is either dead broke or dirt poor."

"Have you considered joining the school's swim team?"

"Given our income, I would be forced to swim in my underwear. I've come to accept my trophy-winning sport is played on the street. I'll never raise a trophy into the air, but every time I score a hit, I'll be respected as a man."

"First, I want to encourage you to reach for your dreams. Back in my day, I played soccer. I never took credit for a winning point, but I enjoyed being part of a team who shared a dream. Before entering the field, we exchanged high fives, and, believing we had a winning chance, we bumped chests. My young team never won a game, but I enjoyed my time on the field. That said, I want to thank you for arriving here on time. This will take only a few minutes," Ted says. "Are you following the rules of your probation? Staying away from drugs?"

"Damn straight," DeShane says, slumping his narrow shoulders. "No need for a urine test. I'm clean. Nice cubicle you have here. Maybe someday you'll have a real office."

"Perhaps. I applaud you and your efforts. Any surprises I should know about?" he asks, rolling over the floor where he searches a file cabinet.

"Nope. I've been walking a straight line."

"Have you given any thought to the CASA program the judge suggested?"

"It's not for me."

"Life is your personal menu. You decide what you want and when you need it. CASA will always be available to you. What about a guardian ad litem?"

"I'm good on my own. There is a whole lot of shit in my head, and we don't want to visit it. I'll say this much … if I had shot my old lady ten years ago when I wanted to, I'd be a free man today."

"Those are mighty big words. We are here to help you work through your issues. If you find yourself changing your mind, I'm here for you."

"No one is ever here for me but me."

"Now, about that urine test. It's mandatory. If you will follow me, please."

Just as they round the corner, DeShane bolts down the hall and out to the street.

15

Believing his presence has gone unnoticed, DeShane returns to the dumpster where he sweeps up the gun and the bag of drugs. Slowing his step, he navigates the city's side streets and cuts through parking lots overgrown with tulip poplars, magnolias, and red maple trees. He bounces a tennis ball he finds parked at the curb until an idling patrol car pushes him into the shadows.

When the walls of his housing complex come into view, he steps over a fallen gate, serpentines overturned garbage cans, and, hoping to enter the housing compound without notice, dodges walkways and patrolled areas. Approaching his building, he jumps over the iron rail leading to his unit.

Eyeing the padlock on the door, he curses the life he was born into and the parents he did not deserve. Knowing he will be left suffering under his mother's soapbox and the never-ending litany of complaints and disappointments she spews with endless breath, he lets a frown own his face. Crouching on bended knees, he searches the unit's only window. Finding the casing sealed and his pockets without a key, he leaves the building and travels along an open field.

Somewhere in the near distance, gunshots ring out. Fearing Pugs and his squad are hot on his tail, a shiver passes through him. More than once, he heard Pugs call this part of town the *Battlefield*. A magnet for crime, the Field's crumbling sidewalks are littered with syringes, a growing parade of pregnant teenagers, and spent shells left behind after drug deals ended with expletives and an exchange of rapid gunfire.

Streets spanning from the far corners of the Field to Warren Road are alive with single mothers carrying cans of wasp spray meant to ward off unwanted advances. Most are high school dropouts or victims of child abuse by a stranger their mother invited into their home when their father went AWOL. Always aware but often unprepared, they shuffle alongside victims of crime and sexual abuse.

Wandering the streets like a nomad, DeShane heads toward the community kitchen on East Bell Street. Steps away from the kitchen's entrance, a kid with a heart full of dreams strums a six-string guitar. The case at his side holds only coins, but his belief in his music carries promise.

Slowing his step, DeShane blends in with the homeless and desperate panhandlers. A quick glance at posted signs advising loitering is not allowed tells him the law continues to go ignored.

Taking a seat at a weathered park bench he shares with a man he knows as Wild Eyes Willy, he studies the man's lived-in face while revisiting the stories the old man once shared. Skipping over his shopping cart burdened with heaps of old coats, empty milk cartons, and paper bags, it takes only a glance for his eyes to fall on a young guy he recognizes from the hood.

"Hey, Slim. Why are you roaming the streets? I thought you were in the clink," DeShane says, eyeing Slim's teeth and their black lesions.

"I caught a lucky break. Opposing counsel mishandled silent witness records."

"What are you doing here?"

"Looking for a car to steal. Me and the boys have a plan."

Hearing these words, Wild Eyes Willy moves to a bench some forty feet away.

DeShane does not ask who the boys are. He knows the pack Slim runs with.

"What brings you here?" Slim asks.

"Killing time."

"Word on the street is Pugs's goons are looking for you. Only a fool would double-cross him. He is living on the edge. He is wanted in drug court for a probation violation," he says, running a hand through his crimpy hair.

"Probably why he never leaves his house."

"He is more evil than any crime lord. Did you hear what he did to Sammie? Pugs cut off his nuts and forced them down his throat. He then chopped off his fingers and fed them to his dog. He likes to carve up those who do him wrong. When he was done slicing and dicing, Dynamite Dean threw gasoline on Sammie just before striking a match. I've been told you could hear his screams for miles. I've also been told that his remains were shoved through a meat grinder."

"Pugs is not looking for me. I just need time away from my old lady. I'm guessing she's on the rag."

"Man, don't make me paint that picture. You ever notice she always has something stuck in her teeth? Your mom is no beauty queen, and she always smells like she's been licking toilets and chewing on dog bones."

"She probably is. You don't get that fat by drinking water. I got a look at her backside when she was washing her hair in the bathtub. I don't think I'll ever get that image out of my head. For what it's worth, she has eyes in the back of her head, and her ears swivel faster than helicopter blades. Hey, is it true if you line the inside of a shopping bag with duct tape, the store's sensors won't go off?"

"That's called a booster bag—the dream of every shoplifter. Better to use aluminum foil. If you don't have a shopping bag, you can use a backpack. Are you thinking about doing some shoplifting?"

"I need a set of speakers."

"Listen, I gotta go. I'm meeting up with my boys. We might do a robbery. If that doesn't work, we're going to take a car for a joyride. You wanna come along?"

"I don't know. I'm on probation."

"We are not going to do anything criminal. Come on. It'll be fun," he says, widening his grin. "We're gonna drive up to Trigger Point. If anyone's watching, we're gonna show off our new ride."

"That's a death sentence. Only a fool would enter that area. Those guys tend to shoot first and ask questions later."

"This is different. They won't know the car or the gang driving it."

16

"**L**et's make a sting," Slim says, waving the .25-caliber automatic pistol he stole in a home invasion. "Let's cruise Parkridge Medical Center's parking lot."

"Over on McCallie?" fifteen-year-old Calvin Toyne asks.

"Yep."

DeShane wants to tell Slim that *yep* is not a word but, knowing he will be taken down, bites his tongue.

"I'm not going anywhere near the Mall of Murder. Some crazy shit happens over there," Calvin says. "I hear they have one in Memphis too."

"Yep. Four shootings last week. How about we visit that high-rise on Sunrise Drive? Lots of cars to choose from," Slim suggests.

"Hey, I saw a police car parked outside Walgreen's. The engine was running," Calvin throws out.

"Stealing that car would keep us behind bars for life. They have surveillance cameras all over the place. Man, you are already on the wanted list for five counts of aggravated battery with a deadly weapon, four counts of aggravated assault with a deadly weapon, and my personal favorite—two counts of negligence involving a deadly weapon. I wonder if there is a reward for turning you in. My pockets could use the money."

"I have shit on you too."

"Road rage is petty compared to assault and battery."

"Are we gonna hot-wire a car?" DeShane asks, changing the subject.

"If you take a car without the owner, it will be reported stolen. I think we should follow someone to their car and toss them into the trunk," Slim says, grinning.

Pondering the plan, Calvin fingers his ear for a moment. "Are we just gonna drive around?"

"First thing we do is go to Cash's house. He might want in on the action. After that, we find a car and switch out the tag. After we hold up a few stores and rob a couple of people, we let the person out of the trunk."

"How are we going to get there?"

"Guessing we will have to walk."

"Are we keeping the car?"

"Do dogs have fleas?" Slim asks, laughing.

"Only in our hood," Calvin says with a grin.

★★★

"How do you all feel about kidnap, rape, and murder?" Slim asks.

"I don't want any part of rape or murder. That will put me behind bars for a lifetime or strapped to the electric chair. Something tells me I don't want to live out my last breath suffering either one," Cash says. "I'm in enough trouble."

"Let's just take a car and throw the owner in the trunk. No murder, no rape," Calvin says.

"Let's start at Kroger. Always tons of cars there," Slim suggests.

"I was just by there. Too many people coming and going," Calvin says.

"How about the hospital?" DeShane suggests.

"Too many security cameras in the parking area. Our presence and our actions would get noticed before we could pop the trunk," Calvin reminds.

Tossing scenarios about in his head, Slim snaps his fingers. "Let's pay a visit to that new apartment complex."

"On Lakeside Drive?" Calvin asks, knowing.

"The one and only."

"I'm staying here," Cash says, kicking off his shoes.

17

Angela Bartoni falls behind the steering wheel of her four-door sedan. Before buckling her seat belt, she cranks up the air conditioner. A glance at the thermostat tells her the temperature is in the nineties and climbing. She considers making a run to the grocery store, but recalling her mother shopped for groceries before returning to her home in Kansas, she heads for home.

She is rounding the corner onto Lakeside Drive when her eyes fall on the young guys walking along the vacant lot skirting her apartment complex. Fearing something is not right, she secures the car's doors. When the guys move to block the entrance, she slams on the brakes.

"Get out," Slim demands with a knock to the car's windshield. "Don't make so much as a peep."

"Please, just let me go," Angela begs. "I have a young child, and I don't have much money."

"Open the damn door, or I'll shoot through the window," Slim says, brandishing his pistol.

"Please, just let me pass. I won't tell anyone that you are here."

"We're taking your car. Now get out and shut your trap."

Taking him at his word, she puts the car in park. Grabbing her purse, she releases the door locks and steps out of the car.

"Gimme your purse and don't try anything funny. I'll use this gun if I have to," Calvin says, leaning against the car's rear fender.

When Angela hands over her purse, Calvin grabs her around the neck and throws a hand over her mouth.

"Get in the trunk. We are going for a little ride," Slim says, popping the trunk.

When she attempts to flee, Calvin tackles her to the ground.

"Listen up, sweet cheeks. If I have to, I'll chop off your arms. Now get your ass in the trunk. Hey, there is a dog kennel in here," Calvin, says, pointing to a large metal cage.

"Shove her into it," Slim says, forcing the gun's barrel at her back. "Grab a license plate and slap it on the rear bumper," he says, shooting his eyes to DeShane.

"You can't trust DeShane to do anything right. He is a doper."

"What do you know about doping?" DeShane asks, wearing a challenge on his face. "And don't go throwing out my name."

"I know doping messes with your head."

"It's my head."

"Cut the crap, guys," Slim says, turning to DeShane. "Put a plate on the rear bumper. I say it's time we have a little fun."

18

"**H**elp! Someone, please help me!" Angela screams in a deafening voice. Wiping sweat from her brow, she kicks at the crate. "Let me out of here! I can't breathe!"

Hearing her cries for help, Slim turns up the stereo and makes a fast and hard turn into a vacant parking lot.

"Do you want me to punch her in the face? That will quiet her down," Calvin says, rubbing his hands together.

"Give her the ole Tyson Fury routine," Slim says.

"Punch her in the gut?"

"Fury was a switch-hitter. Give her face a double uppercut. When you are done there, take a look in her purse."

In the following minutes, Calvin pulls the young woman from the crate, where he gives her face a two-fisted punch. When she falls back into the hull of the trunk, he throws a hand to the trunk's lid.

"Wallet, hairbrush, lipstick, and a teacher's badge from a school over in Highland Heights," Calvin says, searching her purse.

"We're the teachers now. We're going to teach her a lesson she'll never forget," Slim says, laughing. "What's in the wallet?"

"Angela Bartoni's driver's license. Care to guess her age?"

"Who cares? She's already celebrated her last birthday."

"She gave us two credit cards and her checkbook," Calvin continues. "Did I ever tell you that I'm an expert when it comes to forgery?" he asks, lifting his brows. "Get this. My old lady schooled me."

"Old lady? Are you talking about your mom?" Slim asks.

"I come from a family of hardened criminals."

"Where is she now?"

"In the slammer. She got caught forging checks to the tune of almost a hundred grand. She said something about a gopher account. I'm guessing one of these goes to her apartment," he adds, pointing to the patchwork of keys hanging from the car's ignition.

"I thought we were just taking her on a joy ride," DeShane says.

"Listen up, Sally boy. You're still wet behind the ears. I have other plans for her."

"Are you Sally from Onion Bottom? A name like that must keep the chicks away. Word is Pugs has a price on your head," Calvin says, giving him the stare down. "Something tells me your defining moment is waiting around the corner."

Embarrassed, DeShane looks away.

"Might just be that you already celebrated your last birthday too," Slim says, laughing.

"Stick around. We might just make you a hero," Calvin throws out.

"Or a wanted criminal," Slim adds.

"Maybe we should give the kid a break," Calvin says with an ear-to-ear grin.

"Sally, you are about to make it or break it. Listen up, kiddos. Her apartment is our next target," Slim says, cutting the car's engine.

19

"**I**'m not sure about this," DeShane says, parking his feet at the apartment's front door. "I'm already in a big heap of trouble."

"What is there to be unsure about? This is how we roll," Slim says, grinning.

"Other than a big-screen television and a cell phone charger, the apartment has nothing of value," Calvin says, tossing the sofa and taking a knife to its pillows.

"We have work to do. Toss the drawers and check the cookie jar. We might find some cash or weed. Search each and every corner of the bathroom for prescription meds. When you find something, give me a holler. What we don't want, we can sell. Is there an insurance card in her wallet?" Slim asks. "We can always call in a refill."

"Right here," Calvin says, waving the plastic card in the air. "Hey, she lied to us."

"How so?"

"Look around. There ain't no kid living here," he says, inviting Slim to study the small space.

"Maybe the kid is at daycare."

"I don't see any toys."

"Find her passport. Lift the bed and look under the mattress. Pull up the rugs and search her luggage. Tear into every corner of her closet."

"It's an apartment complex. I'm telling you, we won't find a safe or a hidden drawer."

"I don't see a stereo or a set of speakers," DeShane mutters.

"It's a small apartment. Not much room for big-ticket items."

"You still have her checkbook?" Slim asks.

"Yep."

"Calvin, you are gonna write me a check. Make it payable to cash. Grab what you can. We need to get to the bank before it closes," Slim says.

"Wait, I found her Social Security card."

"Are you thinking what I'm thinking?"

"Only if it involves identity theft."

20

"I will need to see your driver's license," the bank teller says. "It's bank policy."

Wearing a smirk on his face, Slim opens his wallet and throws down his license.

"The bank manager will have to approve this. It's more than I'm allowed to cash. If you'll excuse me for a moment, I'll get this taken care of." Before stepping away, the teller grabs the plastic card.

Shifting about, Slim and Calvin watch while the young woman discusses the check with a portly fellow appearing tired and ready to call it a day.

Minutes later, when the teller returns, she is wearing a look of fear on her face.

"I'm sorry, but I am unable to cash this check. The funds are not available."

Fearing the police will come busting through the door with their weapons pulled, Slim and Calvin race from the bank, leaving Slim's license in the hands of the bank's manager.

21

While the day's temperature continues to climb, Angela struggles to remain alert. Warm blood pools in her hair, and her will to live is slowly fading. A hand to her face confirms her nose is broken and her cheekbones and jaw are dislocated.

Passing by an outlet store and the East Lake Academy of Fine Arts, Slim circles back when he nears an auto body shop.

He makes a right turn onto East Thirty-Seventh Street before turning onto Fourteenth Avenue, taking him to East Lake Park. Before stepping from the car, he does several cookies over the thick grass. Slamming on the brakes, he cuts the car's engine.

"Get out," he barks, popping the trunk. When Angela does not move, he pulls at her arm and slams her to the ground.

Calvin and DeShane watch as Slim continues to kick at her abdomen.

Angry that she is not putting up a fight, Slim tears at her clothes. When he pulls the tire iron from the trunk, DeShane doubles over and vomits to the ground.

"Sally, you want some action?"

"The only nipple he has ever latched onto belongs to his mother," Calvin offers. "If you don't want to catch something, you might have at her before Sally gets a piece. I hear he has warts on his privates."

"Warts?"

"Look it up when you get home."

"I'm going home," DeShane says, turning away.

"You best watch your back. Pugs won't give up until he skins you to the bone."

"I need to check on my brother."

"You do that. Calvin, what do you want to do?"

"I wanna go home."

"I'm gonna cut off her fingers. I want her jewelry," Slim says, grinning. "You have a lighter on you?"

"What kind of question is that?" Calvin asks, pulling a lighter from his pocket.

"Burn off her lips."

"For real?" he asks.

"It'll keep her from talking. Drag her over to those tall grasses," he says, pointing toward the lake. "I'm gonna gun the engine and drive over there. When you've had your kicks, drag her over to the river. If the coast is clear, dump her body and her purse over the bridge."

"Hey, Sally," Slim shouts, reaching into the car's trunk. "Here's a roll of twine. If Pugs doesn't get to you first, you might consider a hanging."

★★★

An elderly man walks his dog along the river. When the dog grows curious about something near the river's edge, the old man pulls back on the dog's leash. When the dog presses on, the elderly man leads him over to the bridge.

Observing blood on the bridge, the old man discovers the body. Pulling his cell phone from the pocket of his pants, he calls the police.

Within the hour, the body is recovered from the deep water. An officer notes that the victim's body is beaten and bruised. A plastic library card in her purse identifies the victim as Angela Bartoni.

22

"**S**ome guys came here looking for you," Marshall says in a low voice. "They ganged up on Mom."

"Did they hurt her?" DeShane asks, not caring. "She probably lipped off to the wrong person and barked a growing list of empty threats."

"One guy hit her face with his fist. Blood went flying everywhere. It splattered on the wall," Marshall says, pointing to the space behind the door. "When she tried to fight back, the other guy threw her to the ground."

"Did they ask any questions?"

"After they asked about you, they searched the house. They even looked under the beds. When they were through, they grabbed Mom by the hair and dragged her out to the street. She tripped off the curb and stumbled over the concrete. When she cried out for help, the neighbors came out to see what was going down, but nobody tried to help her. The fat guy called her an example. What does that mean?"

"I don't know," he lies. "Where is she now?"

"Mr. Sweatt helped me drag her back into the house. We tried to put her in bed, but we couldn't lift her. She is face-up on the floor. She looks like she took a beating in the boxing ring. She can't open her eyes, and her lips are swollen. Mr. Sweatt thinks her jaw is busted. He also said she is gonna need something more than a Band-Aid."

"I have to go out. You stay here. I'll be back in about an hour."

"Aren't you gonna check on her? She might need to go to the hospital."

"If you think she needs medical attention, call 911."

23

A glance at his watch lets DeShane know five hours have passed
since he escaped the Crawl. The high he is feeling is wearing
off, and he needs a different thrill. Keeping a leisurely pace, he crosses
over to Stimpson Street and walks the parking lot. He watches a
middle-aged man return his shopping cart to the basket return station
before making his way to a blue four-door Saab.

"Can I hitch a ride?" DeShane asks.

"Where you headed?"

"I wanna get to the expressway. I'm hoping to hitch a ride to
Georgia."

"I'm going to Blue Ridge."

"That's where I'm heading. Not many people know of it."

"What do you have going on there?"

"My old man lives there. He's not right in the head, so I thought
I'd pay him a visit."

"You are a good son. These days, kids your age would rather
spend their free time shooting hoops, watching television, or street
dragging. Your father must be proud of you. Do you live with your
mother?"

"And my younger brother. He wanted to come with me, but my
mom worries that he is too young to make the trip."

"Smart thinking. Maybe next time, when he is a bit older.
I'm Doctor Morris Atwood. My mother hoped I would become a
doctor—a first in our family, but my heart was set on becoming a

mail carrier. I enjoy the outdoors. I can take you to the synagogue, but you'll need to arrange for a ride to your father's home."

"I'm good with that. I will call my uncle when we get there. He offered to come get me, but I wanted him to stay close to my father. Sometimes that uncle of mine takes one toke too many."

"I don't understand."

"When he is not selling black market babies, he is smoking a doobie."

"I'm familiar with marijuana, but what is black market babies?"

"Stolen stones. Mostly diamonds. I don't want my father to serve time for his brother's mistakes. As for me and my dad, every Sunday after church, we tune in to listen to the *Big Joe Polka Show*. It's not my thing, but it makes my dad happy."

"I'll say it again: you are a good son. I always say every parent should have one."

"Do you have kids?"

"My wife didn't live long enough to have children, and I have no interest in remarrying. I have two dogs who insist on keeping me busy. When we can't visit the dog park, they beg to walk the neighborhood. Just between us, those boys of mine are like two old ladies trying to escape the building's knitting group. Running in circles, they keep hounding me until I give in. When they meet up with their dog pals, they play and run for hours."

"I would like to have a dog, but my brother has allergies."

"I understand. I don't like asking, but are you carrying any weapons? Can't be too safe, you know."

"Not even a comb. You don't have to tell me. Crime here in these parts is on the rise. Never know what these crazies will do next."

"I have never considered a comb a weapon until now. Sometimes my barber goes a little crazy with the scissors, but to his credit, he has a steady hand. Son, I didn't catch your name."

"My friends call me Slim, but my real name is Willie Mahoney."

24

The retreat's seventy-acre property offers flowing streams, picnic tables, and miles of hiking trails.

A rabbi's kid from Kansas, Atwood's knowledge of the area runs deep. In recent years, the locals have come to call him their *wilderness operator.*

Stepping from the car and humming a tune, Atwood slows his step.

Hearing footsteps, he turns to find the young man sliding into the driver's seat.

"What are you doing, young man?"

"Give me the keys," DeShane demands.

"I will do no such thing."

Throwing out his voice, DeShane steps from the car. A roll of twine is tucked under his arm, and a sneer owns his face.

"Walk over to that tree," DeShane orders, pointing to a mature tulip poplar.

"I'm staying planted."

"Fine. Have it your way." Before his next breath, DeShane reveals the Glock and, throwing out his hand, pistol-whips the old man. "Now, get over to that tree."

Folding his hands, Atwood makes his way over the grass. "If you're struggling, we can pray together. If you turn your life around, I believe you will find your best days are ahead of you."

"Pray all you want. Now, put your face against the tree. Don't try any funny business. This here gun is loaded, and I'm not afraid to use it."

"Son, please don't do this. I'm here to visit a friend."

"I'm not your son, and I don't care if you are here to swim in the river. Put your face against the tree."

"Please, let me go."

"There is a bullet in this gun with your name wrote on it. I'll shoot you if I have to."

"Written," Atwood foolishly corrects.

"Don't get smart with me," DeShane says, throwing his elbow into the old man's back. Just as he reaches for the twine, he catches sight of a young couple exiting the sanctuary. "Get in the car. We're going for a ride, and you're driving. If you so much as make a peep, I'll blast your ass."

25

"**S**tep on the gas," DeShane orders, waving the gun about like a badass from the hood. His heart is racing, but knowing Pugs and Dynamite Dean are hot on his tail forces him to take action.

"Young man, if you are in trouble, I can help," Atwood offers, taking a hand off the steering wheel.

"I don't need your help."

"The desperation in your voice and that gun aimed at my head tells a different story."

"I'm not into storytelling. So shut your trap and drive."

"My ancestors have blessings for surviving illnesses and managing pain," he offers. "Tell me your name again, young man."

"There's no reason for you to know my name, so shut your mouth and drive. And keep both hands on the steering wheel."

"Where are we going?"

"Turn onto Bear Creek," DeShane says, pointing to the sign up ahead.

"I asked where we are going," Atwood repeats, lifting his voice. "I thought your uncle was coming to get you."

"You'll find out when we get there. I haven't seen my dad since he walked out on his family, and I don't know if I have an uncle. Now is a good time to take back all the *good son* words. They don't mean shit to me or the family I was born into."

"I'm sorry to hear this. Where I come from, family comes first. Young man, I'm needed at the synagogue. It's a peaceful place, and today is the Sabbath."

"What does that mean?"

"It's a day set aside to rest and worship."

"Well, there won't be any resting today."

"You might change your mind should you visit the grounds. There are several gardens on the property—lovely places meant to restore calm to those in need. My wife enjoyed picnicking there. She always said she liked the sculptured plants and the sun on her face."

"What happened to her? I bet she left you because you talk too much."

"I lost her decades ago."

"Did she get shot up?"

"Cancer took her. She passed at home," he says, pausing. "Would you like to visit the synagogue?"

"I'd like for you to be quiet."

"We hosted a blood drive last week. I was told each donation has the potential to save up to three lives."

"Stop with the storytelling. One more word out of you, Mr. Mailbox, and you are going to need a blood drive."

"Did I mention I worked for the post master general?" he asks, not expecting a reply.

"I don't know who that is, and I don't care," he says, shooting him a look. "Where you from?"

"Spencer Mountain, North Carolina. It's a small town alongside the South Fork Catawba River. I moved there several years ago. I have a modest home near the water. Have you heard of the Catawba River?"

"Nope."

"We're a small dot on the map, but it's our dot."

"Why did you come to Blue Ridge?"

"I'm caring for an old friend who doesn't get out much. Poor vision and emphysema keep him homebound. When forced to leave the house, he's on a portable breathing machine. Kipper, his three-legged dog, pulls his wheelchair."

"At least he has a set of wheels. Aren't you a little old for the skull cap?" he asks, eyeing the old man's head covering.

"It's a yarmulke."

"And the thing around your neck?"

"It's a tallit. I wear it to honor God."

"Take it off."

"I can't. I wear it during prayer."

"I said, take it off. You ain't praying now."

"I pray every minute of every day."

"How's all that praying working for you?" he asks, grabbing at the fringed shawl.

"Perhaps, it brought me here to help you," he says with sad eyes.

"Maybe," DeShane says, thinking about it. "You play any instruments?"

"Several, but the guitar is my favorite."

"I have always wanted to learn to play the saxophone. Chicks dig it."

"If you would like, I could teach you."

"I don't have a saxophone."

"I have one you can use."

"I'm afraid playing music isn't in my future."

"Are you from around here?"

"Nope."

"Where is your family?"

"I don't have a family. It's just me and my little brother."

"I have a sister. We're not as close as my mother would like."

"Do you have a dad?"

"My father is a good man," he says, pondering the depth of the young man's question. "He continues to make sacrifices for his family. Joan, that's my sister, is never happy for very long. Something has her believing she is a trust fund baby."

"What does that mean?"

"She foolishly believes our parents are wealthy and she's entitled to their hard-earned money."

"Are they? Wealthy, I mean."

"They get by," he says, locking eyes with DeShane. "Again, I can help if you are in trouble."

"You already said that, and I already answered it. You don't know shit about trouble."

"Oh, but I do. My sister keeps me running in circles."

"What is that up ahead?"

"A cemetery. It's a fascinating place filled with decades of history. Would you like a tour?"

"Sure," DeShane says with a killer's grin.

"The roads up ahead are winding and narrow."

"Be warned, I will shoot you even if you think about pulling one over on me. You understand?"

"I understand. I gave you my word."

26

"**S**top the car and cut the engine. I think I'm going to be sick," DeShane says.

"The winding roads will do that to a person," Atwood says, pulling over to the road's slim shoulder.

"I need to get out of the car for a minute. No funny business, you understand?" DeShane says, waving the gun about.

"I wouldn't dare," he says, throwing up his hands. "When I was a young boy, my mother rubbed my *keppy* when I was sick. It was meant to ease my discomfort."

"Don't go anywhere near my keppy, whatever the hell that is. One false move, and I'll put a bullet in yours."

"*Kepalah* is the true word. It means head. My mother speaks Yiddish, a language rich in expressions," he says with a warm smile.

"Cut the history lesson and save the visit down memory lane for someone who cares. Leave the key in the ignition and get out of the car."

"I thought we were going to visit the cemetery."

"Unless you want a hole in your kepalah, you better get out of the car."

"I was hoping to show you the grounds," Atwood says. "This area is rich in history."

"Do I look like I care about history? And you said the same thing about Yiddish. You are nothing more than a rich man throwing out rich words. Now get out."

"I believe I said Yiddish is rich in expressions."

"Don't get smart with me."

Although hesitant, Atwood opens the door. He reaches for the key, but feeling DeShane's eyes on him, pulls back his hand.

"That wasn't so hard, was it?"

"Young man, can we please talk about this? I'm an old man. I'm not long on this earth."

"Your time here will get shorter if you don't shut up. Now pop the trunk. I'm not asking twice."

Atwood fixes his eyes on DeShane. The smug look he is given in return encourages a challenge, but he does not budge.

"Young man, it is not the railroad or the river that defines and divides us. It is respect, values, and knowing right from wrong." A voice in his ear reminds him to be forgiving.

"The trunk," DeShane says, waving the gun in the air.

Hoping help is on the way, Atwood drags his feet to the back of the car. Looking over his shoulder, he considers making a run for it. He knows the land and its many trails but fears his aging heart and buckled knees might fail him. He also knows there are hungry wolves and mountain lions in the area.

"Quit monkeying around and get in," DeShane repeats, aiming the gun at Atwood's chest. "Drop your wallet on the ground. I need money for my pockets."

"I don't have much, but what I have is yours."

"I'm not asking for your money. I'm taking it. Do you have a cell phone?" he asks, coming in for a pat down.

"No phone."

"Just to be clear, the tables have turned. I'll be taking you for a ride. Shut your trap and get in the trunk."

"For all that is holy, I beg you won't do this," Atwood says, throwing a leg over the car's rear bumper. "Given the temperature, I'll likely die here, but your future will be forever altered. Your actions are criminal. You're a young man. You can turn your life around. If you will allow it, I'll help you. If you continue down this path, you will likely spend the rest of your days behind bars. If you let me go, I'll turn a blind eye. Take my car. I'll walk if I have to."

"I don't have any reason to trust you."

"I am a man of my word."

"Words don't mean shit to me."

"My friend needs me. You must surely know this senseless act of violence will put us both in harm's way."

"What do you know about violence?"

"Many of my ancestors lost their lives in one of the worst acts of violence carried out on human beings."

"Listen, old man. Unless you've lived on the streets, don't pretend to know what it's like," he says, throwing the gun's barrel toward the trunk. "If the ride gets bumpy, you might want to rub your keppy. Some fool once told me it might ease your discomfort," he says, slamming the trunk.

Sliding into the driver's seat, DeShane grabs the wheel with a laugh so loud he worries he might alert the neighbors. A glance out the window tells him he does not have to worry. Other than the old man in the trunk, it appears they are the only people on the road. Placing his hand on the key, he gives it a hard turn. A smile comes over his face when the engine comes to life. When the scent of freedom drifts in through the open window, he closes his eyes and lets the gentle breeze sweep over him. A search of Atwood's wallet puts a rich man's smile on his face. He counts the cash and shuffles through credit cards before shoving the wallet into his back pocket.

A hard press to the accelerator lunges the car forward, forcing him to ease up on the pedal. Gripping the steering wheel with both hands, he focuses on the open road up ahead. He tries to read the posted signs, but fearing he might go off the side of the mountain and fall to his death, he keeps his eyes on the road. Challenging curves force him to move into the middle of the road. Rounding the next bend, beads of sweat form above his brow, and panic begins to seep in. Forced to slow down, he slams on the brakes.

"Let me out," Atwood cries, pounding on the trunk's deck lid.

Lifting off the accelerator, DeShane pumps the brakes before coming to a dead stop.

"If you keep screaming, I will drive like this all the way to Memphis," he yells out the open window.

In the passing mile, DeShane is drawn to a large historical marker planted near a generous ridge. Pulling into a clearing, he throws the car into park. He is about to cut the engine when he hears voices. Hoping to tune out Atwood's loud cries, he bumps up the radio's volume, shifts the car into drive, and driving like he is out to win the Indy 500, makes a bat turn.

It takes only a moment for his thoughts to turn to Pugs. He wonders how long he will have to look over his shoulder for Dynamite Dean, Red, or the other minions who bow to Pugs. It is not like Pugs to join in on the hunt, but something tells him this just might be the exception.

Eager to hop on the open road, he throws a finger to the car's blinker. When all four tires hug the road, he jumps on the entrance ramp leading him to Interstate 75.

27

Atwood folds his hands in prayer and closes his eyes. While his mind races with a myriad of scenarios, his heart worries for the friends and family he will likely leave behind.

Brushing his hand over the trunk's wool pile, he searches for the spare tire's holding compartment. When he finds the small latch, he rolls over on his side. He is set to give the latch a pull when the car makes a hard and fast turn. Tossed about like popcorn in a microwave, he loses his balance and falls hard against the tire hull. Just as he lets go a scream, the music grows louder. A hard slam to the brake pedal throws him into the trunk's hinge. A warm trickle down the side of his head confirms his injury.

"Let me out of here," he yells. "Help me, please!"

28

Approaching Memphis, DeShane eases up on the gas. His stomach is growling, and his bladder is full. Rolling down the window and lowering the radio's volume, he listens for a cry from the trunk. The eerie silence tells him the old man is either unconscious or playing dead.

A right turn has him pulling into a fast-food joint. Cranking the radio to its highest setting, he inches up to the drive-through menu board.

"I want two cheeseburgers and double fries, and a large chocolate shake," he shouts into the metal box. Pulling up to the window, he hands over Atwood's credit card.

It takes only a memory to recall hearing that Marty McKinney, a kid from the hood, moved to Memphis and is renting an as-is foreclosure on Bayliss Avenue in the Kingsbury View subdivision.

29

"What brings you here?" Marty asks through the rental's screen door.

"I need a place to sleep. My eyes are tired, and my pockets are empty," DeShane says, lying.

"You can have the foldout couch but just for tonight."

"Thanks, buddy. I owe you one."

"I have friends coming by. You OK with that?" he asks, tapping at his cell phone.

"Sure. It's your place."

"It's Pugs and Dynamite Dean," he says, letting his words float on the air.

"For real? Did you rat me out?"

"Can you blame me? There is a price on your head. If you haven't noticed, my pockets need money too."

"Ratting me out is a death sentence. I thought we were friends."

"Our friendship ends with a fistful of cash."

"I'm out of here," DeShane says, bolting from the house.

30

While traveling back roads leading to nowhere, DeShane questions his destination. In the coming minutes, one thing becomes certain: returning to the Village is out of the question.

Racing through yellow lights and inching along until he is riding bumpers, he turns off Poplar Avenue onto White Station Road. Exploring the neighborhood, he eyes open garages and children playing on porches. Thinking about it now, he understands he never cared about playing with the kids in the hood. A pinch in his heart tells him Marshall would jump at the opportunity. He considers a quick trip home, but a sixth sense warns Pugs has someone watching his apartment. It is only now he worries he may have put Marshall and his mother in danger. History reminds him Pugs will turn to sadistic torture just to teach him a lesson.

Another turn has him driving west on Summer Avenue. When his eyes fall on the sign leading to a generous parking lot, he takes it.

Always on the lookout, he circles the lot for several minutes before his eyes fall on an older model two-door hatchback.

Staying low, he swaps out the car tags.

31

"**I** understand you are rushing to wrap up the hotel project, but I'm hoping you might have time to run a shopping errand for me," Suzanne says, sweeping breakfast dishes from the kitchen table. "I hate to admit it, but there are times I want to escape household duties. The selfish me wants to enjoy a long weekend in Aspen. Just this morning, the weatherman reported today will be the hottest day we've seen. Temperature is expected to climb over one hundred degrees. That said, I'm glad the laundry service was able to turn my dress around so quickly. Best of all, the orange Jell-O Wade dropped on its collar during a hurried lunch came out without a hitch."

"They do a good job. As for the long weekend getaway, I've been told Santa Fe is the new Aspen. That said, I have to finish the paperwork on the Pederson project. Can our travel plans and my shopping wait until tomorrow?" Glenn asks, throwing out an apologetic frown. "I'm swamped."

"As always, Wade is holding onto your every word." Moving about the kitchen, she eyes their son and the koi pond just beyond the open window.

Throwing her eyes to Caroline, who is now bathing in oatmeal, she hopes Glenn remembers they are celebrating her birthday at school, and later, when grandparents gather around the kitchen table. "Do what you need to do. I'll handle it."

"Is this the truth I'm hearing?" he asks with an easy smile.

"Of course. If you want to discuss this further, I'll need a cocktail with two olives and a twist," she says, matching his smile. "Did I tell you I planned a picnic at the park on Sunday? I know the children will enjoy it. I'm thinking we should go around eleven. After that, we will head to the airport."

"Works for me. Again, I'm sorry I can't get away. Be sure to take pictures at school."

"I was so wrapped up with Grandparents' Day that I forgot about Caroline's birthday," she says in a low voice.

"I forgot about it too. By the way, thank you for including my mother in all of the activities and hoopla. She enjoys spending time with the children."

"No problem. After I drop everyone at school, I'll drive over to American Way. I need to grab paper products for the school's luncheon. If time allows, I'll make a quick trip to the boutique at Laurelwood. Caroline will be so disappointed if she doesn't have several birthday gifts to tear into. By the way, I grabbed cupcakes for her classmates."

32

"**G**et out," DeShane orders.

"I need your help," Atwood begs with sad eyes. "My legs are cramping, and I'm feeling lightheaded. If it's not too much trouble, I would like water."

"I don't have water."

"Young man, I need water."

"Forget about the water. If you want to stay alive, you will get out of the trunk. I'm not asking again."

Throwing out an arm, Atwood pulls himself to the edge of the trunk. Looking into the sun, he rubs at his eyes. "Please, help me."

"This should help," DeShane says, waving the gun in Atwood's face. "Hustle your ass. I've got things to do."

Sitting upright, Atwood lifts his leg over the latch. Although his face grimaces in pain, his other leg soon follows. Planting his feet on the soil, he gives his body a necessary stretch. Offering a prayer in song, he turns to walk away.

"Get back here and stop with the singing. You sound like a squirrel that was just shot out of a tree."

"Young man, you might give singing a chance."

"I'll sing what I want to sing."

"I find that singing offers comfort in times of conflict."

"You must be part mule. If you don't shut your trap, I'll be forced to shut it for you."

"This is how I pray."

"I pray you'll shut up. Now get moving. We're going over to that park," he says, pointing to a gathering of tall trees.

Inching along, Atwood maps out an escape plan. Understanding he will have to make a run for it, he seeks out a path. If he can get to traffic, he believes he will be home free.

"Postal boy, tell me again what you do back home."

"I no longer deliver the mail. When time allows, I often lead my congregation in song. Perhaps like your preacher."

"Look around, preacher man. We ain't in church."

"Would you pray with me?"

"So, you're a comedian too."

"I don't mean to be funny. I'm trying to help you."

"If you don't shut your trap, you'll be the one needing help."

In the passing minutes, DeShane looks back on the life he has been dealt. He lives with cockroach bites, and when his mother lets loose her temper, a tattoo of cigarette burns freckle his arms. Most nights, he goes to bed on an empty stomach and greets the morning smelling of urine. A birthday is never celebrated with cake and ice cream or a gift wrapped in fancy paper. More than once, he was reminded that he was lucky to get new underwear.

His mother has never attended parent-teacher conferences. Each time he begged for her support or for her to encourage his interest in auto mechanics, a class he looked forward to on those days when he attended school, she looked at him with cold eyes. The afternoon he asked her about life insurance, she nearly choked to death on her coffee. Shouting expletives, she gave him an earful. With anger rolling off her tongue, she explained their lot in life.

"People like us don't have life insurance. We rely on welfare checks. What is worse is that your old man doesn't live up to his obligation of paying child support."

All he knows about his father is that he never tossed him a ball or ran alongside him while he was learning to ride the bike he stole from the neighbor's porch. Letting go of the memories, he gives Atwood a hard shove.

"Come on, Mr. Mail Man. We need to see a man about a swing set."

33

"This tallit was given to me by my great-grandfather at my bar mitzvah," Atwood cries out.

"I don't care if he gave you nunchucks and a nunchaku," DeShane says, wrapping the narrow scarf around Atwood's neck. "I hope you're not allergic to twine."

"For all that is holy, please do not do this. I'll likely die hugging this swing set, but your future will be forever altered. As I said earlier, your actions are criminal. You'll spend the rest of your life behind bars. Armed guards will monitor your days in the sunshine, and you'll become just another number in the system. If you let me go, I'll turn a blind eye. If this is about the car, you can have it," he says. "Again, I have forgotten your name."

"No reason for you to know it."

"You're a young man. You can turn your life around. If you'll allow it, I'll help you. I can be your mentor."

"No one has ever helped me. And stop with the mind games. If you keep offering empty promises meant to save your ass, I'll put a bullet in it. And quit calling me young man. I'm a man—neither young nor old."

"I don't know what you're escaping, but I know I can help you."

"You wanna help me?"

"As I said earlier, I am a man of my word."

"Shut up already," DeShane says, shoving the head covering into Atwood's mouth. "That should do the trick."

34

Rolling into the apartment complex, Red slows his speed and revs the engine. When an empty parking space cries out to him, he hurries to take it. Sitting tall in the passenger seat, Dynamite Dean rubs his hands together like a Boy Scout hoping to start a fire. A glance in the rearview mirror sparks a fire in him.

Alone in the back seat, Pugs eyes the building. "What's the unit number again?"

"E-eleven," Red says.

"Sally's mother is a different kind of animal. She is one crazy, messed-up bitch. She scares the bejesus out of me," Dean throws out.

"What about Sally's old man? Is he around?" Pugs asks.

"Not in the picture. DeShane's younger brother lives there too. He's just a kid. No chance he's armed or dangerous. From what I have been told, I'm betting he will pee his pants."

"How messed up is his mother?"

"I'm pretty sure she chases nose candy with a fifth of vodka. Word on the street hints she is always a little loopy and she never misses a meal. A heavy pour and illegal drugs seem to rein her in. It's been said she hurries to drink a year's worth of booze before the calendar turns the page. I'm guessing she will come at us with a cast-iron skillet or her ride."

"Her ride?" Pugs asks.

"Broomstick."

"Beat his old lady to the punch. If she puts up a fight, cut off her hands."

"And his little brother?"

"Make him watch every blow she takes. If that snot-nosed thief is in there, bring him out to the porch. Hold a knife at his throat just like you did with that misfit over in Blue Goose Hollow. One more thing: tell his mother there is a price on DeShane's head. She might rat him out if we give in to her addictions."

35

A hard kick to the door throws out a sea of splinters. Leaving Marshall to fend for himself, Ramona jumps off the couch and makes a run for the bathroom.

Grabbing her by the hair, Dynamite Dean tackles her to the floor. "Where is he?"

"I don't know who you are talking about."

"DeShane."

"I don't know."

"For a poor kid from the hood, he travels the globe like a rich man." Throwing his knees into her back, Dean turns to Marshall. "Is he in this house?"

"No," Marshall says, swallowing hard.

"Do you know where he is?"

"No, but he said he is coming back."

"Red, search the place. Look behind doors, under beds, and roll the couch."

"You better not be lying to me," Dynamite Dean says, pulling the knife from the waistband of his jeans. When Ramona tries to get away, he runs the blade over her face. "A little birdie told me you know where he's hiding. I'm giving you fair warning. I will cut you into pieces if he comes marching in here."

"I swear I don't know where he is. When he walked out, his slim pockets were full of nothing."

"There is a price on his head," he says, placing a fifth of vodka and a clear bag filled with white powder on the floor.

"I'll call you when he shows up. He has to meet with his parole officer twice a week."

"What reason do I have to trust you?"

"I won't double-cross you. That son of mine is worthless and lazy. He's a parasite. He hurries to grab onto a host, and when he's done there, jump onto another one."

"I really want to believe you, but it has been said blood is thicker than water."

"Not in this family. I hate the sight of blood, and I prefer vodka to water. I swear I won't protect him."

"Your kid is a double-crosser and a thief." Sucking in his cheeks, Dynamite Dean lifts her off the floor. "It appears you are dumber than a box of rocks. I'm guessing you drink your vodka out of a lick-log. Now, walk out that door," he says, pointing.

"I'm not going anywhere. I have a son who needs my help."

"Get your fat ass out that door," he repeats.

"I have to be at work in the morning," Ramona cries.

"Forget about tomorrow. I'm making you an example today. And don't get too close to me. Those rings around your belly remind me of Saturn. I'm betting you are probably just as gassy."

In the coming minutes, Marshall cries out when his mother takes a hard and fast fist to her face, a blow to her chest, and when she tries to fight back, suffers broken bones in her arms and the loss of her right ear.

When Dynamite Dean pulls her pants down to her ankles, Marshall cries out for help.

"Little man, do you want a piece of the action?" Dean asks, turning to Marshall. "You just have to work around all that blubber. Something tells me there will never come a time when she can suck in her gut."

36

Riding low and slow, DeShane cruises the hood before parking the Saab one street over from their unit. If his mother gets wind of the stolen car, she will likely give him a long-winded lecture until she runs out of breath. Not to be outdone, she will nail his ass to the wall. Finding the unit's front door off its hinges, he races inside.

"Marshall?" he calls out.

"Where have you been?" Marshall asks, peeking out from behind the couch. "A couple of guys came here looking for you."

"Where is Mom?" DeShane asks, racing over the floor.

"She went with the bad guys."

"Did these guys hurt her?"

"One guy bloodied her face. I think he broke her nose. Blood splattered everywhere. When she fought back, he cut off her ear. It hit the floor with the earring still on it. One of the guys pulled down her underwear. DeShane, he did terrible things to her private parts. She cried out at first, but then she played dead. I could see the soles of her feet as they dragged her out to the car. When they body-slammed her into the trunk, I hid under my bed. She didn't even have time to put the lock on the door."

"Maybe because the door was on the floor."

"DeShane, Mom didn't even put up a fight. They dragged her over the street by her arms."

"What did they want?"

"You. The guy with red hair and bumpy skin said you stole something, and now somebody is really mad at you."

"How many guys are we talking about?"

"Two guys came into the house. Another guy stayed in the car. He aimed a pistol out the window. The guy with the knife called you a double-crosser. What does that mean?"

"I beat them at cards. They are nothing more than a bunch of sore losers."

"I don't know. All three of them were carrying."

"Carrying what?"

"Guns. I cried like that boy down the street when you stole his bike. They laughed at me. I was so afraid, I peed my pants."

"Listen, Marshall, I have to go out for a bit. Go next door and stay there until I get back. Don't say anything about this to anyone. I'll stop at the manager's office. I'm betting they can have the door fixed in no time. Again, say nothing. You promise?"

"I promise, but promise you will hurry back."

37

Careful to remain in the shadows, DeShane travels the neighborhood. Believing his actions will go unnoticed, he edges up to the Village. A quick drive-by tells him Pugs is at home. The garage door is open, and music floats on the air. When his thoughts shift to Atwood, he steps on the gas.

His next stop is a gas station at the corner of Shotwell Avenue and Garfield Street, where squatters and panhandlers hurry to greet him. When he lifts his shirt and gives a glimpse of the gun's barrel, they move about faster than ants rushing to build a colony.

Standing tall and pumping gas, he studies the area. In the car to his left, a young man taps at the car's dash while bobbing his head to music escaping the open window. A double-cab truck darts through the parking lot before rolling to a stop at a tire store. He watches the driver, a big guy sporting a sleeve of tattoos, spit to the ground before entering the store. Minutes later, a forklift drops four tires into the truck's flatbed.

Faster than a speeding bullet, DeShane races over the concrete where he shimmies up to the truck's tailgate. Sticky fingers have him grabbing an electric chainsaw and a leaf blower.

Embracing the life of a rich man, DeShane returns to his car. A bat turn onto Whitwell has him traveling the middle of the road where he cuts off a driver. The next turn has him on Arrowhead Road, a narrow street lined with simple homes built on a workingman's budget.

A glance at a car parked under a tree has him rolling up to the street's edge. Staying low, he rips the car's tag from its rear bumper.

38

"**M**y car has been stolen," Atwood reports to the officer who takes his call.

In the coming minutes, he provides the car's model and its car tag information. In his next breath, he shares the color of the car, its vehicle identification number, and a description of the angry young man behind the wheel.

One hour later, the police department transmits a BOLO teletype bulletin to Georgia, Ohio, Florida, and Tennessee and its neighboring states. The BOLO warns that the young man is armed with a .38-caliber revolver.

39

DeShane circles the synagogue's parking area. His frustration grows when he does not see Atwood. Eyeing the swing set and the bundle of twine, he rolls to a stop and steps from the car.

"Here, boy. Where are you?" he shouts as if calling out for a dog.

Killing time, he walks the compound's grounds and its sculpture garden. Hearing only the beating of his heart, panic begins to seep in.

"That son of a gun got away."

Left with few choices, he follows the road signs leading him back to Memphis.

40

Fighting the onset of hunger, DeShane exits the highway. He circles McDonald's and takes a quick tour of the plaza. While Long John Silver's wets his whistle, he travels the street leading him back to McDonald's. Ignoring posted signs, he secures a space reserved for disabled drivers.

Inside the fast-food restaurant, the manager notices the car and its driver. Fearing a holdup is about to occur, he phones the police.

Hearing a siren, DeShane hurries out to the street where he returns to his car. A turn at the stoplight has him in the drive-through lane at Carl's Jr.

"I want a double burger and fries. While you are at it, throw some bacon on there," he says, throwing out Atwood's credit card, "and make it snappy. I'm on my lunch break."

Accepting the bag, DeShane tears at the wrapper. "My burger is over-bunned."

"That's how they come," the server says.

"Throw on another cheeseburger. And don't add anymore bread."

DeShane's next stop is at a strip center on American Way. While inching the Saab into the slim parking spot, he eyes a storefront's window display. A set of speakers begs him to come in for a visit.

"Can I help you find something?" a clerk asks when he steps over the store's threshold.

"I'm waiting for my friend. He's looking for a stereo system. This is my first visit to Circus City."

"Well, I'll be right over here if you need me," she says, turning away from him. "By the way, it's *Circuit* City."

"That's what I said."

Shrugging his shoulders, DeShane exits the store and returns to his car. Keeping a watchful eye, he travels to the back of the store, where he hides in wait. When an employee props open the door, he edges close. When the time is ripe, he moves at the speed of lightning. Shuffling about like he belongs there, he makes his way to the storeroom. Faster than a speeding bullet, he lifts a set of speakers from the store's holding area. Fast on his feet, he races out to the alley and into Atwood's car.

In the coming minutes, he flies through traffic signs and changes lanes while racing through a changing light. When a car to his left swerves in his direction, he struggles to find the brake pedal. In his panic, he makes a hard turn. While he sits wide-eyed, the four-door spins about, rolls over the curb, and, striking a utility pole, is thrown into traffic where the car crashes into the side panel of a Volkswagen Jetta. Before DeShane takes his next breath, the Saab's front tire suffers a blowout and the rim takes a beating, leaving him stranded in heavy traffic.

Escaping the car, the driver of the Jetta hurries to make sure no one is injured.

"Are you OK?" the young woman asks, tapping at his window.

"You slammed into me," DeShane argues.

"You pulled into my lane."

"I must have been in your blind spot."

"I was in the middle of the intersection. I'm calling the police and my husband. May I see your driver's license?"

Reaching into his back pocket, DeShane pulls Atwood's driver's license from the wallet.

41

"**I** saw the accident," a motorist says.

While DeShane tells the witness the young woman crashed into him, the driver of the Jetta studies DeShane's license. She is quick to notice that DeShane has black hair and dark skin, while the man in the photo has little hair and blue eyes. Doctor Atwood, the man in the photo, appears decades older. A quick glance tells her the man on the plastic card recently celebrated his sixty-third birthday. Feeling something is not right, she grows quiet.

In the coming minutes, two patrol cars arrive on the scene. Following close behind is the young woman's husband.

"Is anyone hurt?" an officer asks.

"I'm a little rattled but otherwise OK," the young woman says.

"Same," DeShane throws out.

"Looks like your car is disabled," the older officer says, eyeing the Saab's bent rim. "Do you have a tow company you can call?"

"No."

"We will call Richard's Custom Towing. The car will be impounded. Is there someone you can call for a ride?"

"My mom is at work. I drop her off and pick her up when her shift is over. I can walk from here." Moving about, he circles the car like he is wearing spurs.

"Perhaps the tow truck driver can give you a lift. I'm sure you know they will hold your car until the accident goes to trial or settles with the insurance companies," the officer says.

Hearing these words, the young woman pulls her husband close.

"Something is not right here. He is not the person on the driver's license," she says in a whisper.

"Are you sure?"

"This license belongs to a man named Doctor Morris Atwood, who happens to be much older."

Taking his wife at her word, he calls the officer to his side.

"Excuse me, officer. I need to speak with you. I'm Haywood Smalley. This is my wife," he says, taking her hand. "I teach at Rhodes College. It appears the driver of the other car should be in school."

"Sir, we are not interested in that at this time. There are no injuries, and we need to keep traffic moving."

"Did you run the plates? Did you run the car through NCIC?" Haywood continues.

"I believe one of our officers has done both."

"Did you check to see if there are any outstanding arrest warrants for the driver?" he asks, hoping the officer will notice the picture on the driver's license bears no resemblance to the young man who is now sitting on the curb.

"We did."

"What about the VIN? Does it match the tag? What about a QV and REG?"

"We have done all of these things. Regarding the VIN, we ran all seventeen characters. The vehicle identification number matches the car's fingerprint."

"What about proof of insurance?"

"In the glove box."

"Did you run a BOLO?"

"Be on the lookout? Of course."

"You and your team need to be alert here. This kid is a bit sketchy."

"I understand your concern, but please trust that we are doing our job. Is your wife's car drivable? As I said to the other party, the impound lot will hold the car until this matter goes to trial or insurance pays out."

"It appears drivable."

"Please understand it's over a hundred degrees out here, and PST, the police service technicians, need to clear this accident. I'll get a copy of the police report for you so you and your wife can get moving."

While clearing the scene, the officer issues DeShane a juvenile citation for failure to yield right of way and lets him go.

42

"The traffic officer hinted that you might need a ride," the tow driver says.

"Where are you taking my car?" DeShane asks, sniffing the air. "I smell cigar smoke and garlic."

"I enjoyed a cigar after breakfast. The car is going to our impound lot. It's about a ten-minute drive from here."

"Is it near Circus City?"

"I'm not familiar with Circus City."

"They sell electronics. My mom works there."

"Are you talking about Circuit City?"

"That's what I said. I can walk from here. I need something to drink."

"I have bottled water," the driver says, pointing to a blue and white cooler.

"I want a soda."

43

"**I** am hoping you will tell me you found my car," Atwood says when the detectives enter his home.

"After an accident, your car was towed to Richard's Custom Towing in Memphis," the seasoned detective shares. "I apologize that the officers on the scene failed to do their jobs. On a positive note, there were no injuries. Here is the paperwork we received."

"Is my car drivable?"

"No, sir. You will need to have it towed to a repair shop."

"Was the young man taken into custody?"

"No, sir."

"The young man who kidnapped me is demonic, angry, armed, and dangerous. Hands down, he is the most troubled person I have ever met. He needs help, guidance, a positive role model, and someone to believe in him."

"While that may be true, he broke several laws," the detective adds. "When you say he is armed, do you recall anything about his weapon?"

"I'm not familiar with guns, but I believe he was carrying a Glock. There was a tube-like piece attached to it."

"Likely a Surefire suppresser."

"His actions tell me he was born into the life of poverty, abuse, and abandonment. I worry he has siblings who fight these same demons."

"These demons often lead to life in prison or an early grave. By any chance, did you get his name?" the younger detective asks.

"He said his friends call him Slim and that his real name is Willie Mahoney. I got the feeling he was lying about both."

"Any idea where he might be headed?"

"It's possible he is returning to Chattanooga. I had the feeling he was running from something. Should you catch up with this young man, I hope you will give me a moment to talk with him. Perhaps I can help him turn his life around."

44

"**D**o you know if you will be able to attend the luncheon?" Suzanne asks. "It would mean the world to the children."

"Tell me again when it starts and where it will be held," Glenn says, holding the phone close.

"Twelve thirty in the school's gymnasium."

"I'll do my best to meet you at school," Glenn says, glancing at his watch. "I gotta go. Love and kisses to all."

45

DeShane drags his feet along American Way, a multilane street. A dry cough reminds him he needs something to drink.

Farther down the street, he eyes Corner Store, a big-box store. Recalling the refund check he found in Atwood's wallet, he steps through the store's sliding doors. He is quick to notice the dome surveillance cameras hugging the ceiling. When he is called up to the café's counter, he throws a wave to the camera while pulling his wallet from his back pocket.

"I want a basket of chicken wings and a large Coke."

Shifting her weight about, the waitress runs her fingers over the register's flat screen. "That'll be nine dollars."

"What? You must be kidding me. That's highway robbery," DeShane says, raising his voice.

"Do you want it or not?"

"I want it," he says, throwing down the refund check.

"We don't accept refund checks here."

"Put it on my credit card," he says, throwing down Atwood's plastic card.

"Here is your order number. I'll call it out when your order is up," she says, handing him the receipt she rips from the cash register.

Minutes later, when the last chicken wing in the basket is down to its slim bone, DeShane meanders the parking lot. This time, he will not be lifting stereo equipment but looking for a car to steal.

46

Careful to avoid eye contact with the young employees who appear to be protecting the electronics store, DeShane takes a seat at an oak picnic table offered for sale outside the big-box store. When a store clerk approaches, DeShane lifts off the picnic table. Shuffling about, he fakes interest in an outdoor grill and a grouping of seasonal plants. When the clerk offers to help, DeShane blows his nose into his hands and wipes them over the grill's large hood.

"What are you doing, man?"

"Giving you something to do. Go away and leave me alone."

Returning to his seat at the picnic table, DeShane observes abandoned carts, hurried shoppers, and rows of parked cars. He sips the soda and slips out of his high-top sneakers. Giving his tired feet a rest, he rubs the ball of his right foot. In the passing minutes, he is drawn to a red sports car, but when the car's owner, a beefy guy who appears to spend most of his day at the gym, shouts out to someone, he continues searching the lot. When his eyes fall on a blue Saab, a winning grin crosses over his face, and his feet return to his shoes.

Stepping over the cracks in the asphalt and skirting around large chunks of broken concrete he believes was once part of the median, he meanders the lot. Careful to stay near the Saab, he moves quickly and under the radar. Jumping over otter puddles a recent rain left behind, he avoids eye contact with the shoppers he meets along the way. With a skip in his step, he circles the lot until he is within arm's reach of the Saab.

Bending at the waist, he peeks through the driver's window. A smile owns his face when he finds the car's interior mirrors Atwood's Saab—the gearshift is in between the front seats, and the control panel has countless buttons and dials.

When he looks back at the superstore's exit, he notices a woman walking his direction. He watches as she glances at the timepiece on her wrist. He is surprised when she does a one-eighty, returning her to the store.

Pulling the tab from an empty soda can he finds in a shopping cart, he uses the sharp edge to loosen the car tag's screws. Moving down the line, he lifts the plate off a Honda Civic. Once he secures the Honda's plate to the Saab, he takes refuge behind a Ford pickup truck.

47

Remaining in the shadows, DeShane watches the young woman as she exits the store. This time, she is carrying several bags. Eyeing her narrow hips, his heart quickens. When she lets go a smile, he finds her easy on the eyes, unlike the girls who walk the streets in his neighborhood and always point at him and laugh behind his back. In the coming hours, he will show those stupid girls the man he has become. It will take only the blink of an eye for them to learn his training wheels have come off and he has moved up to stud status.

Staying low and lurking in the shadows, he times the woman's steps and keeps his eyes on her hands. When she opens the driver's door, he slides into the Saab's back seat.

48

"**D**rive, and no funny business," DeShane orders, brandishing his weapon. "To be clear, I'm not here for a scenic tour." Inching up behind her, he whispers in her ear. "I'll shoot you if I have to."

Finding his face in the rearview mirror, Suzanne shutters in fear. The twisted look he gives sends a shiver up her spine.

"Please let me go. I have a family," Suzanne begs.

"I didn't ask if you have a family."

"Do you see that plane?" she asks, attempting to restore calm. "I recently learned the plane's fuel is stored in the wings."

"That's bullshit, and I'm not buying it."

"It's true."

"Says who?"

"My husband flies a Bonanza."

"Do I look like I care?"

"I am just trying to make conversation."

"I'm not here for conversation."

"Please let me go. I have children who need me," she begs. "The car is yours."

"I told you to drive. I'm not asking again. I'm the one who needs you now. And change the station."

"What?"

"Change the radio station. I'm not listening to that shit."

With unsure hands, she turns the dial—slowly scrolling through the channels.

Growing impatient, DeShane leans over the seat and pushes her hand away. "That's better," he says when rap music escapes the car's speakers.

In a flash, Suzanne's thoughts turn to her children and their love of music. They enjoy singing along with Raffi. They always request that the music be turned up when he sings a little ditty about a baby whale.

"What street are we on?"

"American Way. I believe it travels the city to the Mississippi River."

"What's on the other side of the river?"

"Little Rock, Arkansas."

"What's near Little Rock?"

"Greer's Ferry Landing," she says, catching his eyes in the mirror and the fallen sign leading them to Arkansas. "There is a beautiful church there."

"I don't care for churches. They offer solace to a bunch of hypocrites asking for their sins to be overlooked."

"I find comfort there. Would you like to visit the church? Perhaps your prayers will be answered."

"Don't go preaching to me. You know nothing about me."

"I'm hoping I can help you."

"Did I ask for your help?"

"I think you need help. You should know I'm not afraid of you."

"Keep your thoughts to yourself. As for being afraid of me—it's only a matter of time."

"If it's my car you want, it's yours. I'll pull over and never look back. You have my word. If things are bad at home, I can drop you off at a shelter."

"Are you disrespecting me? And I don't trust you or your words. Whatever is happening under my roof is none of your business. Since you like to talk so much, tell me about your kids," he says, tapping the back of her head with the barrel of the gun while pulling at the collar circling her neck.

"Jack is our oldest child," she says, throwing a hand to her head. "He likes to ride his bike."

"I never learned to ride a bike. Does he look like you?"

"A little, mostly when he smiles," she says, fighting the growing lump in her throat.

"Has he ever been to juvie?"

"No."

"Is he street-smart?"

"He knows to look both ways before crossing."

"Sounds like he's a mama's boy," he says, laughing.

"He's a good son."

"Whatever. What about the other kids?"

"Wade likes pasta, but he doesn't care for vegetables."

"Don't blame him."

"He'll come around," she says, recalling the time he stuck a carrot stick in ketchup before shoving it up his nose. "He likes hot chocolate and a sweet treat from Shipley Donuts."

"Where is that at?"

"It's a doughnut shop in Greenville, Mississippi. Have you been there?"

"Once or twice when no one was watching," he says, pausing. "That's it? Only the two boys?"

"Yes," she lies, not wanting him involved in Caroline's young life.

"What's up with the pencils?" he asks, shopping a box he lifts from the leather pocket behind the driver's seat.

"Jack wants to be an architect. If you look at the floorboard, you will find a drawing pad."

"Sissy."

"My son is not a sissy. He's good and kind, and his future is bright. He would never kidnap an innocent woman."

"Who cares? Your son is nothing like me."

"I'm proud of him."

"Sounds like you're making excuses for him."

"My family is normal. We share breakfast, join hands at dinner, and share stories at bedtime. Why do you want to harm me and change my children's future?"

"I'm guessing it's my purpose in life," he says, turning away. "Do you live near the ocean?"

"Memphis doesn't have an ocean. We have a koi pond in our backyard. The children enjoy watching the fish circle about. When time allows, we enjoy vacationing in Florida. My sons love the water, especially near Sarasota."

"Is it near here?"

"Driving distance. It's in Florida."

"Never been there."

"It's a nice place."

"Is it near Daytona Beach?"

"It's about two hours away. Have you been to Daytona Beach?"

"Where I go and what I do is none of your business."

"Do you have any siblings?"

"I don't know," he says, shrugging his shoulders. "What does that mean?"

"Brothers and sisters."

"Nope," he says, not caring about the lie.

Placing a hand over her heart, Suzanne worries, should she survive this nightmare, the many ways this moment and those sure to follow will forever change her. A voice in her ear shouts she will never again trust a parking lot. A shiver running through her warns she will never subject her children to such fear. Eyeing the young man in the car's rearview mirror, she presses her foot on the gas. Swallowing hard, she considers ramming the car up ahead. Believing the accident and the confusion that will surely follow will allow her to make a run for it, she throws her foot to the car's accelerator.

"Don't run the light and slow down. Who do you think you are? Starsky and Hutch?" he asks, recalling the detectives' Ford Gran Torino. "You best obey the speed limit. If you do anything to attract the attention of another driver or the police, I'll put a round of bullets in your head. Do you understand?"

"Yes."

"What's up with all these Prince Mongo posters?" he asks, looking out the window.

Meeting his eyes in the rearview mirror, Suzanne struggles to put her words together. "His real name is Robert Hodges. He's been running for mayor for as long as I can remember. His claim to fame is that he believes he is from the planet Zambodia."

"Is he?"

"I can't answer that."

In their silence, he catches a whiff of her perfume. It reminds him of a tree he once passed under on his way to school—sweet and fresh. It is nothing like the smell of scotch and bourbon his mother wears. "You smell like soap."

"It's a big day for me. We are honoring our children's grandparents at school."

"I don't have parents or grandparents."

"Where are your parents?"

"Hell if I know, and that's no business of yours. Enough about my family tree and its bare branches. Give me your earrings."

"They are costume. My son gave them to me for my birthday."

"Shut your trap and give them to me. I'll take your necklace too."

"They are meaningful to me."

"Not anymore," he says, reaching over the headrest and throwing out the palm of his hand. "This is my first visit to Memphis. Let's take a ride down Poplar Avenue."

"I don't want to be your tour guide."

"Cut the crap. You will drive where I tell you to drive."

"I just want to go home."

"Quit your whining. Did you ever see the movie *True Grit*? Don't bother with an answer. One more sound out of you, and I'll go John Wayne on you." Exchanging a look in the car's mirror, the silence lingers for a handful of seconds. "Are we on Poplar Avenue?"

"Yes."

"Turn at the next light. And get a move on. I don't have all day."

"Which direction?"

"How should I know? Just don't do anything stupid."

Rounding the corner onto White Station, Suzanne slows her speed when she eyes a group of teenagers traveling the sidewalk.

"What is that up ahead?" DeShane asks, pointing to a campus built from red bricks.

"White Station High School."

"Did you go to school there?"

"I'm not from here."

"Where are you from?"

"Iowa."

"Where is your old man from?"

"Omaha," she says, hoping the lies will put an end to his line of questioning.

49

"**P**ull into that parking lot," DeShane says, pointing to a large compound planted behind a wall of trees.

"There is a church around the corner. Friends and family gather there to celebrate a wedding or the passing of a loved one before gathering at Memorial Park."

"What park?"

"Memorial Park. It's a cemetery in East Memphis."

"Listen up, smarty-pants. I'm on to you. I'm giving fair warning right here and now. Quit messing with my head. Who the hell wants to visit a cemetery?"

"The cemetery, our final resting place on earth, is a place of solace. It offers a healing environment for those who wish to pay respect to those they have loved and lost. There is a growing list of those who continue to seek solace and search for answers when the storm comes at them. I have been told when threatening waves battle the sea, many sailors struggle with fear, while unaware, other sailors are searching for shelter. If you would like, we can go inside. Perhaps we can pray together," Suzanne says, turning her attention to the church.

"I ain't got time for praying. I have bigger fish to fry. Give me your purse."

"I don't have much money, and my purse is a knockoff."

"Knock off of what? And park your tires."

"Prada. I can't afford the real thing. We can drive to my bank. I'll give you all the money I have in my account. Just let me go home to my family."

"That's a great idea. I don't know why I didn't think of it. I say we visit an ATM—one without a security guard or a camera."

While she inches the car into a parking space, he reaches over the seat and grabs her purse. "I don't see a phone in here. Where is it?"

"It was right here. It must have fallen between the seats."

"I want it."

While she searches the space around her, he studies her driver's license.

"Suzanne. Now that's a pretty name."

When she does not respond, he studies the area. He is quick to notice the chapel's brick facade and white trim. The structure sits back from the street, and keeping the front lawn green, a sign directs its visitors to parking in the back. A quick search of her purse has him shopping her wallet. Faster than a common street thug, he shoves her wallet into his pocket.

Although she considers making a run for it, Suzanne's eyes fall on a mourning dove resting in the branches of an aging magnolia tree. Seated behind the wheel, and accepting her life is about to change, she allows her thoughts to take a visit down memory lane. Caroline arrived during the country's most threatening tornado. Power outages shut Memphis down for days. The living room's woodburning fireplace heated their small home, and when the markets closed, they relied on canned goods and peanut butter to get them through. The branches of their tulip poplars were ripped away, and the walkways and streets were littered with debris. Faced with fear, her family hunkered down and prayed. Lost in thought, her trip down memory lane is interrupted when she hears voices.

When a growing group of members she believes are leaving Bible study eye her car and her passenger, Suzanne reaches for the door handle, but catching the young man's eyes in the mirror, she pulls back her hand. It takes only a quick glance out of the corner of her eye for her to understand the church members have noticed the young man in the middle of the back seat. When she does not make eye contact, their excited chatter fades.

Standing on the steps outside the chapel, the crowd of curious onlookers huddle together and speak in low voices.

"Smile big and brush them off with a simple wave," DeShane whispers. "No monkey business, you hear me? If they come over here, tell them that you're with that CASA program and you are working to make me a better person."

"I need to use the restroom," Suzanne says. "I'll only be a minute."

"You're gonna have to hold it." As his words drift between them, he recalls the many times his mother yelled those same words at him, and later to Marshall. Each time, he got a whipping for wetting his pants while young Marshall was asked to do better.

In their silence, Suzanne's cell phone rings out.

"Don't answer it and hand it over."

"It might be my children. I'm expected at their school."

"Don't make me use this gun," he says, pressing the barrel against the back of her seat.

"Please don't shoot me. I just want to go home to my family."

"Give me your phone."

A quick glance at the phone's screen lets her know she has an incoming call from Glenn. Although she struggles to hold the phone, she speaks her concern. "My children might need me."

"Not anymore," DeShane says, throwing out his hand. "Give me your phone and no funny business. I wouldn't want to shoot you. The last thing I need is your blood spraying everywhere. I just washed this shirt yesterday, and I lifted these sunglasses last week. Like it or not, you're driving us to Shelby Farms. I hear there is a lake there."

50

"There is something suspicious happening in the parking lot," Agnes Landram shares with the property's security guard. "There is a woman in a blue Saab. She is seated behind the steering wheel, and a young man is in the middle of the back seat."

"That's odd. Did either make eye contact with you?"

"Although the woman gave us a forced smile, I believe she wants to escape the car. When I stepped toward the car, they both stared straight ahead. The driver turned away like she didn't see me. I can't be certain, but it appears she is in fear for her life. Did I mention she avoided eye contact?"

"Not until now."

"I think we should call the police."

"I'll make the call. If they haven't driven off, I think you should take a picture of them. If you can, take a picture of the car's tag. Although it is rare in this zip code, I fear this just might be a kidnapping."

"A kidnapping in East Memphis?"

"I have come to accept crime happens everywhere."

51

Throwing a finger to the turn signal, Suzanne returns to Poplar Avenue. Travelling west, she turns onto Shady Grove Road. Meandering the winding road, she stops at a traffic light before turning onto Walnut Grove Road. A look to the sky has her admiring an Aero Commander, a low-flying plane hovering overhead. A pinch in her heart has her wishing she were on it.

"Who lives in that house?" DeShane asks, pointing to a large house holding up the street's corner.

"It once belonged to Sidney Shlenker."

"Never heard of him."

"Imagine that," she says in a voice above a whisper.

"What did you just say? Are you disrespecting me?" he asks, believing he did not hear her correctly.

"No. Of course not. That would be foolish of me."

Letting her thoughts drift, she makes a bat turn where she travels the winding road leading to Shelby Farms. She has taken her children to Patriot Lake so many times she can drive the winding roads with her eyes closed. Thinking about it now, perhaps that is what she should do. Fearing she might crash into a car or a cyclist, she brushes off the idea. Returning to the present, she sets her eyes on the car's mirror.

"At one time, Sidney Shlenker owned the Denver Nuggets and was chief executive of the Houston Astrodome's parent company."

"What's he doing now?"

"He suffered a spinal cord injury in a highway accident that left him a paraplegic. He later died of a heart attack."

"He must have been one unlucky guy." A field of flowers west of Germantown Parkway catches DeShane's eye. "What is that?"

"A sunflower farm planted years ago to kick off the corn maze." Suzanne's thoughts return to her children and the Halloween costumes they have spoken of in recent weeks. Jack wants to be a ghost, while Wade is fascinated with the *Lion King*. A lover of the sea, Caroline begs to be a mermaid.

"You know," DeShane says, rubbing his hands together, "I bet you would be a head turner in a miniskirt and a leather bustier. My girlfriend likes cutoff shorts and crystal meth. Damn drugs are rotting her teeth. All she has left are little black stubs that look like coal."

"I'm sure she is missing you. I would be willing to bet she would wear anything to keep you interested."

"One of my girlfriends has a crying-ass baby that's not mine, and her bite is better than her bark."

Left without words and afraid to speak those that dare to roll to the tip of her tongue, Suzanne keeps her eyes on the open road.

"The baby's daddy is known on the street as Charge. Don't know his real name, but he's always flying high on China white and prescription pain pills. My girlfriend tells me he is in rehab more often than the staff. Word on the street is he fathered his own mama's daughter. That would be his kid sister. As for my girlfriend, she's colder than a floating ice cap."

When Suzanne remains silent, DeShane moves in close behind her. "I've always wanted a car with leather seats."

"It's yours. Just let me go."

"What is hanging in that tree?" he asks, pointing.

"It's a bike. It is there to honor Cory Horton. He was a swim coach and a triathlete."

"Why is the bike in a tree?"

"He lost his life in an accident while riding his bike."

"Did you know him?"

"Everyone knew him. He was a good person who brought out the best of everyone he met."

"One day, I'll have a statue in a park. I don't bring out the best in people, but my actions will go down in history." Throwing a hand over the headrest, he strokes her hair. "If you are up for it, we can play cops and robbers. I can't wait to slap handcuffs on your wrists," he says, giving a low whistle. "I can already see us out on the town. We can take NetJet to the Florida Keys. I'm not well read when it comes to history and ancient Greece, but I've read about Florida. While the sun begins to set, you will order a cosmo, and I'll have a Bloody Mary, and later, a scotch and soda—on the rocks, of course."

"I will never have a drink with you, and you will never get away with this. If pressed, I would bet the last dollar in my wallet that you are not old enough to drink. As for your statue, it will be removed, smashed to pieces, and tossed into a dumpster."

"My sweet Suzanne, I'm not liking the sound of your voice. You need to take a chill pill. As for my age, where I come from, drinking does not require an age. How about we throw back a few and talk about wedding venues and our honeymoon destination. I'd like to visit Disneyland."

"We are not getting married, and Disneyland is for children. I'm guessing your empty pockets changed your troubled mind about taking NetJet to the Florida Keys."

"You better watch your mouth. Have you forgotten that I'm the one holding the gun?"

"I've had it with your nonsense and your threats. Your actions and the desperation in your voice tells me you will never reach your dreams. Just shoot me now and put me out of my misery. I pray when the time comes, you will have a swift trial and a short walk to the electric chair."

"I struggle to believe all along I thought I kidnapped a good person. Your words suck the air right out of my lungs. I'm glad your boys aren't here to hear your ugly words."

"Leave my children out of this. I've begged you to let me go home to my family. All you care about is yourself, alcohol you are not old enough to drink, and Disneyland."

"I gotta tell you, Suzanne. I'm liking your fire. Maybe we should stop the car, throw out a blanket, and better get to know each other. After that, we can go shopping for a wedding dress and a veil so long that it kisses the floor. We are going to live on a sweeping estate in a big white house with a meditation garden and a generous landing strip for my private jet. I'm gonna give our house a name. It's gonna have fancy wallpaper and a jungle room filled with furniture like the Brady Bunch had."

"What are you talking about?"

"*The Brady Bunch*. They had a television show. We can go house hunting right after we get married."

"I am married, and I love my husband. My future is with my family. As for your house, I believe you mean you want to move to Graceland."

"Where is Graceland?"

"On Elvis Presley Boulevard. Elvis lived there. I can drop you off there. I understand they have tours available."

"Who is this Elvis dude?"

"Everyone knows Elvis. He was the king of rock and roll."

"Stop with the mind games and forget about Elvis. He doesn't have anything on me," he says, waving the gun about. "Gimme me your ring. And what's in that bag?" he asks, pointing to a brown bag on the car's passenger seat.

"Cupcakes. I'm taking them to my children's school."

"Not anymore. Hand it over."

When Suzanne takes her hand off the steering wheel, she considers stepping on the accelerator and slamming into a row of trees. When she catches his eyes in the mirror, she lets up on the gas.

"I want your ring."

"No!"

"I'll get it one way or another. I'll cut off your finger or take a chainsaw to your arm. I'll let you decide. I'll take your watch too."

"I have babies. They need me. I feed and nurture them. Please let me go. You can have all that I have, but please let me go home to my family."

"Hand over the ring. I'm not asking again. I'll leave that to this here gun," he says, resting the gun's barrel above her ear.

Pulling her wedding band from her finger, she lets go a tear. "This ring is meaningful to me."

"It will be *meaningful* to me, too, when I sell it," he says, tearing into a chocolate-covered cupcake. "What does your old man do?"

"Do?"

"Don't play word games with me," he warns, giving her shoulder a hard shove with the palm of his hand. "What does he do to bring home the bacon?"

"Bacon?"

"Are you getting smart with me? I'm asking about his job."

Swallowing hard, she prepares her tongue to throw out another lie. "He is a janitor at a nearby school."

"I don't trust school janitors. They move about like they are mopping the floor, but I'm guessing they are paid to keep their eyes on the students who drift along the halls between classes. For what it's worth, I've never seen one scrub a toilet or offer a roll of toilet paper."

"My husband engages the students in conversation. He enjoys going to work, especially in late summer when the kids are eager to learn their schedules."

"I hated school, and I didn't give a rat's ass about my teachers, the hall monitors, or a clean floor. What's Bonne Terre?" he asks, eyeing the sign up ahead.

"A bed-and-breakfast resort in Nesbit, Mississippi."

"Have you ever been there?"

"I prefer national parks."

"I didn't ask what you prefer. Have you ever been with a black man?"

"Yes," she says, shooting cold eyes to the rearview mirror.

"Did you like it?"

"I'm referring to you. I don't like this at all. I wish you would let me go. I have a family who needs me. What we share is not a friendship or a walk to the altar. It's an evil plan you have plotted. You are an eyesore on this community. You will never be my life coach. Your actions tell me you are going straight to hell."

"Just when you think you know someone. Listen up, sweet cheeks. Forget about your family. As for hell, I've already arrived there."

"I don't want my family to be without me, and you are wrong about my husband."

"You best accept we are carving out a new future."

"We are not a *we*. I'm married with a family. Tell me, what is it you are running from?"

"I'm not running from anything or anyone."

"I'm guessing you either broke a few laws or crossed the wrong person."

"Keep your guesses to yourself," he says, looking away. "Who is Danny Thomas?" he asks, pointing to a large billboard.

Trembling, Suzanne remains silent.

"I asked you a question."

"He started St. Jude."

"Saint who?"

"Jude. It's a treatment center for young children. The parents don't pay a penny. Donations cover all medical expenses. We can go there if you would like."

"The only place you are going is into the trunk," he says, pressing the gun against her head. "As for me, I'm making a quick visit to Chattanooga. I gotta see a girl about a mattress. Before I do that, I have to visit a tow lot about a set of speakers."

52

Thrown into total darkness, Suzanne kicks at the trunk's lid and searches the trunk's floor. When the car accelerates, she throws her hands to the lid. Panic has her struggling to breathe.

"Help me," she shouts, hoping someone will hear her. The air is thick, and her breathing is becoming labored and shallow. Fighting fear, hope begins to fade. When the music is bumped up, she again cries out.

Folding her hands together, she worries for her children. *Who will feed them? Who will read to them and tuck them into bed? Who will comfort Caroline when I do not show up to celebrate her birthday?*

Closing her eyes, she envisions their young faces. In them, she sees sweet, strong, tender, and determined children. She prays her death will not change them.

What will become of Glenn? Will he always talk of me? Will I be buried back home? If my body is not found, will my family continue to search for me?

When the questions become too much for her breaking heart, she cries into her elbow.

53

Hearing loud voices, Marshall inches open the door. It takes only the blink of an eye to know the naked woman traveling over the sizzling concrete on her backside is his mother.

"Listen up, little brother. When you see DeShane, tell him he is next on our hit list," Red shouts, throwing a foot to Ramona's face. "If you double-cross me, I'll make sure you spend your last days in a cripple's wheelchair and drinking piss from a toddler's sippy cup," he warns, fisting his hand. "If that doesn't scare you, I'll cut out your tongue and shove it up your ass. If you are still breathing, I'll have you exterminated."

54

"Mr. Urling, this is Marcella from school. Suzanne has not arrived, and Grandparents' Day is wrapping up. Do you know if she is heading this direction?"

"Have you tried her cell phone? I tried calling her about fifteen minutes ago, but my call went to voicemail," Glenn says.

"I've tried her cell several times."

"She left early to make a run for paper and plastic products. She is also picking up birthday gifts for Caroline. I'll try her phone again."

55

Fast on his feet, DeShane enters Charmagne's apartment. A glance at his watch reminds him he has only minutes to enjoy their encounter.

The sound of beating drums escaping Charmagne's apartment has his heart skipping a necessary beat. He is disappointed to find Shasta, Charmagne's best friend, parked on the couch. An open bottle of vodka and two plastic cups own the coffee table.

"Hush it up, DeShane. You know I like to hear breaking news," Shasta says in a loud voice. "The city is reporting another kidnapping."

He is quick to notice her voice is as smooth as bourbon. Born decades after Twiggy, DeShane has grown tired of the gossip comparing Shasta to the English supermodel famous in the seventies. It came as no surprise when he overheard a brother in the hood sharing with his ghetto friends that Shasta and Charmagne are known in the hood as Tipsy and Boozer.

Hours after DeShane's release from Oakdale, Shasta made the moves on him. Before the night was over, he stripped down to his birthday suit and slept with her. In exchange for an evening of sex and unlimited street drugs, she agreed to keep her trap shut. If Charmagne gets wind of happenings between her man and her best friend, she will likely take a knife to both of them.

Thinking back on their many one-nighters, a smile crosses over his face. He enjoys his time alone with Shasta. She does not have a crying-ass baby, and instead of smelling like soiled diapers, her apartment smells like dryer sheets. Unlike Charmagne and her constant demands, the only talk Shasta knows is pillow.

Although Charmagne dresses like a Southwest flight attendant in the seventies, it would be the death of him if he were to tell her the apartment's foul odor remains on his clothes for days. She will likely tell him to walk out the door and never look back. He needs her but hates her kid and the changes the little snot brings to their relationship.

While Charmagne's kid plays in the refrigerator box, DeShane shares a joint and the pint of vodka with Shasta and Charmagne.

"I think you were half-lit when I got here. Are you still breastfeeding?" Shasta asks Charmagne. "That kid is high and drunk."

"He's used to it. He acts like he is drunk half the time and plays miserable the rest of the time."

"Are you still tricking?" Shasta asks with little interest.

"I'm guessing it pays the bills," DeShane says in a whisper.

"Catch phrase much?" Shasta asks, throwing out her eyes.

"Back off," he says, displaying a wide grin. "By the way, is that your real hair or are you wearing a nest on your head?"

"That is almost funny. Get this. I stole the vodka from Old Lady Tigret." Letting go a laugh, Shasta allows her thoughts to turn to her boss at the liquor store. "She'll never miss it. She is too busy spitting tobacco and shouting orders. Sometimes I think she believes she is running a German war camp."

"I've lifted alcohol dozens of times from Frau Tigret," Charmagne throws out. "My only punishment is a glare. She's afraid of me and my kind. I'm guessing the knife in my pocket has her turning a blind eye. I believe she has heard I am known as *the cutter*."

"I came by to say I'm disappearing for a while. I have bullets to dodge," DeShane interrupts, avoiding eye contact. "No need to share this with anyone, you understand?"

"Our lips are sealed," Charmagne promises, tossing back the bottle. "I guess this means we are back to dumpster diving. I hope we don't stumble upon a newborn still attached to the umbilical cord."

"What are you talking about?"

"If it can happen in New Orleans, it can happen here."

"Word in the hood hints that you are avoiding a punishment hearing and a butt chewing. It amazes me that you can be so stupid at times. Just so you know, I've been told you're no longer part of the big boys," Charmagne shares.

"The brass?"

"I'm talking brass knuckles. You best watch your back."

56

Suzanne's mouth is dry, and her lips are sticking together. Each swallow burns her throat. The car's speed has her worrying they might crash. Her only hope is she survives it.

The stereo grows louder, and the temperature continues to climb. She recalls hearing the weatherman declaring today will be the hottest day of the year.

Believing the car is switching lanes and picking up speed, she throws her hands to the side panels. Before her next breath, she hears screeching tires and the honking of several horns. In the coming minutes, she feels the dip of several potholes, the rails of a train track, and each time the car leaves the road, she fears the car might roll into a ditch or crash into oncoming traffic. When the car comes to a stop, she screams out.

"I need help! I'm in the trunk. I've been kidnapped!"

When no one comes to save her, panic and fear envelop her. She prays her kidnapper will stop and give her water. Removing her shoes, she kicks at the trunk's lid. A poorly placed kick throws a pain into the arch of her foot. When her cries go unheard, she pounds her fists on the lid until blood falls from her knuckles.

Hearing her cries for help, DeShane pulls into an abandoned parking lot where he slams on the brakes and pops the trunk.

"Knock it off. If you keep yelling, I'll shove a tennis ball down your throat," he warns, eyeing a ball in the grass. "If that doesn't stop you, I'll wrap your head with duct tape. Do you understand?"

While words do not come, she nods in understanding.

"Not one more sound out of you," he warns, waving the gun about. "This is your last warning," he says, slamming the trunk's lid.

Although it was some time ago and the memory is slowly fading, Suzanne's thoughts drift to a time when Glenn encouraged her to join him in a round of golf. She recalls Glenn's disappointment when his ball rolled over the fairway before settling in a pool of water. The puddle he pointed to was a muddy one. *Casual water,* he called it. Thinking about it now, the dark puddle looked like a newly-planted grave. Licking at her lips, something tells her she would give anything for a drink of that water.

"I'm tired of struggling, and my prayers continue to go unanswered. The pain in my chest tells me the fight in me is growing weak and slowly fading. I want only to survive this and return home to my life with my family. His actions tell me the kid at the wheel is angry and troubled. While I struggle to understand his life and the family he will disappoint, I pray he will turn his life around." Pausing, she wipes at her tears.

"There has never been a day when I haven't given thanks for my children. I want to go home. I want to take my children in my arms and tell them how much they mean to me. I want to wrap my arms around Glenn and whisper into his ear my love for him. Dear Lord, please hear my prayers. If there is ever a time I need you, this is it."

When the sense of urgency begins to fade, she cries in a whisper. "I'm here," she says, raking her fingers over the trunk's carpet. Closing her eyes, she accepts her next breath will likely be her last.

57

Believing Pugs and Dynamite Dean are close behind, Hank kicks open the door to Charmagne's apartment.

"Where is he?" Hank asks, waving a gun in the air.

"Who?" Charmagne asks, throwing her son into the refrigerator box.

"Sally."

"He's not here."

"I didn't ask if he was here. I asked where he is."

"I don't know. He came by, but he didn't stay long."

"Is that kid his?" Hank asks, pointing the gun toward the toddler in the cardboard box.

"No."

"Is this the truth I'm hearing, or do I have to beat it out of you?"

"I had my son before I met DeShane."

Doubting her words, he gives her the once-over. "Holy smokes. You have some long-ass arms, and your paws look like they belong on Bert."

"Who is Bert?"

"A dalmatian. That boy of yours looks like Sally."

"Well, he is not DeShane's boy."

"You must be Charmagne," Pugs says, entering the apartment. "Sally once said every move you make is calculated and dangerous. I'm guessing your heart and your mouth mirror Sally's—they know only to lie, cheat, and steal. And why are you dressed like that? Are you a streetwalker?"

"I like shorts, and the lace-up boots get me what I want and need."

"She's always roaching," Hank throws out. "She wears imitation leather boots and the shortest of shorts. She sleeps around, spreads diseases, and battles unwanted pregnancies. I've heard it said she is known as the five-dollar hooker. I've been told she is often asked for a refund."

"When you see Sally, be sure to tell him I was here. My friend here is going to stick around for a while," Pugs says, looking to Dynamite Dean, who mirrors his evil grin. "Start with the cardboard box and everything in it. When the flames grow, toss in the roach."

58

The temperature is climbing and beads of sweat travel DeShane's face as he enters the impound lot. Driving up to the guard station, he cranks up the music.

"I need to get a few things out of my car," he says, entering the lot's small building.

"Can't do that without a release from your insurance provider," the clerk says.

"Not a problem."

Turning on his feet, DeShane returns to the car. Grabbing Suzanne's cell phone, he calls the eight hundred number listed on Atwood's insurance card.

"This is Doctor Atwood. My car has been involved in an accident. It's impounded. The tow lot needs a release so I can get my things."

"Of course, Mr. Atwood. Are you referring to the Saab?" a voice asks.

"Yes."

"I hope you weren't injured."

"Not even a bruise."

"What tow lot should I contact?"

"Richard's Custom Towing in Memphis."

59

Drifting in and out of consciousness, Suzanne's thoughts turn to her mother. It takes only a memory for her to recall the pies she baked and the candy she always kept in a jar near the telephone. Although her heart is breaking, a smile comes to her face when she pictures her mother sipping hot tea from Rosenthal china.

After braiding Suzanne's hair, her mother would wrap the long strand into a bun. She always tried her darndest to hide the thin metal clips.

When errands pulled her mother from the house, she drove an older model Ford Coupe that often traveled up and over the curb. On a good day, when the music was familiar to her, she sang along with the radio, often encouraging Suzanne and her sisters to join in.

Every Saturday, she took Suzanne and her sisters, along with the neighborhood's kids, to the skating rink where they circled the floor until a cry from their stomachs sent them to the large booth where a pepperoni pizza awaited them. Although her mother never let on, it was rumored she would rather be fishing the lake down the street.

A smile comes to Suzanne when she envisions her mother's aging face. Although she continues to argue the expense, her mother has two sets of false teeth. She wears the old dentures during the week. Every Sunday, before leaving the house, she pops in what she calls her *church teeth*.

"Mama, if I make it home, we are going fishing for that trout you have always wanted to catch."

60

"Sally's got a ride," Hank says. "He kidnapped and carjacked an elderly man."

"What's he driving?" Pugs asks, stroking Bert.

"A blue Saab."

"Where did this go down?"

"Right under our noses."

"Where is his victim?"

"The old man was tied to a swing set and left for dead but was able to escape. The description of the young punk who took him for a ride matches Sally. Authorities are searching Chattanooga, Nashville, Jackson, and Memphis. They put out a BOLO."

"We are going to issue our own BOLO—one involving a 637 Lady and orders to shoot to kill."

"Why the Lady?"

"Sally is a titty baby and a pussy," Pugs says, grinding his teeth.

61

A hand to the car's turn signal has DeShane exiting Poplar Avenue and turning into Chickasaw Gardens. He continues along Iroquois Road until his poor driving skills return him to the Poplar corridor.

Crossing over to Union Avenue, he heeds the signs leading him downtown. His heart races when a convoy of police cars appears in his rearview mirror. His mind races with a myriad of thoughts—all involving high-speed chases through side streets and parking lots littered with curious pedestrians. When his eyes fall on the police station up ahead, he returns to Poplar Avenue.

In the coming minutes, he travels Beale Street before turning onto Main Street, where he admires the Orpheum Theatre. His next turn has him on Wagner—a street that mirrors Front Street.

Believing he might need a new set of wheels, he considers dumping the car outside a local pasta joint occupying a two-story building he believes has a view of the river, Mud Island, the city's new bridge, and warehouses and abandoned buildings. Knowing he will need another car, he circles the lot. When the Mississippi River comes into view, he returns to Riverside Drive. Slowing his speed, he admires the mighty river and its steady waves slapping in rhythm against an approaching barge. He recalls hearing from Pugs that this area was once called the Pinch District because of its emaciated immigrants who fled the potato famine. The last time Pugs visited Memphis, he called this part of town the Pinch Gut.

Curious like a kid, DeShane heads toward the Bass Pro Shop but stops short when he understands he cannot leave the car. When he approaches Schering Plough, a manufacturing plant, he lifts off the accelerator. He wonders what is made there until the Coppertone sign jumps out at him. Recalling the shoplifting charges slapped on his mother when she attempted to steal a plastic bottle of body lotion returns a smile to his face.

Circling Kimberly-Clark's parking lot, a Mercedes convertible catches his eye. Thinking he might take it for a ride, he eases off the accelerator. When he catches sight of a security guard meandering the lot, he crouches low and picks up speed.

Down the road, where cars come whistling by, he travels Cleo Wrap's parking lot. Before his next breath, he veers off the paved road where loose gravel hits the car's underbelly.

Wiping sweat from his hands, he bumps up the air conditioner and throws an arm out the window. Lost in thought, he recalls the time Dynamite Dean pointed to a passing car. "That man's driving a four fifty," he said. "All four windows are down, and the speedometer is staying at fifty." Although he had not understood the humor, he had laughed along.

Revving the engine and rounding a tight curve, he hops onto the Hernando de Soto Bridge taking him to Arkansas. Always on the lookout for cops, he keeps the speedometer's needle at fifty-five, the posted speed limit.

Drifting into the fog lane, he takes the exit leading him to Forrest City. In the coming miles, he passes by a working farm and a sandlot. Up ahead, his eyes fall on a forgotten cemetery and a trestle bridge the railroad surrendered to vandals and drifters. Slowing his speed, he travels a rutted dirt road. When an abandoned barn comes into sight, he parks his tires and cuts the engine.

In the silence, he struggles to understand why he was dealt this lot in life. There was a time he wanted his family to be normal. He wanted his old man to shuffle off to work and, at the end of his shift, hurry home to his family. If the weather was nice, he wanted his father to throw him a ball, teach him to ride a bike, and, when his legs tired and his father needed to rest, share a cone from a passing ice-cream truck. He was just a toddler when he understood that the only person who knocked at their door was a bill collector.

Accepting his lot in life, he looks to the sky where he watches the clouds drift on a warm breeze. Looking back on his childhood, he did not care about crayons and coloring books. He wanted to write a book on how to survive the streets and the poison that comes with it. He wanted his writing to be successful and appreciated. His books would not involve love stories and scientific adventures but words to help and encourage kids like him who suffer in the hood to do better and aim higher. He would make enough money to feed the hungry and dress the young kids who raced off to school. Appreciating his generosity, learning would be important to them. His words would speak of family and the role each member plays. Once success was handed to him, he would escape the streets and control the boardroom. It is only now he understands that other than the woman in the trunk of the car, he does not know anyone who has a normal family.

In the coming minutes, his thoughts turn to the public housing he calls home. The walls of their apartment never celebrated a fresh coat of paint or heard laughter and encouraging words. His mother has never asked about his day, and he does not know to ask about hers. In those times when he got sassy, his mother was quick to whip out the belt.

Birthdays were not celebrated with gifts, cake, and ice cream. Instead, his mother counted on fingers the number of years she would continue to be stuck with him. Given his current situation, it is only now he wishes he could return home. Promising to turn his life around, Marshall would look up to him, and his mother would work to be proud of him. Before reality has time to set in, a twin-engine plane flying overhead interrupts his thoughts.

Tapping at the steering wheel, he searches the area. When his eyes fall on a wall of mature trees, he pops the trunk.

"Get out," he orders.

When Suzanne doesn't move, he reaches for her hand. He is quick to notice many of her nails are torn away, and bloody carpet fibers cling to her fingers.

"I'm letting you go."

When she does not respond, he grabs her by the legs and pulls her from the trunk. A quick search of the area confirms they are alone. Although it is a struggle to drag her body through the tall grasses, he continues. When he reaches the row of trees, he pulls her under low-lying branches. When he notices her bare and bloodied feet, he returns to the car where he retrieves her shoes.

Returning to her lifeless body, his eyes fall on the glow of a fallen angel. The afternoon sun gives light to her golden hair. He wants to brush his hand over her cheek, but instead, he touches the curve of her neck. He finds her skin smooth and tender—nothing like Charmagne's dry and cracked skin. Leaning close, he picks up a fragrance his untrained nose does not recognize.

"I'm guessing I better get going," he says in a whisper. In the coming minutes, he fails to notice the sun taking refuge behind a growing cloud.

Returning to the car, he grabs Suzanne's purse and the bags she carried through the parking lot back in Memphis. Curiosity has him searching the bags. When he discovers a rag doll, his anger grows.

"Unless your sons play with dolls, you lied to me," he says, spitting to the ground. Dragging his feet back to the car, he looks over his shoulder. "Way to go, Suzanne. Look what you made me do. Just so you know, I'm already on the hunt for my next victim."

62

The hour is skirting up to three o'clock when police come upon a car in an abandoned elementary school near the river. A look under the hood confirms the battery was stolen. The car's VIN number matches the vehicle registered to Angela Bartoni.

A search of the car confirms the catalytic converter was removed from the car's underside and the car's GPS hardware was ripped away.

63

"**A**s we speak, Miss Bartoni's body and car are being searched for biological evidence," Detective Koutney says, throwing out his badge. "When this is finished, the trace examiner will do her job, which includes combing through critical evidence. You should know the trace examiner is a whole different animal. To ensure safety at the scene, she will follow the homicide investigation standard operating procedures."

"There ain't no such thing," Mahoney says with authority on his tongue.

"Do you see that photographer?" Koutney asks, pointing.

"What is she taking pictures of?"

"She is searching for trace evidence—clues and evidence we might not see. She is skilled at finding skin tissue, body fluids, saliva, semen, and blood—giving us biological evidence. She will study and manage the scene. After absorbing details, she will collect and preserve any and all materials, including footprints and DNA. Fingerprints and human hair are just the beginning. You should know we will ask the court to allow us to take a hair sample from you."

"Pubic or head?" Mahoney asks, throwing out a killer's grin.

"If I have learned anything in my career, it is that both will always reveal the truth," Koutney answers with a challenge on his face. "The team will collect fabric fibers, nail clippings, and soil. They will tweeze the car's interior and its trunk. They will follow the same procedures in the victim's apartment. The man in the lab coat is also a trace examiner. It's been said trace evidence is a whole different kind of monster. He is combing for material evidence left behind after a violent crime. When we are through here, we will know if you sneezed, turned a doorknob, or flushed a toilet. It has been said that the more you know about your criminal, the better you can determine their next move. It is believed the persons responsible for this heinous crime were previously convicted of crimes including statutory rape, drug dealing, extortion, and abuse of children."

"We didn't do nothing," Calvin says, dropping his voice. "They can comb through shit for all I care."

"They will, and you should. Tell me, are they going to find your prints at the house on Browns Ferry Road? The death and damage left behind appear to be the work of a gang."

"They ain't gonna find anything to pin on me."

"Ain't is not a word," Koutney corrects, quoting Judge Judy, his wife's favorite television personality. "As for pinning anything on you, that remains to be seen."

"Seen all you want."

"It appears Miss Bartoni's vehicle was driven through the area, and several small trees appear to have been run over while others were painfully bruised. Tire tracks indicate the vehicle in suspect spun out of control. An empty vodka bottle was left behind. Prints are being processed as we speak." Pausing, he gives Calvin the once-over. "Tell me, Calvin, do you have family? A wife or children?"

"I've never been married, and I can't swear to having children. I've made hundreds of donations, but I've never heard if any of them took. No woman is ever going to tie me down or rope me into marriage. I like the life I'm living, and I don't need anyone telling me what to do and when to do it. That life is for the poor and unfortunate."

"Any chance you know who we are looking for?" Koutney asks. "You should know we also found the victim's body and her purse. Rosary beads were found in a pocket. The list of charges continues to grow."

"I don't know shit about rosary beads. Sounds like something my sister would buy at a carnival. A dozen names race through my mind, but I'm suggesting you set your sights on DeShane Salliver," Calvin throws out, hoping the torture the young woman suffered will be pinned on Sally.

"We've been to his home. No one came to the door," a lesser officer shares.

"Sally is on the run. I've been told there is a price on his head."

"Sally?" Koutney asks.

"That's DeShane's street name."

"Who and what is he running from?"

"A badass guy in Onion Bottom. I don't know what Sally did to piss off this guy, but I'm guessing you would run too if he was after you."

"We located a car we believe was taken by gunpoint. Its driver was forced to go along. Twenty-four prints were found on the car's interior. Tell me about Salliver," Koutney says, flipping the pages of his notepad.

"Sally's a homeboy and he isn't street smart."

"Regarding the list of charges, it includes motor vehicle theft and possession of narcotics. Pathology reports concluded the impact of the car fractured the victim's skull and ruptured the brain. It likely caused immediate death. Injuries to the vaginal area indicate criminal sexual penetration in the first degree and three counts of battery. Should trace evidence find you guilty, you are looking at three counts of resisting arrest or avoiding an officer and assault and murder. I'm sure you are aware tire treads crossed over the victim's torso. The victim also had bruising in the neck area. The fingers on her right hand were cut off, indicating she was wearing jewelry. In the coming days, we will know her last meal. We will also know what she had to drink and any prescription meds she may have taken."

"I want a lawyer," Mahoney says, dropping his voice.

"If you can't afford a lawyer, the court will assign one to you. In the interim, we will contact your parents to make them aware of your arrest, the charges, and that you will be held on remand. You will remain on pretrial detention. If this language is foreign to you, I'll break it down for you in simple words you might understand. You will remain behind bars. You should know a legal team will put together a list of trial witnesses and expert witnesses."

"They don't scare me. I'm not ashamed of my actions or afraid to speak my mind."

"Try not to look smug. Judges hate it. This is not about grand larceny. Given the facts, there is no way you will beat the rap. I'm guessing you and your band of smart-mouth clowns will be forced to face the music."

64

Resting tired bones, Glenn observes the emptiness around him. Once again, he is alone on the compound's third floor. A quick glance at his watch reminds him activities at Caroline's school are coming to a close. When he revisits his conversation with Suzanne, a hint of guilt runs through him. Recalling his hectic schedule, he is quick to brush it off. A born leader, Suzanne always has matters under control. Feeling an emptiness in his stomach, he reaches for his jacket. Knowing the cafeteria's weekly menu by heart, he believes today's special will be a Caesar salad with store-bought croutons. Just as he reaches to close his laptop, the phone on his desk gives a frightening ring.

"Hey, Dad, do you know where Mom is? Caroline is acting like cry-baby duck," Jack says.

"She's at the luncheon," he says, revisiting his conversation with Marcella.

"I can't find her. I've looked everywhere, and now, Aunt Sissy wants to go home."

"My sister?"

"Mom wanted to surprise you. Mom was supposed to bring all the plastic and paper goods."

"I'll try her cell phone again. I'll also call Gail Mann. Maybe she can tell me something."

"Mrs. Mann is here. She's been looking for Mom too."

"Give me fifteen minutes to wrap up here. I'm going to run by the house, and then I'll be on my way."

65

Glenn travels the house on Ashley Cove before stepping into the kitchen. Observing the generous space, he is drawn to the answering machine and its blinking light. Hoping to hear Suzanne's voice and an explanation for her absence, he presses the flashing light.

"Glenn, dear, this is your mother. Suzanne is not here at the school. The kids are beside themselves with worry. One of the volunteers offered to drive us to your house after the function. Don't worry about the children. They are safe and in our care."

While panic tries to weave its way through his veins, Glenn searches the house for clues. Returning to the bedroom, he scans the calendar Suzanne keeps on her bedside table and religiously updates. The pink heart circling today's date puts a pinch in his heart. Rushing over the floor, he searches her closet. His frustration growing, he races down the hall to the coat closet. When he finds Suzanne's suitcase in the closet's dark corner, a sixth sense warns that she did not leave him but has been taken against her will.

66

"**T**his is the police. Please open the door," an officer shouts.

Inching open the door, Marshall throws out his eyes.

"Is DeShane Salliver here?" Koutney asks, displaying his badge.

"No," young Marshall answers in a weak voice.

"Who's at the door?" Ramona shouts.

"The police are here. They are looking for DeShane," Marshall yells over his shoulder.

In the coming seconds, Koutney and a trio of officers watch a big woman ramble over the floor.

"What do you want with DeShane?" Ramona asks with attitude on her tongue.

"I'm Detective Koutney. I would like to question your son about a murder."

"He isn't here."

"Do you know where we could find him?"

"You can be damn sure he is not down on his knees in church."

"If you see him or talk with him, please give me a call," Koutney says, offering his card.

67

While the minutes unfold, Glenn's concerns continue to grow. The ear-to-ear smile on Caroline's face tells him the birthday celebration must go on. Gathering the few gifts Suzanne purchased days earlier, he watches his mother wrap each one with tenderness that brings him to tears.

"Daddy, where is Mommy?" Caroline asks. "We can't have cake and ice cream without her."

"She offered to stay at school to greet the grandparents who missed their flights and are expected to arrive later in the day. She promises she will be home before the candles blow out."

Dragging a chair over the floor, Caroline takes a place at the window. Leaning forward, she rests her small elbows on the window's narrow ledge. Hungry eyes study the street. Each time a car approaches, she presses her face against the glass.

"Dad, do you think Mom might be having car trouble?" Jack asks.

"She will be here soon. I promise," he says, ignoring the scenario his mind hurries to paint.

"Can you drive over to the school and check the parking lot? It's not like Mom to miss time with family."

Shrugging tired shoulders, Glenn makes his way to his mother's side. "I'm no Perry Mason, and Suzanne is no Della Street. Street thugs aren't looking for us. I've been told the bad guys with ill intentions seek out and prey on unsuspecting women. Suzanne is always on her toes. Let's serve the cake and ice cream. While everyone celebrates, I'll head over to the school."

"Glenn, I'm starting to worry," his mother says in a faint voice. "This is all Suzanne has talked about for weeks."

"I understand. I'm worried too. My gut instinct and our history have me believing if Suzanne feels threatened or smells a problem, she will take action. Those who know her understand she has no problem reaching out for help."

"Go look for her. We will keep the children busy," she says, letting her eyes fall on Maeve, Suzanne's mother. "We will be praying for her."

Glenn is caught by surprise when a tightening in his stomach tells him this day will end without answers. He wants to believe Suzanne will come up the driveway any minute and take away their worry, but the pinch in his chest warns a different truth.

68

"**W**e've not heard from her," Glenn shares. "It's not like her. She always sings a lullaby to our children." In the passing minutes, his children look at him with curious eyes and a growing list of questions they want answered. "Suzanne is missing," Glenn says in a low voice for only Drew and Brett Reasons to hear.

"Missing? Are you sure?" A former FBI agent in the Memphis office, Reasons continues to smell out crimes. Although he is officially retired from the bureau, his mindset remains the same. Late in the afternoon, hours before the moon makes its approach over the river city, he owns a corner table at Skinny Dick's, a pub near Mud Island, where the local agents hang out to revisit and discuss cold cases and attempt to solve cases new to the table.

"That's the problem. We don't know what we don't know."

"I have found in my line of work it is the child killers who keep us busy, but this is different," Reasons says. "It's not often a grown woman goes missing, especially one who appears to be in a healthy relationship. It might just be her kidnapper needed a set of wheels."

"What if he wants ransom money?" Glenn asks.

"You will pay it."

"You have to do something before it's too late."

Growing quiet, Glenn recalls the afternoon when he and Suzanne traveled the streets of Memphis's most desirable neighborhoods. When he turned onto Shady Grove Road, Suzanne took a growing interest in the grand estates.

"If one day we are able to own a house in this neighborhood, I want to give our home a name," she said.

Slowing his speed, he had turned to his bride. "What is it you would name our meek castle?"

Settling deep into her seat, she brushed her hand along her throat and turned to him with a dimpled smile. "Villa Urling."

Caught up in the memory, Glenn does not hear Brett call out his name.

"I'm sorry. What were you saying?" he asks.

"I'll contact the police. I'll demand action and request that a team is sent to your house."

"I don't want to worry the children. As you can see, we have family visiting."

"I'll ask them to cut the sirens and turn off the blues. Is it possible to talk in the garage?"

"At this point, anything is possible."

"I need you to be on top of your game," Reasons says. "Sadly, we are living in a time where we have more guns on the street than people."

"Is this your way of telling me that my wife might not be coming home?"

"Glenn, I love you, man, but I think you will agree we have no way of knowing how the coming hours, perhaps days, will play out. I do believe if Suzanne is in danger, she would want you to shield your children from the pain and fear you are suffering. When questions come at them, they will turn to you for answers."

69

"**N**o word yet, Mr. Reasons. We are looking for her car," an officer says.

"I was hoping you would say you're looking for my wife," Glenn throws out.

"I'm sorry, sir. That is what I meant to say."

A uniformed officer observes the house while another officer flips open a notepad and clicks a pen.

"Does your wife have any health issues?"

Ringing his hands and skipping his eyes over the empty space where Suzanne always parks her car, Glenn paces the garage floor. "Nothing serious. She plays tennis. When necessary, she takes an aspirin for the pain in her lower back."

The officer's face turns sympathetic. "I'm sorry, sir, but these are questions I have to ask. Did you argue this morning?"

"We don't argue. Did I mention we have three young children? Believe me when I say Suzanne is happy to listen to me even when she's heard the same story a dozen times," Glenn says with a look of disbelief. "You are wasting precious time. We had a conversation this morning about running an errand for her. It wasn't an argument. She asked me to pick up a birthday gift." A tear begs for understanding and forgiveness. "If only I had known how this day would play out." Biting back tears, he swallows hard and struggles with the catch in his throat. "I would do anything for her." His heart folds, and the scenario his mind hurries to paint is a scattered mess. "Anything."

"Unfortunately, we can't put out a BOLO until twenty-four hours have passed," the officer says.

"Suzanne Urling is in trouble!" Reasons says, raising his voice.

"We will do what we can. You have my word."

"I need more than your word. I demand action."

70

Prepared to conduct his own investigation, Glenn throws down his wallet. One by one, he places his credit cards in a straight line. Believing he can track Suzanne's movements, he grabs the telephone. It is after the third call that he makes a connection. Rubbing at tired eyes, he calls Brett Reasons.

"She used our MasterCard to make two purchases at Corner Store."

"The big-box store?"

"Yes."

"Here in Memphis?"

"Near Mendenhall. I'm telling you, something is terribly wrong. Suzanne is in trouble."

"Don't cancel the card. It's a tracking tool. I'm calling Dennis Ivy. He's with the FBI. Screw the twenty-four-hour hold. One way or another, I will see to it that we get that damn BOLO."

71

Keeping an eye on the car's side mirror, DeShane steps on the gas. Some forty miles away, Paragould is on his radar. In the coming minutes, he drives through a fast-food restaurant, where he orders a pulled pork sandwich and a double order of fries.

Waiting in line at the drive-through, his thoughts turn to Marshall. He wants to believe his baby brother is missing him, but knowing his mother's tongue, he doubts anything good has been said of him. A smile comes to him when he pictures his brother with a mustard sandwich he would be willing to share with him if he turned the car around.

He hates when his mother and her drama worm into his thoughts. If there was ever a woman who should never have had children, she takes the trophy. He never met her parents, but he once overheard his mother say his grandmother washed dishes and his grandfather dirtied them.

The few things he knows about his mother include that she walks along flat-footed, eats like a horse, and lives with an ample supply of regrets. She has never taken him to the zoo, offered a hug, paid for him to attend the school's field trips, or encouraged him to reach for the stars.

Parking his tires at the drive-through window, he hurries to hand over Glenn's MasterCard.

72

An advertising billboard has DeShane on the road to Paris, Arkansas. Using Glenn's First State Bank credit card, he checks into a roadside motel.

"How long will you be staying with us?" the clerk asks, accepting the credit card. "This part of Arkansas has several places to visit," she adds, sliding a travel flyer over the counter.

"Just tonight."

"If time allows, you might consider visiting our zoo. It has a train and a carousel. Exotic animals are not my thing, but my grandkids spend hours watching their playful interactions. They really enjoy the bearded dragon, the red-knee tarantula, and the fennec fox."

"All zoos are the same. If you've seen one, you've seen them all. For what it is worth, I hate tarantulas."

"Are you familiar with Magazine Mountain? It is beautiful this time of year."

"I hate mountains. The twists and turns do a number on my stomach."

"Perhaps you would enjoy Eiffel Tower Park. It draws in the tourists and world-famous photographers."

"Why is that?"

"It is a seven-foot two-tiered water feature."

"I feel the same about water features as I do about winding roads and tarantulas."

"To each their own I always say. Here is a park tag for your car. You wouldn't want it to get towed."

73

"**M**r. Sweatt, this is DeShane Salliver," he says, speaking into Suzanne's cell phone. "Can you get a message to Marshall?"

"Where are you? The police have been here looking for you. They must have asked me a hundred questions. For a minute there, I thought I was either on trial or in a deposition. They hinted that you are in a big heap of trouble," Sweatt shares.

"My new job has me on the road, and the police don't know what they are talking about. I am as clean as a whistle."

"I don't know, DeShane. The look on their faces put a fear in me. Your brother is home now. Should I get him?"

"Yes, please. If my mom is there, don't let on that I'm on the phone."

Minutes pass when DeShane hears a commotion in Sweatt's apartment.

"Hello?" Marshall says in a weak voice.

"Marshall, it's me."

"Where are you?"

"I'm with Dad," he says, not caring about the lie. "He needs my help."

"I need you too."

"Listen, Marshall, you are going to be OK. Promise me you will stay on the right side of the law."

"I promise. When will you come home?"

"Coming home is not my lot in life. I'm like Dad. We were born into a different lot in life—one that encourages us to travel the globe and its twisted back roads."

"I wanna be in your lot with you," Marshall says, fighting back tears.

"We can talk about this later, little buddy. Just promise you will stay out of trouble."

"I promise."

"I'm proud of you, Marshall. Your heart is as big as the moon, and your soul is pure."

"My heart hurts without you."

"Hang in there, buddy. I'll call when I can."

74

"**M**y MasterCard was used in West Memphis, Arkansas, and my First State Bank card was just swiped at a Holiday Inn in Paris," Glenn hurries to share with Reasons. "Suzanne made a phone call about an hour ago."

"To?"

"Don't know. She appears to be in Arkansas. I'm tracking the phone's movement on her iPad."

"Stay near your phone. I'll alert Ivy."

While Glenn waits for word, he revisits the vignettes of his life with Suzanne. The day he laid eyes on her remains etched on his heart. She was far more beautiful than the models who posed for magazine covers and traveled the runways in the latest fashions. She didn't need makeup and the newest trends. She was blessed with the gift of beauty and the warmest smile he had ever laid eyes on.

The way she moved about and the ease she displayed in small groups and growing crowds told him she would never settle for less than status quo. The sparkle in her eyes told his heart she was one of a kind. When she became one with his kind, he placed her on a pedestal.

Growing quiet, his thoughts drift to the many times Suzanne spoke of visiting Sedona. Although he wanted to be near the water, he agreed to travel Arizona's Red Rock Scenic Byway, explore steep canyon walls, and hike the areas many trails.

Minutes after checking into the hotel, Suzanne threw a canvas under her arm, grabbed an art easel, and steadied a paint palette in the bend of her arm. In the coming days, she was over the top with hiking trails and the picturesque red-rock buttes. On the last evening of their vacation, they shared champagne under the stars. Ring in hand, Glenn got down on one knee and asked for her hand in marriage.

Believing Suzanne would want a large wedding in a cathedral filled with flowers, chandeliers, and rose petals peppering the aisle, he was surprised when she hinted at an intimate wedding with family and close friends. Eight months later, they exchanged vows in front of family, loved ones, and friends they had held close for almost a lifetime. The photographer captured every smile, hand squeeze, and the kisses they exchanged when they thought no one was watching.

75

"**I** have the worst hangover," Chip Wagner shares. "I rolled out of bed this morning. After catching my foot on the bedside table, I took a crash landing on the floor. It took all I had to strap on my camo vest and lace up my field boots."

"What was the occasion this time?" Andy Hanson asks, shifting his Mossberg Patriot Predator over his left shoulder.

"Same as always. I was thirsty."

"You're always thirsty," Mitch Powell throws out with an easy laugh. "Andy, how is your father?" he asks, approaching Cloud Springs Road.

"I asked him to join us today, but his knee continues to play tricks on him. I'm not sure how much longer he can farm this land. This stretch of land holds some great memories. When I was just a tadpole, we picnicked out here. The air seemed fresher, and the sky appeared shades bluer. My mom would throw together a basket of home-cooked meals, and when the day was warm, a thermos of cold water made the journey."

"I always say there is nothing better than great memories," Chip says. "Is that your dad's Vortex Crossfire?"

"It took some arm twisting, but he agreed to let me use it."

"That's a great rifle. I'm betting you'll tag a dove or two," Chip says, admiring his Browning BAR. "If you use your scope, you might get a jackrabbit," he adds, eyeing a family of rabbits near the lake.

"I can't kill rabbits. I had two growing up—Tigger and Chompers. Chompers's given name was Fluffy, but when she ate her young, I tagged her with a new name that better described her."

"Rabbits make great pets. They don't bark, whine, or sneak into your bed in the middle of the night. Speaking of whining, I got all kinds of grief this morning. Nicole wanted me to stay home with the kids. I have to say, I didn't know my wife is so long-winded," Mitch shares.

"I haven't met a woman who isn't. Hey, what is that up ahead?" Chip asks, pointing to the tullie patch abutting the levee. "And what am I hearing?"

"Bobwhite quail. I've been told you can hear them a mile away. Someone drove through here," Andy says, setting his eyes on the tire tracks. "I hope they aren't hunting. This is private property."

"Don't look now, but I think that's a body up ahead," Mitch says in a weak voice.

"A body? How in the hell did a body get out here?" Andy questions, picking up his pace. "I'm guessing this explains the tire tracks. She must have been left here," he says, eyeing the scattering of shopping bags near the woman's feet. "Don't touch anything. I'm calling the sheriff's department. We will let them take it from here."

"Did you see her face?" Mitch points out.

"And gnats are swarming," Chip adds, swatting at the air.

"Should we call for an ambulance?" Mitch asks with fear in his voice.

"I believe you will agree it is a little late for that," Andy says, turning away from the lifeless body.

76

Assigned their route, two officers out on patrol spot Glenn's car at a hotel outside Paris. Believing the driver who stole the car is on the premises, one of the officers calls for backup. Parking his tires, he enters the hotel's lobby.

"I need to know the room number of the person who checked in using Glenn Urling's credit card," the officer tells the desk clerk.

"He is in room two sixteen," the clerk says, studying the computer's screen.

Taking the stairs two at a time, the officers find the door to DeShane's room propped open. A glance inside gives a glimpse of the older model RCA television. Although the volume is turned off, movie credits cross over the screen.

"Check the bathroom," the senior officer instructs in a low voice. "Wear gloves and don't touch anything."

77

"**T**his is a homicide investigation," Koutney advises. "We will follow the standard operating procedures—principle, policy, and procedure," he adds, addressing rescue personnel, evidence technicians, and homicide detectives. "As first responding officers, you will document who, what, when, and where," he says, throwing his eyes to the man who is wearing a serious face.

"Remember to record your arrival time at the scene along with weather and lighting conditions. Patrol units will establish a command post. The lead investigator and his team will be first on the scene to record and photograph all evidence before moving or altering the scene. In addition to crime scene photos, we will request an aerial survey. There will be a crime scene sketch and steps taken to protect the evidence. This includes tape, vehicles, and ropes. Dell," he says, addressing the older officer who wishes only to remain in the shadows. "No smoking. This scene is not to be altered in any way. That said, stay alert and be prepared. I've heard it said a threatened animal can sniff out danger. Remember, stick with open-source reporting and follow the rules regarding electronic crime scene investigations. I am off to a possible crime scene, but you can be damn sure I'll be back."

78

The police circle DeShane, who sits lazy-eyed and slumped over on the hotel's commercial ice machine. While his eyes search the sky, his feet are parked on the machine's slanted steel doors. Shifting his weight about, he tries to get comfortable in the clothes he pulled from a dryer in the hotel's laundry station.

When an officer approaches, DeShane moves the straw about before taking a sip from a fast-food cup. Observing the officer, it takes only a glance for him to notice the officer walks with a limp.

Aware eyes are now on him, the officer throws a hand to his hip. "Are you DeShane Salliver?" he asks.

"Did you get shot up?" DeShane asks, pointing to the officer's leg.

"Golf injury. Only a fool would take aim at an officer of the law. Please understand I ask the questions. Your duty is to answer them."

"I've heard it said a fool is born every day. Besides, I'm just curious."

"Are you DeShane Salliver?" Koutney asks, arriving on the scene.

"Yeah."

"How old are you, young man?"

"Sixteen," DeShane answers with sass on his tongue.

"Have you ever done time?"

"Once or twice."

"Given your young age and that you are a juvenile, I'll need a parent here before I question you. Would you like us to call your parents?"

"Nope. Question me all you want."

Aware his body camera is recording their conversation, Koutney pulls a rights card from his pocket. "Would you be willing to waive your rights?"

"Yep."

"Before I can proceed, I'll need you to sign this waiver," he says, offering a clipboard and a pen.

"No problem."

"What brings you to Paris?" Koutney asks. Turning to his team, he raises his voice and shouts out orders. "If he attempts to flee, go after him with a pit maneuver. It won't be pretty, but we will get the job done."

"I'm just chillin'," DeShane says. "Last I heard, chillin' isn't a crime. We don't see skies like this in my neck of the woods."

"What has you so hot that you need to chill?"

"It's hot in these here parts."

"Where is home for you?"

"You can be sure it is not here."

"Please do not cop an attitude with me."

"I'm guessing it comes as no surprise that I was raised in tenement housing. There was never a time I didn't wish I was born into a real family. You know, in a family with parents who encouraged us to do better. My mother knows only to nag and remind us of our faults and disappointments. When the opportunity presents itself, she blames me for my father jumping ship."

Rubbing at his chin, DeShane throws out words he hopes the police might find challenging. "Why are you asking me all of these questions? All I'm doing is looking for my father. I don't think searching for a loved one is a crime."

"As for our questions, it comes with the job. Do you have any assumed names or aliases?"

"Nope."

"Does the name *Sally* mean anything to you?"

"Nope," he says, chewing at his lip.

"Where are you headed?"

"Wherever the road takes me."

"What is your date of birth?"

"Unless you are planning to buy me a birthday gift, I don't see where my date of birth is any of your business."

"Do you have a driver's license?"

Pulling his wallet from his pocket, DeShane offers Atwood's license.

"This license is issued to Doctor Morris Atwood. Do you have a driver's license?"

"No."

"Where is your car?" Koutney asks, scanning the parking lot.

Pondering the question, DeShane throws his eyes to the parking area behind the hotel. "The blue four-door."

"The Saab?"

"Yep."

"I'm going to need the key."

"Not without a warrant."

"We have a warrant and a trunk to pop. Where did you get that ring?" Koutney asks, pointing to DeShane's pinky finger.

"This sweet, young thing I met in Memphis asked me to run away and marry her. Pop the trunk all you want. All you are gonna find is the spare tire."

"Where is she?" Koutney asks, eyeing the dirt on DeShane's shoes.

"Who are you talking about?"

"The *sweet, young thing* who asked you to run away with her. We believe you kidnapped her and stole her car."

"I didn't steal her car. This is nothing but racial bias."

"This is not about the color of your skin or a stolen car."

"I don't know what you're talking about."

"You used her credit cards."

"She was hungry, and the car was running on empty."

"Where did you last see her?"

"In the country somewhere. I believe there was either a lake or a river nearby. Listen, she begged me to run away with her." Displaying the diamond ring he ripped from Suzanne's finger, he holds out his pinky finger. "She proposed to me. The first time I felt her breath on my face, I knew she wanted me. Did I mention she has legs like Carol Burnett? Long, lean, and full of promise."

"Not until now. Where did this proposal take place?"

"At a picnic table. I was grilling hot dogs on a park grill. Believe what you will, but I'm speaking the truth. I know girl talk when I hear it. Once I allowed my eyes to skip over her age, we exchanged vows right then and there. We didn't have a preacher or a man of the cloth, so I'm not sure if we are legally married."

"Are you having me believe you had consensual sexual intercourse with her?"

"Come on, man. Is this something you want to hear?"

"I'm searching for facts."

"I've been straight-up honest with you."

"Something tells me I should study your words. This is a good time to fess up," he says, allowing his words to float on the air. "Where did you go to get all that dirt on your shoes?"

"When my wife said she had to pee, I pulled over, unlocked the door, and encouraged her to explore the pasture. I waited a bit, listened to some music, and after about twenty minutes or so, I yelled out for her. I waited a little longer, but when she didn't come back, I shifted the car into drive and took off."

"Is that the last time you saw her?"

"Yeah. I called out her name. Even called out our married name."

"What name might that be?"

"Mrs. Salliver," he says, not recalling her name, "but I figured she got cold feet and decided to throw me under the bus and go back home to her family. I was OK with it."

"Were you involved in the murder that took place in Chattanooga?"

"Nope."

"Tell me what you know about Angela Bartoni."

"I don't know her."

"Your prints were found in and on her car."

"I told you I don't know her. Why can't you accept the truth? Don't make me say it again."

"I am sure you are aware Miss Bartoni was brutally murdered. She suffered a basilar skull fracture and discoloration of the skin. Her neck was broken between the C5 and C6, and there were several fractures down her spine and major contusions to her head. I am sure you are also aware there was a tremendous amount of bleeding. All parts south succumbed to severe and brutal damage. By that, I mean rape—likely a gang bang," Koutney shares, letting his words linger. "I was told her car was found near your neighborhood. Again, it looks and smells like the work of a gang. I'm sure you know it has been said there is danger in numbers."

"Is she the chick who asked us to help her with her car?"

"Are you wanting me to believe she asked for help?"

"Her car was stuck in a ditch off the side of the road. She got out of her car, waved us over, and asked Slim to take the wheel. I'm guessing she thought he was Jesus."

"Does this Slim have a last name?" he asks, skipping over the insult.

"He's a brother from the hood. As for his last name, you will have to ask him. Me and another homeboy rocked the car back and forth. That's probably how my prints got on her car. When the tires finally caught traction, the car lunged forward. Next thing we know, it slammed into the lady, and she fell to the ground. The car kept going with the lady trapped under it. It was so bad, I had to look away."

"Did you call for an ambulance?"

"No."

"Notify the police?"

"Nope," he says, turning away.

"Anyone check her pulse?"

"I don't know. I went home. I didn't want any trouble. I'm still on probation."

"In Arkansas or Tennessee?"

"Tennessee."

"If you are on probation, why are you here?"

Shifting about, DeShane turns away. "I told you. I'm looking for my dad."

"Are you wanting me to believe you left the young woman for dead?"

"I didn't know she was dead. I figured she broke a couple of bones."

"And Suzanne Urling? Did you leave her for dead too?"

"I told you. I think she went home to her family," he says, opening his face with a yawn. "I couldn't keep her forever."

"My question is a simple one. You don't need to explain your actions to me. It's not my job to beat the truth out of you. As for your visit here, what were you doing down by the river?"

"I was frog digging and noodling for catfish."

"Frog digging and noodling for catfish?"

"Is that a crime?"

"The term is frog gigging. What were you doing in a dove field? Dove digging?"

"I don't know what you are talking about. People don't dig for dove. What if I told you we were cow tipping and snipe hunting?"

"I don't believe anything you say. I am sure you are aware you trespassed on private property. I've been made aware a body has been found. That said, we will need to swab your body," Koutney shares, staring him down with cold eyes. "I've been told hell has a place for people like you."

"It can't be any worse than the streets. Do I have the right to use the bathroom? I want to wash my hands."

"Not at this time. Your hands will be swabbed for trace evidence. We will also go over your body with intimate DNA swabs. Are those your clothes?" Koutney asks. "They look too big for you."

"Yep."

"A guest at the hotel reported his clothes were stolen. Officers found dirty clothes in your room. Along with your underwear and the clothes you are wearing, these items will be turned over to the crime lab."

"Will I get them back?"

"I can't answer that, but it's likely they will land in a court of law. The officers also found drug paraphernalia, crack cocaine, marijuana, and nearly nine hundred pills believed to be fentanyl. Are you taking prescription meds?"

"Until last month, I was taking Ritalin."

"Why did you stop?"

"Unless you are writing a book full of false narratives, I don't see why my actions are any of your business."

"I'll accept that for an answer. When the time comes, I'll pass your words on to the judge assigned to your case. That said, DeShane Salliver, you are under arrest for the murder of Angela Bartoni. If the second body is identified as Suzanne Urling, you are in a big heap of trouble," Koutney advises. "Possession of illegal drugs, theft of clothing, and unlawful use of credit cards will be added to the growing list of charges. I'm sure you are aware capital murder comes with a life sentence."

Hearing the list of charges, DeShane reaches for the Glock. When the officers pull their weapons, he throws up his hands. "Cool your jets. The hood don't take a liking to officers who arrest the innocent."

Koutney puts on gloves and throws out his hand. "I'm going to need your weapon." Turning to the officer at his side, he places the gun in a clear plastic bag. "Run the gun's serial number through the federal database. Check to see if it matches the description of the gun used in Atwood's kidnapping."

"Sir, you are not going to like hearing this," the officer says. "It's a ghost gun. It appears the serial number has met up with a metal grinder."

"Rest your bones and take a chill pill. I bought it at an army surplus store," DeShane offers.

"It takes a lot of work for a man of your young age to be a successful criminal."

"You should be relieved that I don't know a hill of beans about chemical warfare."

"You should know it is street rats like you that carved out my future. Much like your brothers from the hood, your criminal history and your recent actions tell me you are not that bright." Turning to the officer at his side, Koutney drops his voice. "See what you can do with the serial number. It might just be the good guys catch a break."

Hearing these words, DeShane gives a devil's smile. "You will never know what happened. Where I come from, we take care of the problem before you know you have one. As for the ladies you mentioned, I've heard it said you can only turn a light switch on if it's off."

**79**

"Throw on gloves and secure the door with crime scene tape. When you are done there, search every inch of this room," Koutney tells his team. "Use the zone method. Place his belongings in clear plastic bags. Remember, one item per bag. We can't risk contamination. Every inch of this room—the bathroom, the windows, the bed, the closet, the telephone, doors, and the platform under the bed—are to be fingerprinted and photographed. Note the case number, photograph the print, and note who found it. If necessary, use alternate light sources and fuming. You know the drill. It's important that you stick with it. As for trace evidence, use fluid collection kits and HEPA vacuums."

"Am I on weapons?" a lanky officer asks.

"As always. After photographs are taken, record the make, model, and the caliber. When you've gone through the checklist, package any and all weapons and submit them for ballistic analysis. Let me know if you find the victim's cell phone. For legal purposes, it might help us track Salliver's movements. Again, you know the drill. If you need me, I'll be in the lobby. It's time to question the front desk clerk."

"What about the car?" a team member asks.

"I've requested another team to get on it. When they are through, the car will be towed and held for trial."

80

"**W**hat can you tell me about the young man we saw sitting on the ice machine?" Koutney asks, throwing out his badge.

"From a distance, we could see his knees parked on the ice dispenser," the clerk says, pointing a firm finger toward the window.

"I understand he used Glenn Urling's credit card to pay for the room."

"He checked in just before happy hour," the clerk shares. "Is there a problem?"

"The FBI is on it," Koutney says, skipping over the question. "Was anyone with him?"

"I didn't see anyone," the clerk says, studying the computer screen. "When asked to present a credit card for payment, he offered a First State Bank card."

"I'm going to need your name and a contact number. It is possible you will be questioned by other law enforcement officials."

"Not a problem," she says, sliding her information over the counter.

"Thank you for your time. You have been most helpful."

81

Minutes after the call, the first responding officer arrives at the open field. A contingency of black-and-whites with flashing lights and an ambulance follow close behind. The officer's first job is to document who, what, when, and where. He will take statements from the hunters who were first on the scene. He records the time of his arrival, the exact location of the crime scene, the time the call came in, his ID and unit number.

Once it is determined that the victim is deceased, a unit uses crime scene tape, vehicles, and rope to cordon off the area. Having worked hundreds of crime scenes, the first responding officer sticks with the grid method, which is the most effective search method in almost all situations.

"I'm Officer Kirk," he says, approaching the three men outfitted in camouflage clothing. "I understand one of you made the call. I need to ask if any of you touched the body or moved any evidence?"

"I'm Andy Hanson. I made the call," he says, toying with the zipper on his vest. "We didn't touch her. When we didn't hear a cry for help, we believed she passed long before we arrived." Pointing a finger at the path their boots carved out, he forces his eyes to skip over the activity growing around them. "We walked through the grasses. Our boot prints are visible. I'm guessing the tire tracks were made by the person who left the body out here."

"What brings you here on such a hot day?"

"My father owns this land, and he lets us hunt out here."

"Are those your trucks we passed by?"

"The GMC Sierra with the big mud tires and the four-foot antennae belongs to me. My son is sleeping in the cab. The Silverado belongs to Mitch, and Chip owns the Toyota Tundra. This is Scooter Pankow," he says, placing a hand on Scooter's shoulder. "He's along for the ride."

"Anyone else with you?"

"Just Bullet, my golden retriever."

"And the palomino over there?" he asks, pointing.

"That's Dilly. She's been with the family for years. As for shooting, I think we will return to clay pigeons."

Hearing a plane, all eyes turn to watch an air ambulance making its approach for landing.

"Excuse me for interrupting. I'm Detective Koutney." Before continuing, he turns to watch the crime scene photographer who appears to be heading his direction. "Gentlemen, if you will, please separate and do not talk with anyone or touch anything. I'll be back to get your names and document what you witnessed. We have warrants coming to search your vehicles. Would you like to retain counsel?"

"That won't be necessary," Andy says. "We are innocent and as shocked as you are. Is it OK if I sit with my son?"

"Of course. I'll have an officer stay with you."

Making her approach, the photographer handles the digital SLR—a single-lens reflex camera—as if it is made from glass.

"Detective Koutney, are you ready for me?" the photographer asks. "I have recorded lighting conditions, current weather conditions, and the temperature. I have also documented tire treads and the damage to the grasses and dry riverbeds."

"Good work. Your focus is now on the body."

82

The county's most famed medical examiner aims his Hasselblad H6D-400c MS camera on the hits to Suzanne's face. Should he determine an immediate viewing is needed, an instant camera falls from his shoulders. Much like the crime scene photographer, years on the force have him recording lighting and current weather conditions. A glance at his watch gives him the exact time of documentation. Searching his camera, he notes the camera's film type. A senior on the job, he notes the time when the violent crimes unit arrives and when the homicide investigation begins.

In the shadows, several officers huddle close—each growing quiet while giving thanks the victim is not family.

Hearing an engine, the first responding officer turns to watch the medical examiner's van approach what is now considered the crime scene.

83

"**M**r. Urling, I'm Detective Koutney, and this is Officer Whiting," he says, turning to the officer at his side. "Our cars are parked around the corner. Would you mind stepping out here?"

"Thank you. I don't want to cause a scene until we have answers."

"I understand. Do you have family in town or nearby?" Koutney asks.

"My mother and my sister. Suzanne's mother is here, also. Our three children are here. Do you have any word about my wife?"

"What can you tell me about the days leading up to your wife's disappearance?" he asks, skipping over Glenn's question.

"If you are trying to pin any foul play on me, you are out of line. I love my wife. I would never wish harm to come to her."

"I'm sorry, sir. I'm not pinning foul play on you. What can you tell me about the morning of your wife's disappearance?"

"Our morning started like most mornings. My wife prepared breakfast for our children while I studied the morning paper. Before I reached the comics, Suzanne asked if I had time to run an errand for her." Recalling how the morning had played out, he grows quiet. "We were planning to celebrate our daughter's birthday."

"I'm sorry," Koutney says.

★★★

Standing near the window, Glenn's mother places a hand over her heart. Understanding the words the officer delivers does not promise the outcome they expected, she whispers for Suzanne's mother to come to the window.

"Maeve, my son needs me. Please stay with the children. Perhaps you can take them out to the backyard."

"Am I to understand my daughter won't be coming home?"

"I'm so sorry," she says, wrapping her in her arms. "I was praying for a different outcome."

84

In the coming hours, Suzanne's body is delivered to the St. Francis County Coroner's Office. Before an exam takes place and reports are written, her body is laid out on an examination table positioned under a surgical lamp.

A cardboard tag is attached to Suzanne's big toe. Hanging by a string, the tag includes what the medical examiner believes to be the victim's name along with her hair and eye color. The tag's flip side shares the assigned case number.

Before touching the body, the medical examiner circles the table with a PathCam. After photographs are taken and documented, clothes are removed and examined. His assistant stands ready with a tray of instruments.

MA-Light supply units shed light on the autopsy table. Chrome parabolic mirrors attached to the ceiling surround the light supply unit. The neon lamps overhead are splash water protected. A table within arm's reach holds a Stryker autopsy saw.

Satisfied that he may continue, the medical examiner pulls the plastic sleeves from the body's hands. Before continuing, he places the sleeves in a clear plastic bag. Knowing the camera will pick up the faintest detail, he focuses the PathCam on every inch of the body. He zooms in on abrasions, scratch marks, and skin and fibers held hostage under fingernails partially ripped away from the bed. With skill to be admired, he moves his findings to glass slides he pulls from a tray.

Taking a deep breath, he turns toward his assistant. Exchanging a look they have shared many times in moments like this, he steps up to a cabinet mounted high on the wall. Keeping with routine and the possibility the victim was sexually assaulted, he reaches for a rape kit—a box that years earlier was referred to as a Vitullo kit. It is possible that the evidence collected from the victim will put her assailant behind bars.

The examiner's next job is to perform a body rinse, which includes a shower head and hose to wash the skin, where he will continue to look for bruises, scrapes, defense wounds, and bites.

Satisfied with the first set of findings and the rinse, the examiner places the body in a white lightweight body bag with a full zipper down the front before placing it in a chamber drawer kept at 14 degrees Fahrenheit to reduce decomposition.

"We will examine internal organs and the brain after positive identification. As always, they will be returned to the body before burial. That said, I'll start toxicology reports," the medical examiner says, dropping his voice. "We are ready for the family to help us with identification," he shares in a low voice.

"Breaking bad news to the families is the worst part of this job," the assistant says.

"Tell me about it," the medical examiner says, rubbing at the lines in his face. "I've been doing this for decades. Believe me when I say it never gets easier."

"The criminals take some blame. They are armed with live ammunition and years of hate and distrust. They have learned to hone their skills, which oftentimes makes our job more difficult."

85

Although the drive to Forrest City is a short one, Glenn's heart grows heavier with each passing mile.

Hoping to buy time and pray for a different outcome, he circles the parking lot several times before claiming a spot near the building's entrance.

"Take a deep breath, Glenn," Brett says. "I understand this is the most difficult moment in your life, and there is little doubt you will get the results you are hoping for."

"I want to wake up from this nightmare, gather my family, and get the hell out of here."

"Something tells me the coming minutes—whatever the outcome—will be life-changing."

"I know I sound selfish, but I pray it's not her body waiting inside. If I ever get my hands on the person responsible for her death, I'll kill that little bastard."

"You would be leaving your children without parents."

"Suz did the parenting. My job was to provide for them."

"That's parenting, Glenn."

"It didn't hold a candle to her loving touch." Fisting his hands, he pounds at the car's dashboard.

"I understand your pain, but for now, we need to tweak your mindset."

"My mindset is my business."

"If the outcome we fear waits behind those doors," Brett says, skipping his eyes over the parking lot to the building's entrance, "your mindset will need to make a change. Should we walk into the worst-case scenario, I ask that you allow your heart to grieve. There may come a time when you will need to paint on a different face—one your children will trust."

"My love for my wife tells me I can't hide my pain." Turning away, Glenn wipes at his tears. "I can't live without her. Suzanne has always been my rock."

"I've never been in your shoes, but I believe this moment might be the first step toward closure."

"Closure? Hell, it is uncertainty I'm battling. I keep asking my brain to make this go away. I know only to fear what will come next."

Turning away from his best friend, Brett reaches for the car's door handle. "Delaying the inevitable won't change the outcome."

"Sadder words have never been spoken. I have to say, this is a different kind of darkness. It's funny what we remember. I wanted to buy a house in East Memphis, but Suzanne loved our little house. She wanted to live near the soccer fields where our children could ride their bikes and kick balls with their friends." Turning away, he looks to the sky. "The walls of our home have absorbed years of joy and laughter—tender moments I fear will come to haunt me."

"I'm sorry, Glenn."

"If what I am fearing is waiting inside that building, I'm afraid I'm going to need more than strength and guidance."

86

At the onset of its construction, the exposed brick walls of the county coroner's building were intended to offer a working relationship with higher governments. The foyer's southern wall offers a million-dollar view of the atrium and framed black-and-white photos of county judges and state representatives the city's voters deemed honest and worthy.

The walk to the holding area is a long one. With each step, Glenn struggles to breathe. Entering the generous space, the smell of rubbing alcohol and antiseptic rush at him. He is caught by surprise when the scent of saltine crackers drifts through the air. In his next breath, he is quick to notice the floor is pristine, and the walls are the color of virgin snow.

A clear bag holds what he fears may be Suzanne's personal possessions—several tubes of lipstick—L'Oréal's gold tube, a liquid stick, and a black tube. It also holds a prepasted toothbrush and a slim package of disposable tissues. Before the day is over, these items will be turned over to the authorities.

Glenn's eyes fall on the trio of uniformed officers standing in the shadows. Their silence fills his ears. Moving over the floor, he makes his way to the gurney, where his eyes fall on the tag hanging from the body's toe. When the coroner pulls back a corner of the sheet, Glenn collapses in grief. Falling to his knees, he screams out in pain and his head begins to spin. Fearing he might faint, he grabs hold of the gurney.

Taking hold of his friend's elbow, Brett pulls Glenn from the floor. Their embrace lasts only seconds, but the silence they share offers Glenn a shoulder on which to rest his head.

"I've been told trauma is a unique and private moment in a person's life. I know it's going to take time, but healing is dependent on the condition of your soul," Brett offers in a soft voice. "We can't undo what has been done, but we can walk you and your children through this pain. In their eyes, and in yours, we must find a way to keep Suzanne's memories alive in their hearts and in their lives."

"If it were not for our children, I would not get out of bed. Suzanne was my life … my reason for living. I need to hear her voice. I want to hear the beating of her heart, smell the nape of her neck, and see life in her eyes." Unable to bite back tears, he lets them flow.

"I'm going to step out so you can have your privacy," Brett says, placing his hand on Glenn's shoulder. "If you need me, I'll be right outside the door."

"Thank you for your respect. I would like to believe it brings some comfort to my heart—which is no longer whole."

87

"**E**tta James knew my heart when she sang out for all the world to hear that she would rather go blind than see you walk away. She nailed my love for you in 'At Last' when she crooned those seven simple words—*at last, my love has come along.* Never have truer words been spoken. What I wouldn't give to hold you one last time." Taking Suzanne's hand, Glenn places it next to his heart. With tenderness unknown to him until now, he gently strokes her face. "Oh, Suz. I am so sorry." Letting go a tear, he wipes at it with the back of his hand.

"Here we are in a place I wished would have remained distant and unknown to us. I know it sounds odd, but I always believed you would be the one to arrange my passing. If I had known we would be here today, I would have wrapped you in my arms and never let go. You are my first thought in the morning and the last each night before I close my eyes. The pinch in my chest warns this pain I'm feeling will never go away. I need you in my life. Our children need you. My heart will not easily heal. I'm left without answers and resolutions. Every time my brain paints a vivid picture of what that monster did to you, I shout out my hate for him and heaven's misguided angels. Those little bastard angels should be stripped of their wings. Last night, I looked back on the days leading up to our wedding only to find that our future has been ripped from us."

Keeping her hand, he leans in close. "If I am allowed to pass along one meaningful act I learned from you, it will be your gift of patience.

I can't speak for our children, but what I believe we will miss most is the love you have given us. You didn't deserve to die this way. I wish it had been me to suffer. Better still, why didn't that piece of garbage take his own life? He must know he will never escape his lot in life and its growing poverty. The world would be a better place without him. The taking of your life was not God's will, but Satan's. Hell's worst evil slipped through the cracks of society. I can't help but feel angry, bitter, and frustrated. I'm left questioning everything I've had faith in. I would give anything and all that I am to erase your last hours."

Lowering his face, he takes a deep breath. "I wanted to believe, with all of your responsibilities, that you lost track of time. If prayers are to be answered, I would ask for one more lifetime with you."

Letting his tears flow, Glenn rubs his hand along her face. "You were always the one I wanted. You always gave me the courage to move forward in our endeavors. The universe performed a miracle when it allowed our paths to cross." Pausing, he takes her hand. "It pains knowing I will be denied celebrating a lifetime of monumental moments with you—the marriages of our children, the anniversaries we were meant to celebrate, and the births of grandchildren we were to welcome with baby showers while giving thanks. Although we won't be together, I will forever celebrate our anniversary. This moment puts an end to uncorking a bottle of our favorite champagne while toasting to our many blessings. Oh, Suz, I would give all that I have to wrap you in my arms and whisper into your ear my love for you." Lowering his face, he rubs at his eyes. "Ours was the last great love story." Placing his face in his hands, he takes a deep breath.

"You have always been and will continue to be the shining star that illuminates my darkest hours. I have been far more blessed with you in my life than I deserve. I love you with my whole heart." Growing quiet, he takes a trio of deep breaths.

"When I look into our children's eyes, I'm forced to pretend my broken heart is still whole. A tug at my heart reminds this is what they need. In my quiet moments, I fall to my knees and bury my face into my hands. I don't believe I will ever be able to change anything in the house. Those rubber shoes you wear when tending the garden will continue to shadow the door in the breakfast nook. Your clothes will always hang in the closet alongside the straw handbags you just had to have, and your shampoo will continue to own the shelf in our shower. This morning, I held your bathrobe against my face. It continues to carry the scent of the perfume you bought when we stayed at that resort just outside Aspen. When I'm not wiping away tears, I'm holding onto the hope that keeping it close will comfort my soul." Lowering his head, he lets the tears stream down his face.

"Intimate conversations and late-night moments we shared race through me, and although I hear your words in my head guiding me through life, my heart will always hurt because I will never again kiss your lips or feel your arms around me. With every breath I take, I find myself missing you. I miss your smile. I wish I could whisper a prayer and in a single breath, bring you back to life. If I may ask anything, let it be that you are at peace." As the words roll off his tongue, he fights the urge to race out the door.

"All I want is for you to come back home—home to us." The sudden tightening in his chest leaves him short of breath. Resting his head against hers, he runs his fingers through her hair. "I love you, my sweet angel. I pray heaven's gates opened to you before …" Unable to continue, he pauses. "It kills me to let you go." Lowering his face, he lets his tears fall. "I would give anything to bring you back to our family. I prayed for a different outcome, but my words went unheard. On our wedding day, I vowed to love you until death parted us, and as long as God puts air in my lungs and love in my heart, my vow stands tall and true. I love you, Suzanne—forever and always. There will never be another love like ours."

Closing his eyes, he allows his shallow breath and broken heart to visit vignettes of their life together. Although he fights the memory, he revisits the day they picnicked at the park.

Under a spring sky, her eyes danced to music he wanted to hear. The first time he felt her skin, he vowed to honor and protect her.

"God placed you, an angel on this earth, in my care. Never forget that I love you. These years with you have been the best years of my life. Until we meet again, fly high, my sweet angel."

88

"**I**t must have been a three-ring circus up there. I'm not talking about the bearded lady and the monkey on her shoulder. It's as though heaven's angels took a day off." Reading the autopsy report, Glenn curses the heavens. "That monster left her for dead. His selfish acts and disrespect for life robbed our children of a future with their mother. My heart tells me that in every monumental moment in their lives, her absence will be felt." Although he struggles through the pause, he locks eyes with Brett. "You want to know what angers me most about that piece of garbage? We are supposed to be more alike than different." He pauses when a bitter taste rushes his throat. "I'm no Boy Scout, but I respect the gift of life. That punk kid destroyed and changed many lives when he took Suzanne's. I have to believe a different blood travels his veins."

"Glenn, you are not like him."

"His sorry ass knows only to lie, cheat, steal, and kill. I bet if I were to pound on his chest, I will hear only an echo. His actions tell me he is heartless."

"While I agree, you need to tell your children," Brett reminds in a low voice. "They are your first priority."

"What I know about priorities, I learned from my parents."

"Regarding your parents, you should consider yourself blessed. Many of the parents today choose to take the easy way out. Your children and their needs come first. It will be a step toward healing."

"I've never once prepared breakfast for my children, and I don't know their favorite snacks. Suz must have told me a thousand times the children's after-school activities."

"Your children will guide you through this."

"I suppose. I hope God allows me to see Suzanne in the lives of our children," Glenn says, rubbing a hand over his forehead. "I've been listening to Ray Charles. Instead of hearing *Georgia*, I keep hearing Suzanne's name."

"Perhaps the passing of time will bring peace to your soul."

"As much as I fight it, I have to accept that I am forced to live a different life—one without the love of my life. It might just be that I move my family far away from here. I've always dreamed of living near the water. A fresh start might just be what we need to heal."

89

"**J**ack, Wade, Caroline, please come sit with me," Glenn says, patting the sofa with an open hand.

"Is this about Mom?" Jack asks, turning serious.

"I want to sit on Grandma's lap," Caroline says in a soft voice.

Maeve looks to him—not for permission but understanding.

"That's fine, Caroline," he says in a voice above a whisper.

Grabbing a tissue, Glenn's mother takes a seat near the fireplace.

Believing it is not her place, Sissy returns to the kitchen, where she falls into a chair at the table.

Biting back tears, Glenn places Wade on his lap.

"Mommy was involved in an accident. The doctors tried their best, but they couldn't save her. No one could," Glenn shares.

"What kind of accident?" Jack asks, fighting the lump in his throat.

"A car was involved." Turning his eyes to the floor, Glenn hopes his half-truth will put an end to their questions.

"Did Mom suffer?" Jack asks.

"Given her injuries, it is likely she knew she would not survive."

90

S oon after his booking, DeShane is moved to an inmate holding
facility where he is charged with three counts of kidnapping,
three counts of auto theft, two counts of intentional touching or
application, three counts of intentional confining or restraining
individuals without consent, and aggravated rape and murder.

"How old are you?" the guard asks, circling the cell.

"Turned sixteen last month," DeShane answers, shifting about.
"I think this birthday made me a man."

"In the eyes of the court, you are a minor. Have you ever been
in trouble before?"

"Trouble seems to follow me. Does it really matter now? My luck
is so bad, I'm thinking I must have busted a mirror or two."

"It's not for me to comment. I'm a guard. Those in power called
your mother. I've been told she can't get here."

"Don't matter. She's never been here for me."

"She wanted you to know she was fired from the cannery, and
she needs to look for a job. She also wants you to know that if you
ever darken her door, she will shoot you if you attempt to take one
step over the threshold. She said something about your time here is
expiring."

"Whatever. She knows only to sweep me under the rug. As for losing
her job, I'm guessing she got caught with her hand in the till again."

"On a different note, your father is here. He would like to have
a few minutes with you. We will be moving you to a holding cell."

91

"**T**hanks for seeing me," Vern says, lifting off the bench.

"You are not welcome here," DeShane says, keeping his eyes on the floor.

"Over the years, I've come to learn the skills I need to silence my demons. When I learned of your struggles, I thought I could help lead you back to the right path."

"Listen, old man, you don't know anything about my struggles. You know only to be absent from my life."

"I understand you are in serious trouble. I thought it was only right for me to be here. I get that you are angry, but I'm hoping to right my wrongs and ask forgiveness."

"Just when I thought my life could not get any worse, you come here trying to get back into it. What in the hell is wrong with you? I'm guessing guilt brought you here. To be clear, you have never been here for me, and don't go thinking that being here today changes how I feel about you. You are and will forever be dead to me. For what it is worth, I've grown up believing you died from food poisoning, diabetes, or several shots in the back during a prison escape. When you are forced to answer to your faults, you will deserve nothing but a public hanging."

"DeShane, please let go of the past. I'm here because I care about you."

"Care about me? You are out of touch with reality, and I'm not buying your bullshit story. Your absence denied me of any award-winning moments I should have had in my young life. When you decided to leave my mother, you left me too. In case you have forgotten, you have another son, and he has no memories of you. That should put a smile on your face. I have never needed you, and I don't need you now. You could not save a drowning fly. When you walked out on us, you not only left my mother to raise us, you also surrendered your role as a parent. And guess what? I'm OK with that."

"I didn't leave you and Marshall. I left your mom. All she knew was to hound me. She wouldn't let me visit you and Marshall. I asked her over and over if I could take you to lunch, the park, or on a fishing trip. The answer was always the same. *Not ever.* My hands were tied."

"There are lawyers and child advocates who could have helped you."

"I wasn't in a good place. I was living on the streets and begging for food."

"How were you gonna pay for our lunch?"

"I don't know, DeShane. Dine and dash maybe."

"Please just go and leave me alone. This shouldn't be too difficult for you. I'm guessing you always wear sneakers."

"What are you talking about?"

"You always run away from your obligations."

"With or without me in your lives, I wanted to believe my sons would learn from my mistakes. I hoped you and Marshall would be good students, followers of the law, and earn an education that would take you out of the ghetto. I wanted the best for you."

"You want me to believe abandoning us was the answer? The time to be an example and role model has expired."

"Again, my hands were tied. I wanted you to love and respect your mother, but believe me when I say that woman put me through hell. If I could go back and do it all over again, I'd escape the hood and take you and Marshall with me."

"There is no going back."

"This is it then?"

"You will never be back in my life. If I ask anything, let it be that you go away and stay away from me and my baby brother."

92

"**I**'m Newton Lewis. I am a defense attorney, and I've been assigned to represent you," Newton tells DeShane. "Everything you say to me will be recorded."

"Whatever."

"Judges don't like to hear *whatever*. Let's talk about Suzanne Urling."

"Who is she?"

"You took her against her will. Later, you left her for dead."

"You got it all wrong."

"I want the truth."

"I'm giving you the truth. She talked all cute—flipping her hair over her shoulder and waving her wedding ring in my face. I kept telling her I just wanted to go home. She drove by this big hotel—the Peabody, I think. Believe me when I say she is nothing like the girls I know."

"What do you mean?"

"She smelled good. You know, like a brand-new bar of soap fresh out of the box. If you've seen her, you know she's good-looking enough."

"I don't understand."

"She had curves in all the right places. I'm guessing she wore fancy panties."

"Let's shift gears. I want to hear about your family. Let's start with your mother."

"Her cotton undies could pull a double-wide semitrailer."

93

Struggling with the handcuffs bound behind his back, DeShane maneuvers the courthouse. Camera flashes threaten to blind him, and microphones rush his face. Reporters from local news stations look at him in disbelief and disgust. He doesn't care. He is sixteen. It's likely he will get a slap on the wrist and ordered back to juvie.

DeShane is quick to notice the walls of the courtroom are covered with chipped paint while a tired ceiling fan fails to move the air.

"Have those seated in front of me been sworn in, given their rights, and searched for contraband?" the judge asks.

"They have, Your Honor," the bailiff says. "All rise," he calls out. "This court is now in session."

"It's time to unveil the truth," the judge says, observing the faces staring him down. "First on the docket is *The State versus DeShane Salliver.*"

"Your Honor, along with Newton Lewis, we represent DeShane Salliver," a psychologist tells the court. "DeShane Salliver has no redeeming qualities. As you are aware, he committed several heinous crimes. I'm afraid he is a fast-growing cancer society can't cure. His actions speak that he is programmed to act this way. It appears he does not show remorse or accountability for his actions and has no respect for life. Off the record, I would say he is pure evil. He is accused of extensive criminal activities, including burglary, drug charges, unlawful possession of a firearm, and kidnapping and murder. It appears he has the makings of a career criminal. Perhaps a serial killer.

When we look at crimes and question criminals, we identify motive, means, and opportunity. His devil-may-care attitude tells me he has an ax to grind. If I may do so, I would recommend he is placed on suicide watch with guards checking on him every five minutes."

"I'm sorry to hear this. Are his parents supportive?"

"They are marginal. What they offer is minimal."

"Suicide rates among youths held in detention centers are a major concern," the judge says, nodding in agreement. "Failure does not prevent them from making another attempt. Unfortunately, many of those under suicide watch manage to take their own lives. That said, I will grant pretrial detention and suicide watch. We should all hope for success. DeShane Salliver, please step up to the podium," the judge orders. "First, let me advise you that Willie Mahoney and Calvin Toyne have been charged for the same charges you are facing regarding the kidnapping and murder of Angela Bartoni. To be more specific, it is likely they will receive twenty-five years imprisonment for especially aggravated kidnapping, twenty-five years imprisonment for especially aggravated robbery, and twelve years for aggravated sexual battery. It is also likely each will receive life without parole. I have been made aware traces of your blood were found in a home invasion in Chattanooga on Browns Ferry Road. I don't have to tell you a dead body was discovered in the house. I understand charges regarding the kidnapping and carjacking of Doctor Morris Atwood will be addressed at a later date. It's possible he will be called to testify."

Looking to the judge, DeShane questions the role government plays in his life. A young man at sixteen, he understands he will never be free. Onion Bottom is far from the land of opportunity, and the last he heard, opportunities are not available to boys like him.

"As a student of the Tennessee Code Annotated, I will tell you that a kidnapping occurs when one knowingly removes or confines another unlawfully so as to interfere with their rights and liberties," the judge shares. "It becomes aggravated when the victim suffers bodily injury. When the victim suffers serious bodily injury or a firearm is used to accomplish the kidnapping, it becomes especially aggravated. This is known as a class A felony. Violent crimes need to be addressed as such. They can't be watered down or swept under the rug. It's time to stop the revolving door. Gun crimes need to be tackled head-on. If you, an armed felon, had not been on the street with access to a weapon, Angela Bartoni and Mrs. Urling might still be alive. When this type of criminal activity happens, victims and victim families feel they are either silenced or unheard. It has been said that the law has a process for a reason. I hereby order you to remain in jail on a no-bond hold. In addition, I hereby order that you will be held in solitary confinement with minimal contact with other individuals."

94

Dressed in a safety smock meant to prevent suicide, DeShane walks the floor of a special management cell set apart from the jail's general population. He has heard all he needs to know about prison life. One thing becomes certain—it is not for him. Pacing the cell, he holds his face in his hands. He is unaware his cries are heard down the hall until someone calls out to him.

"You're a pussy. Cut out that shit. I'm trying to sleep here," a voice shouts.

When DeShane allows his future to flash before his eyes, his legs begin to fall out from under him. Not to be outdone, his palms grow sweaty and the pounding of his heart hurries to drown out the voices around him. When his thoughts shift to his mother, he understands there will be hell to pay when she gets wind of this. When his baby brother comes to mind, he hurries to block out his face. A pinch in his stomach warns Pugs will punish Marshall for his actions.

Understanding the pain his brother will surely suffer, he drops his face into his elbows. An uneasy feeling in his stomach warns his life journal will have few pages and end without a plot. Once again, his thoughts return to his mother and the anger and regret she carries. If he is granted a single wish, it would be to forget not only her face but also her name.

In his next breath, his thoughts turn to the kids at school and the gang he runs with. It is only now he understands they are like him.

Most live in a single-parent environment where the father is absent and, oftentimes, unknown. Single mothers left to raise the kids often spend their days fueled with resentment and anger. Having suffered his mother's wrath, he understands she is not the exception.

95

"**I**s your father present in your life?" the doctor asks DeShane during his standard behavioral and medical assessment test.

Turning away, DeShane pretends to study the charts on the wall. His eyes fall on an armed officer in a lightweight jacket who stands near the door. He is quick to notice the cameras mounted near the room's ceiling. It has been only days since he last saw his father, and already he understands his father's face is slowly fading from his memory.

"I asked if your father is in your life," the doctor repeats, lifting his voice.

"He walked out on us."

"I understand he came by to see you. How did that go?"

"I asked him to leave and stay out of my life. What little I know about my father I learned from my mother," DeShane shares, tenting his fingers. "If her lips are moving, you can be sure she is lying. When she hops on her broomstick, I'm reminded he left us because I was a rotten kid. I understand he fled in the dead of night. When it comes to family, I've been told all I know is to disappoint."

"Until his visit here, had you ever searched for him?"

"Nope. He is long gone. If you were married to my mother, you would go away and never look back."

"Perhaps I could help you reconnect with him on a level where you feel comfortable."

"When he flew the coop, he became dead to me. When he believed it was best to walk away from his family, I let him go. From there, he went ghost on us."

"Do you ever think of him?"

"He is not worth the memory. As I said, he is dead to me. Just when my memories begin to fade, I'm reminded of a time when I tripped over my shoelaces. Although I struggle to recall her name, the lady down the street came to my rescue. Bending at the knee, she placed me on the curb. Laces in hand, she went through this crazy-eight routine I hurried to put to memory. I remember thinking this was a job for my parents. Months later, I heard this lady suffered a heart attack. Supported by a walking stick, she crossed over the street to wish me a merry Christmas. Can you believe that? *Merry Christmas.* I have never once heard these words from my parents. When it comes to holidays and special occasions, my mother pretends she doesn't speak or understand English." Turning away, he hurries to erase her face and the memories.

"Our unit never has a wreath on the door or a tree for us to decorate. Last Christmas, Marshall, my little brother, got pajamas and a plastic bag filled with second-hand socks my mother likely lifted from a thrift store. He was so excited about the socks until he learned they were several sizes too small for his growing feet. He spent hours giving those socks a determined stretch. Our gifts were never wrapped in holiday paper topped off with a ribbon or a bow. Instead, they sat cold and exposed on the kitchen table. One year, I got a package of underwear and a toothbrush my mother likely lifted from the house she once cleaned on South Third Street."

"Is it possible for your heart to forgive your parents? It's possible they were raised in conditions far worse than those you have endured."

"Forgiveness is not in the cards. Right or wrong, their actions carved out my future. When it comes to my mom, I have spent my life preparing for hand-to-hand combat. I learned from her to fight back with a smart mouth and a two-fisted sucker punch. And I'm done talking about my old man. He doesn't deserve being called dad or father. Truth is, he doesn't deserve shit."

"I'm curious about the gold chain around your neck."

"What is there to be curious about? It's gold, and I like it."

"And your watch?"

"It's blinged out and circles my wrist."

"Does it keep time?"

"Not anymore."

"Before you leave this room, you will need to surrender both. Now let's talk about Marshall," the doctor says, shifting gears.

"He's a good kid. His teachers always say his heart is in the right place. It is his hands we have to worry about."

"Help me to understand."

"That kid can shoplift just about anything. He once walked out of a store with a box of chicken broth, a bag of Russell sprouts, and a set of pots and pans."

"How did your mother react when she learned of this?" he asks, not correcting him about the sprouts.

"She whipped up a pot of vegetable soup."

"Did your brother's actions go unpunished?"

"Yes, but I was. That soup was awful. I swear I had food poisoning."

"Does Marshall look up to you?"

"I can't say that he looks up to me, but I believe he trusts me."

"What do you mean when you say that he trusts you?"

Pondering the question, DeShane draws in a deep breath. "I'd kill for him."

"Would you? Kill for him, I mean?"

Shifting about, DeShane studies the floor beneath his feet. "In a heartbeat."

"When you think about Marshall, what do you see in his future?"

"The kid isn't street savvy, but he's smart. Book smart too. Given his name, I picture him protecting our streets from people like me and the gang I run with. The thing about Marshall is he can be whatever he chooses to be. He could be a doctor, lawyer, or a man of the cloth. That said, that damn kid is always hungry. He would be a great chef. I'll say this: mustard and mouse fur will never be on the menu."

"How can you be so sure?" the doctor asks, letting go a laugh.

"They are always in our refrigerator, and he never goes near them."

"I'm sorry to hear this. Have you ever self-harmed or had thoughts of suicide?"

"No and no," DeShane answers. A challenge on his face backs up his words.

"Why the kidnappings?"

"What are you smoking, man? I'm sure you've been told you are out of touch with reality," he says, eyeing the man's receding hairline.

"Not that I recall."

"You got it all wrong. The Bartoni chick wasn't on my radar. She just got in the way. Same with the older woman. It was never about kidnapping her. I wanted to learn how to hot-wire a car and build a car bomb."

"For what reason?"

"I would slide deeper into the ghetto and be feared as a man."

"It appears you are broken, bruised, and filled with anger."

"Can you blame me? Hell, I am a black kid who can't walk the streets at night, enter a movie theatre, or travel the bus without curious eyes staring me down."

"Many of our country's greatest heroes are black. In your short time here on earth, you've made several poor choices. Taking the lives of innocent women raises the bar."

"As I said, you got it all wrong. These women got in the way. I just wanted a set of wheels. They made me the victim."

"You do understand you kidnapped them and left them for dead?"

At a loss for words, DeShane sets his focus on the floor. "I've been told weakness invites invasion and opportunity."

"Do you believe these women were weak?"

"They gave me the opportunity."

"Let's talk about Doctor Atwood. Do you believe he gave you opportunity?"

"Not answering."

"That's fine. Let's get back to the car bomb for a moment. Do you see this as a hobby or your life goal?"

"I don't understand the difference."

"A life goal puts money in the bank."

"If you are doing it right, so does a hobby."

96

"**Y**our Honor, I conducted an evaluation that explored DeShane Salliver's behavioral patterns, relationships, and family history. He believes he has been cheated and robbed of life's simple pleasures. While it appears he suffers delusions, he rejects mental health therapy. He suffers with antisocial personality disorder and exhibits signs of mental and physical abuse," the doctor advises. "Psychotherapy that includes treatment for substance abuse, anger management, and aggression is often used to treat this disorder. Unfortunately, there are no medications approved by the Food and Drug Administration to treat his symptoms. Given his young age, it is my opinion that he undergoes treatment as soon as possible. Without treatment, he is a threat to himself and others. Given his heinous crimes and his lack of respect for life, I see him as a flight risk."

"Any redeeming qualities?" the judge asks.

"Not at this time. Further questioning might tell us he is a sociopath. It appears he lacks empathy for others and knows only to act on impulse."

"DeShane Salliver, addiction treatment will be provided to you if needed," the judge adds, throwing down his gavel.

97

Accepting he will live out his final hours in a cold cell without a soft pillow or a blanket to warm his weakening spine, DeShane throws his hands over his ears.

Fighting the silence, he allows his thoughts to drift to his childhood. Although he has spent most of his life trying to erase the memory, he hated when his father bailed on him. Believing his father would return home, he waited at the door. When this grew tiresome, he sat on the building's concrete stoop.

Thinking back, he cannot recall a single time his mother offered words of comfort or took him in her arms. Thinking about it now, the same could be said of his father.

Although the words his mother uses to describe his father continue to haunt him, deep down he wants to believe there was a time when his mother had love in her heart for his father.

98

Sticking with routine, two jail guards look in on DeShane around eight o'clock. Passing by his cell, they find him humming a tune.

Although DeShane appreciates the three hot meals a day and a dry cot, he fears for his future. In his alone time, he regrets leaving the lady in the field. It is only now he wishes he had thrown her into the river along with her cell phone. It may have taken weeks for a search party to find her body. By the time the sheriff issued an all-points bulletin, he would be long gone.

In a quiet moment, he recalls the spelling bee he won in the third grade. The winning word escapes him, but the way his friends treated him remains etched on his heart. When they abandoned him, he threw the blue ribbon into the trash.

Letting go of the memory, he understands if he is released, he might just have to escape into the shadows. It takes only a breath for his thoughts to turn to Marshall and the life he will likely fall victim to. Accepting that his own future promises a fate worse than death, DeShane fills his lungs with thick air. Filled with worry and desperation, he understands the time to take action is fast approaching. When his mother's face comes to him, he spits to the floor. Silencing his demons, he steps up to the window.

Minutes later, when a guard makes a welfare check, he finds DeShane hanging from the window. Knowing seconds matter, DeShane is rushed to the center's infirmary.

99

"**T**his is total bullshit. His ass belonged on Rikers Island. I wanted him to experience Riker's fight night, illegal drugs, and an evening with an infamous organized street gang that lives by its own set of rules. Hanging himself was the easy way out. I was hoping for a little frontier justice. Perhaps a shot of vecuronium in his arm. If allowed, I would be first in line to witness his execution. He was a scab on society with no conscience or a chance at healing. Hell, I was told he was on suicide watch. I wanted him locked up for life and accountable for his actions. Unless he is sentenced to eternity in Satan's hell, he will never be punished for his crimes," Glenn cries out.

"I've heard it said that bail reform should be blamed for senseless murders and violent crimes," Drew says.

"Death row was too good for him."

"Are you getting any sleep?"

"Only long enough to have the same nightmare. Last night, I rolled out of bed and damn near broke my hip."

"You need to pull it together. You have three young children who, in different ways, need you now more than ever. You are not the only one missing Suzanne. They are missing their mother. In the years to come, when they learn of her kidnapping and murder, they will look to you for answers, comfort, and strength. Those times are going to be difficult and painful, but you will be forced to go through them. Jack and Wade will look to you for guidance in every decision in their lives, especially when they speak of marriage and the young women they trust to enter this family. Given their resemblance, I'm betting you'll see Suzanne in Caroline. The walk down the aisle on her wedding day will be tough. Those who gather to celebrate will no doubt be wishing Suzanne could be there to witness Caroline's big day. Something tells me she will grow to be the spitting image of her mother. When the pain hits, and it will, you will become Caroline's hero. She will understand that in the years since her mother's death, you've worn both hats."

"I wanted to give Suz the world and some amazing memories to go with it. She was named after her grandmother."

"I respect and admire the tradition of passing down family names."

"She always made my soul laugh and my heart smile. She was a natural beauty."

"I've seen pictures."

"If you had met her once, you would remember her for a lifetime."

"I understand."

"When I asked for her hand in marriage, I got down on one knee and gave her three options: forget about me, write as often as you like, or come along with me. I was hoping our lifelong journey would be longer."

"Again, I understand."

"I don't know, Drew. I struggle to get through the days. I've come to accept that the world around us is not as safe as we once believed."

"Your children need to know it's safe for them to play outside and that there are good people in this world."

"How can I do that when I no longer believe it? Our community is devastated. I'm devastated. Nothing about this is easy. That kid's selfish actions changed dozens of lives and changed my family. You know, Suzanne's pajamas are still under her pillow, and I sleep with her robe tucked under my chin. She was the queen of multitasking. She is, was, the first to volunteer at the children's school, all the while making sure our needs were met on the home front."

"You need to understand your children, these precious gifts, will always be tuned into real words—not excuses, anger, or regret. They might not say it, but they need to hear all the good things about their mother, your marriage, and perhaps how you arrived at their given names. They need healthy stories about their mother they can later pass on to their own children. You'll want to share photographs, especially those including party hats and helium-filled balloons. Like a flourishing garden, be the first to plant good memories."

"Thank you for believing in me."

"You might consider authoring a self-help book—one offering comfort, acceptance, and guidance to those who walk in your shoes."

"I don't want to *author* a book. I want my wife. I want my wife here for our children. I'm lost without her. I can't eat. I can't sleep. I'm finding I can't put words together to form a simple sentence. I don't even know what the children eat for breakfast or their favorite snacks. Suzanne must have told me a hundred times the children's after-school schedules."

"The children will help you."

"I stare at the telephone, hoping the next call will bring peace to my soul."

"Peace might not arrive in a phone call. If you allow it, I promise it will come."

"Every time my thoughts drift, I fear I'll suffer a heart attack."

"I promise there will come a time when you will smile again."

"I'm not so sure. The pain in my heart has me feeling like Bread."

"Bread?"

"The rock band. 'I'd give up my life, my heart, my home. I would give everything I own, just to have you back again.' If I ask anything, it is that you won't judge me. I'm guessing you've never lost anyone to a violent crime."

Lost in thought, Drew lets his eyes fall on the open window.

"I surprised Amy with a three-week honeymoon. She wanted to visit Paris and experience its history and beauty. I suggested we stay close to home. Hours after we exchanged vows, we hopped on a plane to Mexico. I'll never forget the smile on her face when we arrived on Isla Mujeras. We snorkeled the reefs, dined at the finest restaurants, and she was over the top when I surprised her with a sailing excursion that offered great views of Playa Norte beach and its sea turtle sanctuary. We also explored Punta Sur and Garrafon Reef Park. We were living in paradise until we visited Copper Canyon."

"I've never been there," Glenn shares.

"Copper Canyon is a series of massive canyons in the Sierra Madre mountains. It is known for its hiking trails, but we explored Divisadero, a popular tourist spot offering breathtaking views into Urique Canyon." Again, Drew looks away. "Amy needed to use the restroom. My mistake was not going with her."

"I don't understand."

"Members of a drug cartel took her right out from under me. I spent hours canvassing the area and calling out her name. I finally reached out to the police. Four months later, they found her drugged up and pimped out in the green-tinged gorges of the Copper Canyon area."

"I'm sorry. I didn't know."

"I haven't told many people."

"What did you do?"

"I brought her home. It took only a breath to understand she didn't want to be there. She is in an institution now. I understand she continues to wait at the door, expecting someone to save her. When her family reaches for her or tries to hold her in their arms, she screams for help. She still cries out for someone to rescue her. At this point, all we can do is pray for a miracle. It's possible she is still blaming me while I'm blaming myself. There isn't a day that goes by that doesn't have me regretting that we didn't visit Paris."

"I'm sorry, Drew. I know it's painful."

"What I'm trying to say is be here for your children. Hold them, hug them, and make them feel safe. Take pride in telling them stories about their mother. Keep her memory alive. Display photos of better times throughout the house. I believe you will find it healing for all of you. This is more than a bump in the road. Your children need you, not just today but until their hearts mend and laughter envelops them again."

100

"While in custody, your son committed suicide," the officer shares with Ramona. "Prior to his death, he was facing charges involving the kidnapping and murder of Angela Bartoni. His prints were left behind. He was also charged with the kidnapping and carjacking of an elderly man."

In the awkward silence, Ramona reflects on DeShane's short life. "I'm not surprised. He was always angry. I always thought he would spend his last days in the slammer. He was always up to no good. From birth, he was hardwired. Dodging bullets and surviving the streets became his life goal. What did he do to this woman?"

"Angela Bartoni suffered severe bodily injury and rape. Hours later, he carjacked and kidnapped Suzanne Urling. She was a wife and mother. He threw her into a hot trunk."

Hearing the charges, Ramona sits in shame. "He did all of these crimes?" she asks in a gravelly voice.

"Suzanne Urling's death left three young children without a mother."

"So he moved up from slashing tires and smashing pumpkins," she says, pausing to blow a smoke ring to the ceiling. "You know, I can't say I'm surprised. That son of mine knew only to toot his own horn and argue his actions and opinions. He was always angry and eager to hop on the food chain. He was misguided, but at the end of the day, he was my son. I'll agree he was dealt a bad hand."

"I don't understand."

"He lived the life of a caveman. He knew only to kill or be killed. I always knew he would end up a wanted man, but I never thought his growing list of crimes would include murder." Again, she fills the air with smoke. "Just goes to show you never really know what a person is capable of doing. He came home from school one day. I believe he was in the seventh grade. His little lost soul could hardly control his excitement. PE coach convinced him to sign up for track. DeShane needed six dollars for running shoes. Keep in mind, we were living much like we are now—hand to mouth and on a shoestring. That night, when I got home from work—back then, I worked at Benny's Diner—that was before I got caught with my hand in the till. Not a proud moment, but it's the truth. Sometimes my hands get a little sticky. Anyway, I reached into my pocket. DeShane's eyes flew wide open when he saw all the coins. We sat at the kitchen table separating the quarters, dimes, nickels, and pennies before placing them in dollar stacks. When we finished counting, I placed those coins in the palm of his hand and gave it a loving squeeze. I asked him to do his best," she says, painting a false picture and stretching the truth.

"His smile was so big you would think he won the lottery. The high didn't last long. The following week, he quit the track team and started running with the wrong crowd. Unaware he skipped over the opportunity, I asked him about his accomplishments. He always brushed me off with the shrug of his shoulders. It wasn't long before he moved up from petty theft to stealing bikes and smashing storefront windows. What is sad is he thought that committing crimes was the only way he would ever fit in. A doctor once told me DeShane battled his own silent demons. While I nodded in agreement, I didn't understand his words. I accept that we all have our troubles, but DeShane's troubles were different. Every time I held him in my arms, I tried to show compassion, but he always brushed me away and shot me down," she says, playing the role of the victim. "I was always left scratching my head. He once told me I was too old to understand the struggles a young black man faces. I remember telling him the same struggles apply to all men—regardless of the color of their skin—white, green, black, or blue. Did I mention he always wanted velvet gloves?"

"Not until now."

101

"I'm Viviana Craig. Today, we gather to celebrate the life of Suzanne Urling. Suzanne was one of a kind. I laughed when she told me she had hundreds of recipes for peaches. She enjoyed reading and had a passion for music. She took pride in Glenn, her husband, and their children. On an afternoon when she arrived before the dismissal bell, she told me being a mother is the best gift in the world." Pausing, she looks about the room. "Suzanne will be deeply missed by all of those who were blessed to know her."

Traci Richards, Suzanne's best friend since elementary school, is the next to take her place at the podium.

"Our Suzanne didn't watch much television, but I learned early on in our friendship not to call her during *Judge Judy*." Allowing the laughter to play out, she lets a genuine smile open her face. "Suzanne enjoyed trivia games and cheering for her alma mater's football team. She was a dear, sweet friend. I believe I speak for all of us in this room when I say her presence will be missed."

"I'm Gail Mann. I considered Suzanne to be my best friend—a trusted confidante. Always one to dodge the spotlight, she lived her life as an activist for those less fortunate. As a lifelong friend, I will say her laugh was infectious, and her ear-to-ear smile was genuine. Suzanne will long be remembered for her many passions and her deep-rooted integrity. There was a time in my marriage when I reached out to her for advice," she shares, throwing her eyes to her husband, who appears to be shrinking away. "In our brief conversation, I came to understand the love she shared with Glenn and their children was not only special, but forever and always. She was a strong woman with a gentle heart, and she will always live in mine." Exiting the stage, she shoots cold eyes to her husband.

Luci Falls is next to step up to the podium. "I'm the art teacher here. When Suzanne shared with me that she took an interest in art in her younger years, the smile on her face lit up the room. She was over the top when she told me she intended to study art history at the University of Memphis when Caroline entered middle school. She enjoyed painting sunrises and sunsets. I have to say, her best work of art was a charcoal drawing of her children. She had it framed and gave it a wall in their home's dining room. If you have seen it, I believe you will agree it is worthy of a grand museum."

Allen Rizer, the school's headmaster, makes his way to the podium. In the silence, he adjusts the microphone.

"Suzanne Urling was one of a kind. She never spoke a negative word or acted out in anger or disappointment. She was always first to volunteer her time in all things she felt passionate about. What I admired most about her was her love of family. She always put them first. In the coming months, we will introduce the Suzanne Urling Scholarship Fund. Once a staple on this campus, Suzanne's legacy will continue."

In the coming minutes, the room grows dark, and a large screen lights up the stage. In a moment of silence, the film shares the sympathy notes Glenn and his family received in recent weeks. A video of Suzanne at home with her children soon plays on the big screen. It is followed by a video of her with her family at the lake, where she is seen waterskiing, swimming, and boating. In the following video, she is caught laughing when Jack does a belly flop off the floating dock. In the next clip, the camera zooms in on Suzanne riding inside an equestrian center. A voice lets the viewers know she is riding Oconee, a sixteen-hand quarter horse.

102

S eated near the airplane's window, a young man shifts about.
"I need a drink," he says when the flight attendant makes his
way to his seat.

"What may I get you?"

Knowing his children's eyes are on him, the man looks down at
his lap and drops his voice. "A vodka martini with three olives."

"Of course."

"My wife is down below ... in cargo. I would like to be with her. I
know she hates being alone. She must be cold and confused. If you will
allow it, I'll only stay with her for a few minutes ... just long enough
to assure her we are here and we will not let anything happen to her."

"Sir, I will talk with the pilot in command, but I can't make
any promises. Your request would require us to make an emergency
landing. The Federal Aviation Administration has a responsibility
to keep air travel safe for all passengers. There are consequences for
such a request."

"You don't understand. My wife is down below. I need to be with
her. She wants me to hold her hand."

"Sir, I am sorry for your loss, but you need to stay here. Are these
your children?" he asks, looking at the sad faces hanging onto his
every word. "They need you here."

"Make that martini a double," he says, turning away from the
frightening expressions his children offer.

Seated across the aisle, Glenn reaches for his children.

103

Folding his hands, Glenn steps up to Suzanne's casket.

"I reach for you, but the cool sheet reminds I'm sleeping alone. Each time the pain strikes, the children come to my rescue. There are moments that come without spoken words, but the hugs we share provide what we need to hear. If anything good comes from this, let it be that you are at peace. Suz, I loved doing life with you."

104

"**D**ad, I've been invited to Jason's birthday party. It's this Saturday at the Putt-Putt Fun Center."

"On Summer Avenue?"

"Yes."

"I don't think that is a good idea, Jack," Glenn says, turning away.

"His parents will be there, and they offered to pick me up and bring me home."

"Son, there will be other parties."

"I'm guessing I'll never get my driver's license, Wade won't play soccer, and Caroline will never be allowed to date."

"When you are older, you will understand. I can't risk losing my children," Glenn says with sad eyes.

"Dad, I understand your fear. It's hell for all of us. We know to be careful and aware. Mom would not want us to sit back and watch life go by. She would encourage us to be outside exploring, learning, and laughing again. I'm guessing she would want us to go to sporting events and see a movie. She would want us to have a network of close friends. There will be meaningful moments in our lives we will want to celebrate with you and our friends."

105

"**D**rew, I think I need to question the officer who let that piece of trash slip through the cracks," Glenn says, addressing his good friend and the firm's general counsel. "Once Atwood notified the police that he was kidnapped and his car was stolen, the public safety officer should have made an arrest. They bear some fault in Suzanne's death."

"I'm thinking you should aim higher. Traffic cop has little to offer. You know, you might give some thought to suing the honey pot."

"Which is?"

"Corner Store. Their pockets are loaded, and receipts confirm Suzanne was on their property when she was abducted. Last year, an elderly woman was killed in the parking lot of a shopping center known as the Mall of Murder. Four shoppers had been killed in that same parking lot before her death. You might consider hiring Chas Warner. He specializes in premises liability law. Be sure to tell him I sent you."

106

It is a little after five o'clock when Glenn and Chas meet up at the Oyster House, a two-story establishment squeezed in between a print shop and an architectural firm on South Main.

"Tell me about Suzanne," Chas says in a low voice.

"I was introduced to her through a mutual friend. Keep in mind, I was kind of shy. Throughout my childhood, I was constantly reminded my imagination knew only to stretch and grow. Soon after entering school, I was told my father was next in line behind our country's president. Like any kid, I went to great lengths to toss my father's name about. Each time I filled my VW with gas, I yelled out a cheer for my dad. It didn't take long for me to realize that my fellow pumpers wanted only to fill their tanks. When I shared this story with Suzanne, she smiled from ear to ear." Revisiting the conversation, a smile crosses over his face. "We agreed to meet up for dinner. She arrived with a faux fur falling over her shoulders and smelling like lilacs after a spring rain. Her smile lit up the room, and her hair was the color of corn silk. She had a smile larger than this planet and perfect teeth to go with it. I know it sounds cliché, but her heart was bigger than the moon. She volunteered at our children's school. I believe she was room mother four or five times. Last year, she spearheaded the school's largest fundraiser. Although she understood it would be time-consuming, she took on Grandparents' Day. Every time she spoke of the children's events, her eyes lit up like a kid at Christmas," he says, reminiscing. "She refused to sit on the sidelines. She always said the bleachers were meant for those parents who worked long hours so their children could receive a proper education."

"Admirable and insightful," Chas says, listening with great interest.

"That big heart of hers was always in the right place."

"Would you say she was always aware of her surroundings?"

"Hell, she looked both ways before crossing the street. Sometimes twice. It wasn't that she was fearful or gullible, but trusting. She always looked for the good in people. To her credit, she usually found it," he says, choking back tears. "I bet she tried convincing herself that this piece of garbage had a better future awaiting him." He sits back and looks Chas in the eyes. "Suzanne obeyed the laws. She never ran a stoplight or earned a parking ticket. She once questioned a charge for a library book she was told was overdue. Instead of arguing, she placed a ten-dollar bill on the counter. Knowing all eyes were on her, she strolled over to the romance section, pulled the thin novel from the row of books, and returned to the front desk. The next thing she knew, she had every woman in the library circling around her. In the passing hour, they discussed Maureen, the book's main character. Before parting, they promised to stay in touch." Thinking back, he lets go a laugh. "The following week, she returned to the library. With the help of her new friends and a cork bulletin board, she announced the first meeting of the East Memphis Book Club." Pausing, he glances out the window. "I've said it before, and I'll say it again. It must have been a three-ring circus up there. I'm guessing heaven's angels were on sabbatical. I hope they are blaming each other and themselves for ignoring her cries. If only one person had done their job, my wife would be alive today."

Harry, the restaurant's owner, slides over the floor and greets Chas with a handshake. Chas's favorite bartender, a young woman who is always willing to share pics of her dogs, gives a wave from across the room.

Eyeing his assistant, Chas leans in. "I hope you don't mind, but I asked my associate to join us. Celia is the firm's engine. We call her Della Street. Trust me when I say Perry Mason has nothing on her."

Although Glenn nods his approval, he is well aware it will cost big bucks to have Chas and his team in his corner.

"This case involves especially aggravated kidnapping, aggravated rape, especially aggravated robbery, UTMV—unauthorized taking of a motor vehicle. That said, our golden key is premises liability," Chas says, locking eyes with Glenn. "Are you familiar with the Chelsey Hauste case?"

"No."

"When it came to Chelsey Hauste, a gang of thugs took torture and murder to its highest level. Just recently, a prominent Memphian was followed into her home in broad daylight. She took three shots to her torso. Shooter was apprehended when he attempted to use her credit cards. Just last week, a man jumped over a wall and kicked in the back door of a house in a gated community skirting Collierville. I should mention a vacant lot was on the flip side of the wall. Once inside, he hears voices coming from a room down the hall. He walks in and finds the couple watching television. He orders them out to the garage and into their car. About five minutes into the ride, the wife starts quoting the Bible. After about twenty minutes, the bad guy decided he had heard enough. He drove them back to their house and let them go. Police are still looking for him."

"Listen, Chas, I don't think I'm ready to talk about this."

"I understand. Don't talk. Just bend an ear. I think it's important for you to understand your loss is different and will be presented and treated as such."

"I agree with you."

"Bad things happen all the time. Some can be fixed without going to court, while others deserve compensation when negligence is involved. Do you know the difference between compensatory damages and punitive damages?"

"Educate me."

"Compensatory damages are awarded to make the plaintiff whole. Punitive damages are awarded to the plaintiff when the defendant is negligent in his conduct and is meant to deter similar future behavior.

For example, an incident took place last August. The defendant, a minor, went to the apartment complex where Cezar Tepote lived. High on drugs, the minor started shooting up the place. Several neighbors were injured. Turns out the complex didn't have any security—no guard, no gate, no cameras. Tepote sued the building's owner and its management company."

"You are going to have to explain to me what it is we have in common."

"Wrongful death and premises liability. If forced to choose, I would bet the fiver in my wallet that premises liability promises a winning case."

"That's crazy. This makes no sense to me. No jury would make the connection. Hell, I continue to fight the nightmare. As hard as I struggle to understand the law, I can't piece it together. Law or no law, I lost my wife."

"I'm not talking slip and fall, dog bites, falling objects, or snow and ice removal accidents and incidents. I'm talking the real deal. The property owner's duty to make their premises safe." Chas steadies his eyes and his face turns serious. "Urling versus the big-box store," he says, displaying a million-dollar smile. "Do you recall when Ford Motor Company introduced the Ford Pinto? I believe it was 1972 or '73. Early on, they had a real problem with the fuel tank. It was dangerously vulnerable to combustion. When the car was rear-ended, it burst into flames. The cost of either replacing or modifying the fuel tank would have cost, at a minimum, eleven dollars per Pinto. With over eleven million Pintos on the road, it would have cost Ford a hundred and twenty-one million dollars. After playing with the numbers and tossing about the odds, Ford held its position. They ignored the fuel tank problem that ultimately yielded a seventy-million-dollar savings for the company. We are going to lead by example. In short, we are going to make new law."

Placing his elbows on the table, Glenn leans forward. Words don't come, but his interest shows.

"Governing case law," Chas says.

"You will have to explain this to me."

"Law established by judicial decisions. Precedent, if you will. A form of following reason and decision-making formed by case law. It allows us to follow a case decided by a court to help resolve future legal issues. It could be said that we are playing the odds. The million-dollar question is how many people need to lose their lives before property owners work to protect them?"

"I don't understand."

"Accountability. We've done our homework. That said, we are prepared to challenge the court. If and when the time comes, we are prepared to cite *Jackson versus Glory Wells Hospital*. Are you familiar with the case?"

"This is all new to me."

"Daughter sued the hospital for negligence after her mother died during surgery. We will also cite *Langston versus Schmidt*. It is an older case. A violent attack and attempted kidnapping took place at a shopping center. What's worse was the plaintiff had been shopping at a neighboring store, and when first responders asked to use their telephone to call the police, their request was denied. We will also study *State versus Dwayne Schmitter*, and *State versus Carl Lacey*. I'm also studying a Texas case—*McLiven versus Big-Mart*. To be clear, the McLiven case does not involve premises liability. It involved a defective cell phone. The plaintiff alleged that Big-Mart violated Texas's Deceptive Trade Practices Act when it failed to remove and deactivate the phone's magnetic inventory control security chip. Plaintiff was stopped in the parking lot and was asked to return to the store for questioning. That is small potatoes. Speaking of small potatoes, we can discuss *Fulks versus Gasper*. It involves Avery, the family pet that was mistakenly placed on the euthanasia list. The family sought damages for Avery's intrinsic value. Let's talk about *Barry Harvey versus Corner Store*. Kidnap and murder by two men who escaped prison and kidnapped Faye Harvey. In this case, the suit alleged that jail officials were indifferent to training and ignored instruction and supervision of their officers and that the jail was understaffed when the inmates made their escape from a Kentucky prison. The Harvey family is also part of a federal lawsuit filed against the county jail. As for the kidnap and murder of Faye Harvey, the lawsuit accuses the property owner of negligence and carelessness that resulted in her death. The suit also alleges they failed to adequately monitor and control its premises. There is a lesser case in South Carolina's Florence County. Fortunately for the plaintiff, it ended with a large settlement."

"Kidnap and murder?"

"Rusty nail injury."

"For real?"

"A shopper familiar with the store stepped on a rusty nail. The nail pierced her shoe and went into her foot. The wound was treated, but an infection followed. After three amputations, the plaintiff lost most of her right leg."

"And the settlement?" Glenn asks.

"Millions. *Millen versus Messersmith* is another rusty nail case. Nail penetrated Millen's hand. He ended up with pain in his neck and shoulders. I'm going to shift gears for a moment. Are you OK with that?"

"I believe so."

"Tell me about your mother," he says, hoping to learn Glenn's mindset.

"She is a good woman. Back in the day, when my father was still alive, she always wore an apron and the simple ring my father placed on her finger when they exchanged vows. They didn't have much, but they were happy. When my mother wasn't in the kitchen, she was out in the garden where she pulled weeds and pruned branches. My father adored her. My mother continues to be a positive role model. She is on her own now, but she stays busy with bingo and canasta, and she has a large circle of friends."

"I would say you are very blessed."

"Until I lost Suzanne."

"I understand," Chas says, rubbing at his chin. "I'm going to shift gears again. A woman was recently awarded one million dollars in damages after she was falsely arrested for stealing groceries she purchased using one of the big-box store's self-checkout lanes. Why all the money in these cases? Premises liability. I would like to know what these stores take in every day. If this goes as planned, we just might find out."

"Suzanne's loss of life is worth far more than these cases."

"We will make sure the jury understands this from day one. We will cite previous cases, those similar to ours. I suggest we start with the Harvey case. There is a security firm in Little Rock we might consider. I'll reach out to them this afternoon."

"I need a drink," Glenn says, wanting to change the subject.

"I believe you have one coming."

"I would rather have a Bordeaux. Nothing grapey. Something with the flavor of soil."

"I'll have what you are having. If it helps to calm your nerves, a wise man once said do not let reality take up too much space in your head."

"Who is this wise man?"

"His name doesn't matter. That said, leave the tough questions to me. Keep in mind we just have to tip the scales of justice and avoid a rusty nail. Are you familiar with Lang and Farnsworth?"

"I don't believe so."

"We will retain them to determine the value of Suzanne's life. This will be the figure we seek in court. Their testimony will be presented to the judge and likely questioned by opposing counsel. There is one more issue we need to discuss. While I represent you, do not step one foot into Corner Store, and don't shop the store online. We can't purchase so much as a pack of gum or a can of Fix-A-Flat. I will ask the same of my wife. I'm hoping you will ask the same of your mother, Suzanne's mother, and your sister. We can't have them believing their premises are safe while we are suing them. One last thing, and please don't take offense. It is possible it may take years to settle this case. That said, it is my duty to advise you that remarriage terminates loss of consortium."

107

"**I**'ve accepted a new case. It's a difficult matter with lots of legs, and I will need your help," Chas says to Kristen, his wife. "You might want to pour a glass of wine and take a seat next to me."

"This sounds serious. Do I need to worry?"

"You need to be aware."

"Do I need to pour a double?"

"I trust a single pour will do," he assures her, taking her hand. "It's a premise liability case. My client lost his wife to an unimaginable crime. She was at the wrong place at the wrong time. The circumstances and the facts are beyond evil. There are several underlying issues. The one that concerns me most is your safety."

"Chas, I'm not liking this. You promised you would retire at the end of the year."

"I understand, but please hear me out. Before I go any further, this case is going to require long hours at the office and some travel. I'm afraid St. Lucia and Italy will have to wait."

"Oh, Chas, we've been planning these vacations for months."

"We can always reschedule. This case is a cash-making machine."

"For you or your client?"

"We will be set for life."

"Do you believe your client's wife should have made better choices?"

"I can't answer that. As for our children, I want you to take them to South Padre Island. I'll drive over with you, and when you are ready to come home, I'll come for you."

"This is our annual vacation. It won't be the same without you. Need I remind that you missed our last family vacation?"

"I'm sorry. You know I enjoy our time there, but I'm needed here. Perhaps you can invite your sister and her family and your mother. Your mother always enjoys her time at the Nature Center. She never skips a meal when it comes to dining at Blackbeards'. I'm sure your sister will enjoy the boutiques. The beach is always a favorite. As for the kids, nothing beats the bike rentals and the fireworks on the Fourth of July."

"It pains me to ask, but what makes this case different from the others?"

"My client's wife was kidnapped from a big-box store. She left behind three young children."

"I am so sorry for their loss. How are they holding up?"

"My client is hanging in there. I can't speak for the children."

"He needs to be here for his children."

"I understand. We will seek damages from the store. I know you have never shopped there, and I'm asking that you don't start now. It would hurt our case if your face appears on a security camera or our credit card gets in their system. That said, I want you to steer clear of American Way."

"Not to worry. I avoid that part of town at all costs."

"I know. I just want you to understand the position I am in."

"Our children are missing you. If you have not already noticed, they are growing up so quickly. We've arrived at a place where you vacation with your Saturday-morning foursome. I'm thinking I should take up golf. On those days I find myself feeling lonely, I foolishly pin the blame for our growing distance on your golf buddies. Do you have room for one more in your group?"

"I'll squeeze you in. I promise I'll make it up to you and the children. When this case settles, we will go away for the summer. I'll let you and the children choose the destination," he says, planting a kiss on the tip of her nose.

108

"**C**elia, assign what you are working on to one of the paralegals. Gently remind them that nothing leaves this office without my signature. Your focus is solely on Glenn Urling's case. Study my list of witnesses and the role they played. If I missed someone you feel we should depose, run it by me before scheduling a deposition. I've added DeShane Salliver's mother to the list. I'm still sitting on the fence with her. It's possible she will be both a wealth of information and a hostile witness. Let the front desk know we are not accepting calls from her. Should it come to it, any and all conversations with her will take place in the presence of a court reporter. If need be, tell her I am in a deposition. It is likely I will be. As for the big-box store, Richard's Custom Towing, and the traffic officer, put them high up on the list. Their testimony is crucial. We do not need to depose Atwood, but we will want a copy of his sworn statement to the police," Chas says with a straight face. "We are going to set up shop in conference room B. We will need file cabinets, roughly one hundred file folders, and a babysitter."

"Babysitter?" Celia asks.

"Someone to guard the room. Also, arrange to have a magnetic key lock placed on the door. We will need five cards. Every person entering the room must sign in, record the time of entry, and what they studied. Exit time will also be documented. At the end of the day, I want a record of comings and goings."

"Do you want the usual file cabinet routine?"

"Absolutely. Line them up against the wall. The first one will hold correspondence, expenses and bills, and our in-house legal notes. The second cabinet will hold copies of premises liability cases we've handled with success and copies of similar cases we might cite. The next cabinet will hold papers, photos, and letters or emails Glenn will provide to us relative to Suzanne and their children. The remaining cabinets will be used as usual—discovery, request for production of documents, subpoenas, and depositions. As always, keep the files in alphabetical order. Make several copies of the accident report, the aerial survey, and the crime scene sketch of the hunting field. I want cell phone records and all charge receipts, including those belonging to Atwood. Contact the St. Francis County Sheriff's Office. We want a copy of their file and their interviews with the hunters and Pankow."

"I received crime scene photos this morning," Celia shares. "My visit to the store yesterday confirmed they sell firearms and ammunition in roughly half of its forty-nine hundred stores. Just recently, the store made the decision to raise the minimum age to purchase firearms and ammunition in their stores to twenty-one years of age. Salliver didn't qualify unless he purchased a firearm with false identification."

"It's possible he stole the gun. Regarding the crime scene photos, open a file and make several copies. I'm not presenting Polaroids. It is going to be tough for Glenn, but I want the photos blown up. That said, we will need an easel. Have we received the store's guidelines for onsite employees?"

"A certified copy arrived yesterday."

"We will question the store regarding their inside and outside security. Have you opened a file regarding photos of the Urling's car? I might ask the same of Angela Bartoni's car and Atwood's. One more thing before I forget. I want several copies of *Medina versus Rangel, Ltd.*"

"I'm on it. I received a list of the store's parking lot crimes and a copy of their parking lot guidelines."

"We will address the parking lot crimes during the store's deposition."

"Let me warn you. The list is long."

"It is likely we will need an extension table, a chalkboard and chalk, and several printers."

"I'll need a paralegal."

"Clear Karen's calendar. She will be working with us on this case."

A knock at the door interrupts their conversation.

"Excuse me, Mr. Warner," his secretary says, inching her way over the floor. "I believe you will want to see this," she says, handing him a stack of papers. "There has been a shooting inside another Corner Store."

"Where?" Chas asks, accepting the papers.

"Butler County."

"Celia, make copies of these papers and contact the authorities in Butler County. Make a request for any and all documents and photos they are able to share. I believe it is time to depose Corner Store's director of security."

"Will we be working with the FBI?"

"Not unless we need to. Glenn has connections with the FBI. That's a conflict of interest if I ever saw one. That said, I tend to find them arrogant and a pain in the ass."

"I hope you don't mind my asking, but what made you decide to practice premises liability law?"

"Friends of mine were traveling cross country—coast to coast," Chas says. "A few days before their departure, the wife fell and suffered a hip injury, forcing her to walk with a cane and leaving her husband to do all the driving. Weeks into their adventure, they checked into a motel—one with a flight of stairs and an exterior door overlooking the parking lot. Husband helps his wife up the stairs to their room. Once she is settled, he returns to the car to retrieve their travel bags. He is standing at the trunk when two armed thugs approach him." Pausing, he recalls the story as it was told to him.

"When minutes pass, the wife steps out the door. When she sees her husband arguing with two guys, she ambles down the stairs," he says, again pausing. "Waving their weapons in the air, the thugs forced my friends into the car's back seat. High on drugs and smelling of liquor, they took the couple on a joy ride. When they found the couple's camera in the glove box, the thugs took pictures of themselves they would likely have shared on social media and with the boys in the hood. Fortunately, they failed to notice when the camera fell to the floorboard. When the driver stopped at a red light, the couple escaped the car, taking the camera with them. They went straight to the police. Thugs were arrested within the hour."

"I can't begin to imagine their fear," Celia says, folding her hands together.

"When Kristen learned of this, she vowed to never travel outside our zip code."

109

"Thank you for meeting with us," Chas says to Ron Lang and Carl Farnsworth. "This is Glenn Urling."

"I'm sorry for your loss," Carl says, offering his hand to Glenn. "That said, we've arrived at a figure we believe is fair."

"I don't believe there will ever be a dollar amount that will bring my family closure. Each time we gather, a heavy silence envelops us. Although the words are not spoken, we continue to mourn our loss. Suzanne should be here. Instead of her presence, we continue to fight a growing emptiness," Glenn offers with sad eyes.

"I'm sorry, Mr. Urling. I have never suffered such a loss," Carl says.

"I pray you never will. This is a pain worse than hell."

"Let's take a seat at the table. Would anyone like something to drink?" Chas asks, reaching for the water pitcher.

"I'll have water," Ron says.

"Carl?" Chas throws out.

"Thank you, but I'm good."

"Glenn?"

"Maybe later."

Settling into the chair, Carl pulls a file from his briefcase. Reaching across the table, he provides Glenn and Chas with a slim folder.

"We determined Suzanne's life value as a wife and mother. Given her young age, we estimated she would survive another 60 years," Carl states with a straight face. "As for legal fees and the added expense of any and all expert witnesses, we used the hourly rates provided to us, along with the cost of depositions, interrogatories, witness and filing fees. We also considered travel and hotel fees and pain and suffering. The figure highlighted in red is what we estimate to be the value of Suzanne Urling's life. Regarding the number of billable hours we estimated, please be advised that figure would likely change should you go to mediation and negotiate the terms outside the courtroom."

110

"**A**re you having me believe that after all this time we have a calendar conflict? We are set to go to trial in four days," Chas says.

"I'm looking at four weeks," Judge Carnahan advises.

"Four days."

Judge Carnahan raises brows, taps a pen on the desk, and gives a heavy sigh. "Game on."

★★★

Four days later, Chas arrives in Carnahan's courtroom with multiple boxes, three lawyers, four paralegals, and expert witnesses.

Tables are set up, and file cabinets are placed behind Celia's chair. Cardboard boxes are arranged according to the file list and subfile list. As directed, a trial witness index is placed in Chas's chair.

"Your Honor, as you can see, we are a bit short on space. Is it possible to move to the Supreme Court room?" Chas asks, pointing to a row of extension tables and printing machines anchoring a wall opposite the room's floor-to-ceiling windows.

"Denied," Carnahan barks. "I'm sure you are aware you are not the only case on my docket. If I miss lunch with my wife one more time, there will be hell to pay. For all that is holy, please get your team prepared for court. The last time I missed lunch with my wife, I was forced to eat a tuna sandwich. Have I mentioned I hate tuna?"

"Not until now. For what it is worth, I prefer chicken. If you will look around, I believe you will agree we need more space."

"Your request for more space does not fall into any category. Your request is not a legal motion. That said, the symphony of growls coming from my empty stomach tells me your request is denied. I'm calling a recess."

"Your Honor, a delay will cost my client more money."

"I believe you will agree this is not my problem but yours."

111

"I suggest we refile in federal court," Chas says to Glenn.
"More delays, more money."

"We will nonsuit it."

"What do you mean?"

"The plaintiff drops his suit under terms or circumstances that do not prevent another action being brought on the same set of facts. It is not a proud moment, but it has been said we live in a time when strippers and celebrities use their fame to off-balance the law. Returning to the law, we stick with the truth and argue opposing counsel failed to bring sufficient evidence to the table, and their client's negligence put Suzanne's life at risk."

"How does that help us?"

"We come back with a bang they didn't see coming."

"What is this bang?"

"A previous client and dollar signs."

112

In a corner conference room overlooking the Tennessee River, a team of lawyers entertain the idea of deposing Glenn Urling.

"I don't think we want his words on record," a partner advises.

"He should be going after Salliver's family," a young partner says.

"Salliver lived in public housing. He was riding the struggle bus since the day he was born. Truth be known, he was the worst-case scenario of his environment. In his short time here, he was a blight on society. I'm guessing his mother never gave him pearls of wisdom."

"So what do we do?"

"What we always do."

113

Mediation with Judge Stone kicks off at 9:00 sharp. It is said she is a fair and just judge, and rumor has it she scores below par every time she plays the links—which she often shares is never often enough.

"These are high stakes. Be careful what we gamble. Words to the wise—when people talk too fast, ease the flow," Chas whispers to Glenn. "Morgan Evans is here with Kerry Hoffman. I'm guessing Hoffman will do all of the talking and Evans will remain stone-faced. We might have to negotiate the settlement, but we are staying near the range we discussed with Lang and Farnsworth."

"Are they here?" Glenn asks.

"They are outside the courtroom. If need be, they are available to share how they determined the value of Suzanne's life. If you are ready, let's do it."

★★★

After a lengthy chart presentation from Lang & Farnsworth, the case settles later in the afternoon for an undisclosed amount.

114

"**F**ollow that boy," Pugs orders. "He is Sally's baby brother."

"See that ring of keys?" Dynamite Dean asks, pointing. "That little shit has convinced the teachers and the staff that he is the school's new janitor. I hear he is pushing gummy bears, candy samples, fentanyl, and crystal meth."

"How did he pull off the janitor role? He's just a kid."

"Claims he is in training with his father."

"Take him out back. Remind him bad things happen when his brother makes poor choices. After he pees his pants, throw a match to him. When you are through with him, grab the keys. We are taking over his business."

115

"I want a divorce," Kristen says. "This is becoming too much for me. You are never here, and when you are, you are locked away in your study. Most nights, you sleep there."

"That is not true. We just enjoyed a nice dinner with our children. Have you been hitting the wine again?"

"Could be worse. I could be shooting up heroin and throwing back a pint of whiskey."

"It wouldn't surprise me."

"I was in the Urling's home today."

"On Ashley Cove?"

"The one and only. My mind hurried to play out scenes of the day Suzanne didn't return home and the days that followed."

"How did it come about that you were in their home?"

"We attended a classmate's birthday party. Turns out the birthday girl's mother is a teacher. When the house went on the market, she and her husband offered the asking price. She was well aware of the home's history and wanted to restore love to the house. As she spoke, a chill ran through me."

"Forgive me if I don't see the problem."

"Of course you don't. You don't see me. This case changed you and continues to haunt me. I'm always looking over my shoulder, listening for footsteps, and checking the back seat of the car before sliding into the driver's seat. Door locks are pressed before the key turns over the engine."

"As it should be."

"I worry that I'll instill these same fears in our children."

"Again, I don't see the problem."

"I want them to be aware of their surroundings, but I don't want them to live in fear."

"How can I fix this?"

"You can start by sleeping in our bed."

"Agreed."

"You can ask your clients to keep their phone calls to the house at a minimum. Perhaps we can have lunch together after you play golf."

"I'll do whatever it takes to keep our family together."

"Promise?"

"You have my word," he says, taking her in his arms. "I'm sorry I have disappointed you. Please know I love you with all of my heart."

"And I love you. Although it has been a struggle, I'm writing again. Unlike my other novels, I spend hours waiting for the right words to come to me. It is as if I am living in a fog while escaping a storm."

"It makes me happy to learn you are writing again. I'm sure the struggling will soon pass. Is it a children's book?"

"It's about Suzanne Urling."

"What are you talking about? You just said all of this is becoming too much for you."

"It is. I am hoping I will find healing in writing her story. Glenn's wife was a victim."

"While I agree she was a victim, I don't think you should continue. Much of what you know is privileged information."

"Privileged? I'm living this nightmare with you. I live in fear for our daughters. They are both young and naïve. I've watched this horror film play out with you. I feared I would be called to testify. Unlike you, I am not bound by any attorney-client privilege."

"Please rethink this."

"I have, and I will continue writing. I find that writing lets me escape. It also fills the void I have been feeling not only in my heart but also in my life."

"Do we need to revisit the divorce you mentioned?"

"I was hoping to hear I have your support."

"You always have my support."

"I'm finding that we are stuck here in the this and that."

"What are you talking about?"

"This is not the time for half measures. Our marriage needs a better recipe."

"I'm listening."

"My heart tells me your heart has moved on without me. I'm guessing you haven't heard I ordered a set of clubs and scheduled lessons with the club's summer interns."

"You don't golf."

"I've never been invited. To be fair, you have never hit the open road in running shoes."

"If it will save our marriage, I'll take up running," he says, taking her in his arms.

116

"**I**f I may, I would like to make a suggestion," Chas says. "Be careful whom you allow into your heart and into your life. Your children need all of you, not just today, but until your family is whole again. I believe you will agree it's time to heal and change directions."

"I continue to feel like my bones are breaking," Glenn says, folding his hands together. "Every time my eyes fall on a blue Saab, my heart breaks. As for my family, we will never again be whole. We are a puzzle with one piece missing."

"Perhaps you can ask your heart to make this missing piece the most memorable."

"I wish you had met her," Glenn shares in a voice above a whisper. "She was one of a kind."

"I can only imagine your joy when you see her again."

"Something tells me I'll be counting the days. I wonder how much longer I'll wait at the door, reach for her in the middle of the night, and sweep a hand through her clothes in our closet."

"I trust your heart will guide you."

"There will never be another love like ours."

Printed in the United States
by Baker & Taylor Publisher Services